"Now, there's the Sara—

"Don't you dare throw that word around. If you loved me, we wouldn't be in this situation." A surge of emotion tightened her chest, and she silently cursed herself for letting him get to her.

Hands on his hips, Mike sighed. "Look, I know you have every reason to believe that, but it's just not true. I've loved you since the first moment I laid eyes on you."

She paused. God, how she wanted to believe him. But if he'd truly loved her as he claimed, he'd never have been able to stay away for so long.

She swallowed past the lump in her throat and reached into the dish drainer for something else to dry.

"All right, I'm done playing. Come on, we're going for a ride." Mike reached out and grasped her elbow.

"I'm not going anywhere with you," she said, yanking her arm free. "If you want to talk, we'll talk, but we're doing it right here." She threw the towel down on the counter and crossed her arms over her chest to hide her shaking hands.

"You either follow me to my truck, or I'll toss you over my shoulder and carry you there. But one way or another, we're taking a ride."

She gasped. *Arrogant son of a...* "If you touch me, I'll scream bloody murder."

"Then I guess I'll have to gag you as well."

He took a step toward her. She took a step back.

"You stay the hell away from me." She took another step back and bumped into the table, quickly grasping it for support. Her pulse sped up, though she feared it was as much from excitement as anger. Damn him for making her...*feel* something.

"Not a chance. I made that mistake once, I won't make it again."

Reviews for Donna Marie Rogers

There's Only Been You

"Love lost and found is the basis of this wonderfully heartwarming read. Throw in a years-old lie and a strong sense of family and it only gets better and better."
—4 Stars, RT Book Reviews

"Donna Marie Rogers delivers a tender tale of love, family, and second chances."
—5 Bookmarks, Wild on Books

Meant To Be

"The plot kept me spellbound throughout the entire book. Rogers has the ability to keep her readers on the edge of our seats."
—5 Hearts, The Romance Studio

"The material is tightly written, well plotted and fast paced, and the characters are unforgettable."
—5 Books, Long and Short Reviews

Welcome To Redemption Series

"With their easy, breezy style and skilled characterizations, Rogers and Netzel have created a town that readers won't want to leave."
—4½ Stars - RT Book Reviews

OTHER TITLES

Jamison Series

There's Only Been You, Book 1
Foolish Pride (Extra Peek Short Story)
Meant To Be, Book 2

Golden Series
(Contemporary Western Romance)

Golden Opportunity, Book 1

Welcome To Redemption Series
(with Stacey Joy Netzel)

A Fair of the Heart, Book 1, Donna Marie Rogers
A Fair to Remember, Book 2, Stacey Joy Netzel
The Perfect Blend, Book 3, Donna Marie Rogers
Grounds For Change, Book 4, Stacey Joy Netzel
Home Is Where the Heart Is, Book 5, Donna Marie Rogers
The Heart of the Matter, Book 6, Stacey Joy Netzel
Never Let Me Go, Book 7, Donna Marie Rogers
Hold On To Me, Book 8, Stacey Joy Netzel

Writing as Liza James:
Only Man For the Job
Mischief in the Dark
Branded
Game On
Lying Eyes
Hot For Teacher

DEDICATION

To all the amazingly supportive women in my life,
whether friend, family, or both.

Thank you, I love you all.

This is a work of fiction. Names, characters, places, and incidents are either the product of the author's imagination or are used fictitiously, and any resemblance to actual persons living or dead, business establishments, events, or locales, is entirely coincidental.

Copyright © 2013 Author Edition
There's Only Been You by Donna Marie Rogers
First Published 2008 by The Wild Rose Press

All Rights Reserved. No part of this book may be used or reproduced in any manner whatsoever without written permission of the author except in the case of brief quotations embodied in critical articles or reviews.

Edited by Stacy D. Holmes
Cover art by The Killion Group
Formatted by Author E.M.S.

ISBN-13: 978-1490482842
ISBN-10: 1490482849

There's Only Been You

DONNA MARIE ROGERS

One

Sara Jamison believed in premonitions about as much as she did the Easter Bunny. Yet, from the moment she'd opened her eyes that morning, she'd felt the strongest sense of impending doom. Okay, so maybe she *was* being a bit melodramatic, but the unexplainable nervous energy she'd been trying to work off for the past few hours just didn't seem to be dissipating.

She pulled the last pan of cinnamon rolls from the oven with an appreciative sniff and slid it onto the cooling rack, then tested the tub of icing in the microwave to see if it was of drizzling consistency.

Perfect.

Grabbing a spoon-shaped spatula, she walked out to the front of her shop, *Sara's Bakery*, and slathered the hot icing onto a cooled pan of cinnamon rolls.

The bell above her bakery's door chimed, and Sara darn near jumped out of her shoes. *Good lord, woman, get a grip!*

She looked up in time to see her oldest brother, Garrett, enter the shop. He strode toward her, the scowl twisting his face sending her already racing heart into overdrive.

Hello impending doom. "What is it? What's wrong?"

Garrett stalked behind the counter and stole one of the

fresh, gooey buns from the tray. He took a huge bite before meeting her gaze, those big brown eyes simmering with barely concealed fury. But still, he remained quiet.

Exasperation warred with panic as she watched her brother struggle to get that infamous temper in check. She set the icing down and moved to the coffee maker to pour him a cup of her house blend.

"Thanks." He leaned back against the counter and took a few sips from the cup she'd handed him, his brow knit in thoughtful contemplation.

She glanced up at the big cupcake-shaped, neon clock that hung over the blackboard menu and prayed for patience. "Garrett, would you spill it already? You're starting to scare me."

"John Andrews was found dead yesterday in his living room. Looks like he had a heart attack while watching TV."

Her pulse spun out of control. "My God... Has his son been contacted yet? Is Mike coming home for the funeral?" She stared at her brother, silently begging him to say no.

"They tracked him down last night. Andrews should arrive in Green Bay sometime today." Garrett massaged the back of his neck. "Turns out he's a cop. A detective on the Southside of Chicago. How's that for irony? That abusive sonofabitch and I ending up in the same profession."

Sara slowly shook her head, the shock of her brother's news almost too much to comprehend. She turned around to pour herself some coffee, but realized her hands were shaking and braced them on the counter. "He hated his father. Maybe he won't come."

"He's coming, Sara."

"You don't think he knows..."

She heard him blow out a hard breath. "It's unlikely. No one else knows, how could he?"

"I don't know." She wasn't exactly convinced.

"Listen, even if he does, so what? He's not likely to contact you. Don't forget the reason he skipped town in the first place—he's a gutless worm. Just like his father."

The look in his eyes grew fierce, and her heart missed a beat. Garrett had a devil of a temper, especially when it came to his family. The last thing Sara needed was for him to work himself into a fury and go looking for a fight.

Specifically, go looking for Mike Andrews.

"Garrett, you keep that temper of yours in check. Especially around Ethan. I don't want him to suspect something's wrong. He's a very intuitive little boy."

His harsh expression softened at the mention of his nephew. "Yeah, he's a sharp kid all right. Always knows when something's bothering me." His brow furrowed. "It's annoying as hell."

Sara managed a small smile. Her son had no doubt inherited that particular talent from his Uncle Garrett—although she'd keep that observation to herself. "You're right, it is."

They were both silent for a moment. Her brother took a few more sips of his coffee, then poured the rest down the sink and tossed the dark pink, paper cup in the trash. He stood beside her, hooking an arm around her shoulders.

"Listen, the Andrews' place is all the way on the east side of town, so there's not much of a chance you'll run into him. And before you know it, he'll be on his way back to Chicago and the rock he crawled out from under."

"I sure hope you're right."

"'Course I am. Now," he said, gently pulling her with

him until they faced the back of the display case. "On to something important."

"You promised to bring back sweet rolls for the entire station again." She cocked an eyebrow. "Didn't you?"

He grinned down at her. "Yeah, but don't look at me like that. I'll pay for 'em this time."

She gave her head a small shake. "Don't be silly. I wouldn't have this place if it weren't for you. Your sweet rolls are on the house, just as they've always been." She folded up one of the big white boxes and began filling it with an assortment of what she knew were everyone's favorites.

"You have this place cause you work your ass off. I only co-signed the loan." He reached in and filched a raspberry-filled bismarck from the box. "Besides, you were meant to own a bakery." He gestured with the half-eaten donut, raspberry jam coating a good portion of his upper lip. "These are even better than the ones from that little bakery out in Pulaski."

"Glad to hear it since they're still my biggest competitor."

She'd loved to cook for as long as she could remember. Even before Uncle Luke moved in with them following the deaths of their parents nearly eighteen years ago. And after one bite of the young bachelor's Spam casserole, she'd dug out her mother's old cookbook and barred her well-meaning uncle from the kitchen.

Baking, however, became her specialty. By the time she'd turned fifteen, the kitchen had become the busiest room in the house. There was always hot coffee in the carafe and fresh-baked something or other coming out of the oven. Her brothers' friends had even hung out on a regular basis, waiting to see what she'd pull from the oven next.

Which was how she'd met Mike.

"Don't forget to throw in a couple of cherry honeymooners for Muriel," Garrett said, popping her from her thoughts. He swiped a napkin across his mouth. "She threatened to kick my ass if I forgot 'em again."

Sara's lips twitched at the thought. At five-foot-nothing and a hundred pounds with a brick in each hand, Muriel Spencer was even tinier than Sara. Yet, every single person down at the station tripped over themselves trying to please her. Of course, Sara couldn't blame any of them. Muriel was one of a kind—a firecracker with a heart of gold.

And a perfect match for Uncle Luke.

"Don't wet yourself; I'm getting them right now." She stuffed two of the precious cherry-topped honeymooners into a bag, set it on top of the box, and slid both toward him. "Who's picking Ethan up from school today, you or Nicky?"

"I am. Ethan wanted to be picked up in the squad car on the last day of school." Garrett grinned, looking very much like a little boy himself.

"Thanks," she said, forcing a smile. "I appreciate it. Just drop him off here, and he can watch cartoons in the storeroom 'til I finish up."

"Sounds like a plan. I'll see you later." He picked up the box and strode out the door.

Sara collapsed against the counter as soon as he drove out of the parking lot.

Good God, Mike's coming home!

It was a miracle her knees hadn't buckled under the impact of Garrett's news. But she knew her overprotective big brother never would've left if he'd known just how unsettled she'd been. And she certainly didn't want him getting into trouble at work.

The shop's bell rang again just as she stuck the tub of icing back into the microwave. She took a deep breath and composed herself. *Later*. She'd dwell on Mike's imminent arrival later. Right now, she had a bakery to run.

Her neighbor, Nancy Martin, walked through the door, keys jingling in her hand.

Sara arched a brow. "Wow, you're out and about early."

"I have tons of running around to do today. Thought I'd hype myself up on caffeine before hitting the stores. Besides, it's gorgeous out there—already seventy degrees. And it's supposed to hit eighty by noon."

Sara smiled, although it took some effort. She'd never felt less like making idle chit-chat. "Well, then I'm glad I decided to do Shelly's cake first thing this morning."

"You did? Cool." Nancy plopped her purse and keys on the counter and blew out a dramatic breath. "I still can't believe my baby's turning five." She leaned in to peer at the half-iced tray of cinnamon rolls, and a mob of strawberry-blonde curls spilled forward. "Man, those suckers smell good. I'll take one to go, and a cup of your house blend."

Thankful the coffee machine was playing nice today, as it had been giving her trouble on and off all week, Sara poured a paper cup of the aromatic, vanilla-flavored *Icing on the Cake* and snapped on a plastic lid. Then she slid one of the gooey cinnamon rolls into a bag. The usual rush of pride swelled her chest when she read the words *Sara's Bakery* in dark pink print on the front of the bag.

"Your cake's in the big cooler. I'll be right back." When she returned, she set the rectangular white box on the counter and proudly flipped open the lid.

"Holy Bubble Guppies, Sara! It's perfect," her friend declared. "Shelly's going to love it." She dug out her wallet. "How much do I owe you? And don't say 'nothing'. We've already been over that."

"Twenty-seven fifty." Sara reluctantly accepted the two twenties Nancy handed her and counted out her change.

"I can't wait to show Shelly." Her neighbor slung her purse over her shoulder and picked up her goodies. "Her eyes are going to light up like sparklers."

Sara came around the counter and walked ahead to open the door for her. "If she's even half as excited as you, I'll be thrilled. See you at the party."

As Nancy walked out the door, three more cars pull into the parking lot, and she recognized one as Teresa McKay's. She'd struck gold the day Teresa walked into the shop looking for a job. Professional, friendly, and an absolute favorite with the customers. Jay Rogers, her only other full-time employee, had been with Sara since day one. He came in six nights a week, working until the sun came up frying donuts, baking cinnamon rolls, muffins and other pastries.

In the beginning, she'd worked side by side with Jay, baking all night, then working half a day behind the counter. Thank God for her brothers and uncle who'd taken good care of Ethan while she'd been busy getting her business off the ground. Now, *Sara's Bakery* was a thriving success, and she no longer had to spend so much time away from her son.

Life was almost perfect.

Almost.

The fact that she hadn't been on a date in more than

two years was a bit depressing. She'd always insisted her lack of a social life was no big deal. She had her son, her family—all she needed for life to be complete.

Yeah, sure, keep telling yourself that.

Okay, so truth was she'd been ready for some time now. Ready to find a good man she could fall in love with and settle down. A man who would love Ethan almost as much as she did.

Her thoughts unwittingly returned to the news of Mike's father's death. She tried not to let her nerves get the better of her, but it was hard. Although she'd never have admitted it to Garrett, a small thrill shot through her at the thought of seeing Mike again.

She gave herself a mental head slap. Mike Andrews deserved her contempt, nothing more.

With Herculean effort, she managed to drag her thoughts back to business.

By two o'clock, Sara had all her cake orders filled and everything packaged except a few pies that had just come out of the oven. She tried to get some paperwork done, but found it impossible to concentrate, so she told Teresa she had personal business to take care of and had to leave for the day. She gave Garrett a call as she packed up a few bakery boxes to take home.

Half a block from the house she saw her brother's squad car pull into the driveway. God, she couldn't wait to hold her son. Of course, he'd squirm and protest, but he'd just have to deal with it because she needed it today. She'd give him the squeeze of his life, order his favorite pizza, and all would be forgiven.

She parked on the street and made her way up the walk as Garrett unlocked the front door. Ethan ran inside with a quick wave in her direction, but his uncle waited, holding the door.

"Thanks again for picking him up. I wish I'd been ten minutes earlier, I could've saved you the trip." She walked into the kitchen of the home she'd shared with her brothers since birth and carefully set the stack of bakery boxes on the table.

"It was no problem, don't worry about it." He followed her to the table and started rummaging through the boxes. His eyes lit up when he came across the chocolate chip cookies, and he dug a couple out.

He's as bad as Ethan, she thought, unable to hold back a grin.

When little mister 'speak of the devil' ran through the kitchen, Sara caught him around the waist and pulled him against her in a ferocious hug.

He squirmed, just as she knew he would, and when she reached down to kiss his cheek, he whined, "Come on, Mom, leggo! My show's about to start!"

With a wistful smile, she released him.

Garrett ruffled Ethan's nearly black hair as he ran past. "Hey, don't let it get to you. He's seven. Boys that age don't like their mothers to cling. It's just the way it is."

"I know."

Garrett searched her face. "You sure you're all right?"

"I'm fine, really." She made a shooing motion with her hands. "Now, get your butt back to the station before someone puts an APB out on you."

Sara set the coffee carafe on the kitchen table. "Anyone ready for dessert? I have apple or coconut custard pie, and chocolate chip cookies."

Her younger brother, Danny, leaned back in his chair and blew out a heavy breath. "I couldn't eat another bite."

"I want chocolate chip cookies," Ethan announced.

Uncle Luke poured himself a cup of coffee. "I'll have apple, please."

"I'll take coconut," Garrett said and reached over to snag a couple of the cookies.

Sara cut and served the pie, then gave Ethan two cookies on a napkin. She looked at Nicky. "Apple or coconut?"

"No thanks."

Hmm. The second oldest of the Jamison siblings had been quiet all through supper, which wasn't exactly late-breaking news in itself. Nicholas, known as Nicky since childhood, had always been the quieter one of the bunch. But it wasn't like him to turn down pie.

"So, how'd your big meeting go?" Garrett asked him. "You getting that promotion you were hoping for?"

Younger than Garrett by nearly four years, Nicky leaned back and raked his fingers through his dark blond hair. "They offered me a promotion all right."

"And...?" Garrett prompted.

Nicky's gaze bounced around the table before he admitted, "It's in New York City."

Stunned silence followed his announcement. Chaos erupted a moment later.

"Well, you turned them down, right?" Garrett demanded.

"Yeah," Danny chimed in. "I mean, you aren't seriously considering moving all the way to New York, are you?"

"Is New York City as far away as China?" Ethan's eyes were as wide as dinner plates.

His uncle's smile seemed a little sad. "No, big guy, China is much farther away than New York City."

Sara placed her hand on Uncle Luke's shoulder for support and stated, "You're going to accept the job, aren't you?"

"Look, it's more than three times the money I'm making now," he said, his tone defensive. "How can I turn that down?"

She blinked rapidly to hold back the tears welling up in her eyes.

Uncle Luke set his fork down next to his half-eaten pie.

Garrett took a sip of his coffee and set the cup down with a decisive thud. "You are *not* moving to New York City, and that's final."

Nicky rubbed his temples, as if sadly resigned. "Don't be ridiculous. I'm twenty-eight years old. If I want to move to New York, I will."

"But, Uncle Nicky, I-I don't want you to move away."

"Ethan," Sara began with a reassuring smile, "why don't you go downstairs and watch TV." Her baby was already upset enough, and the grim faces around the table weren't helping matters any. When he hesitated, she added, "Go on. I'll be down in a minute. We can watch a movie."

"But, Mom, I want—"

"Ethan, listen to your mother." Garrett rarely spoke to his nephew in such an authoritative tone, and her son raced down the stairs without further complaint.

Uncle Luke picked up the carafe and topped off his coffee. His eyes seemed to have grown weary as he thoughtfully stroked his neatly trimmed salt-and-pepper beard. "Garrett, Nicholas is a grown man. You can't just order him around like you did when you were kids."

"I'm not trying to be the bossy older brother here. It's just...shit, I can only deal with one crisis per day. And New York City, Nick? Can't a computer programmer make a decent wage right here in Wisconsin?"

Sara certainly hadn't prepared for this particular reality—one of them leaving the proverbial nest. She and her brothers had lived in this house their entire lives, and the thought of Nicky moving so far from home was more than she could handle at the moment.

"Crisis? What crisis?" Danny demanded.

Garrett took another sip of his coffee before meeting her gaze across the table, as if to offer support.

"Mike Andrews' father died yesterday," Sara said, fighting to keep her face expressionless. "Mike's on his way home as we speak."

Their uncle reached over and grasped her hand, his gaze full of concern.

"No shit." Danny looked back and forth between her and Garrett. "You don't think he'd show up here, do you?"

Little brother echoed the question that had been running through her mind all day, keeping her stomach tied in such knots she'd barely been able to eat supper. *Would* Mike have the nerve to show his face here? The thought frightened her as much as it excited her, and she hated herself for such weakness.

"I think the threat of getting the shit kicked out of him will probably keep him away," Garrett said. "But we can't take any chances. Especially for Ethan's sake."

Sara decided it was time she spoke up. "Look, I appreciate all your concern. But I'm a grown woman and more than capable of taking care of myself. *And* my son."

All four men exchanged glances.

Sara rolled her eyes. She really hated when they did that—made her feel like a little girl who needed protecting. She knew they all loved her dearly and only wanted to protect her and Ethan, but sometimes they could be a bit overbearing.

Like right now.

"Sara, we know you can take care of yourself." Garrett's tone was annoyingly placating. "But what would you do if Mike showed up on our doorstep and got a good look at Ethan? Hell, even a blind man could see the resemblance."

Her pulse picked up speed. She didn't even want to *think* about what could happen if Mike and Ethan came face to face. "You don't need to worry. I'll be careful."

With a heavy sigh, Garrett rose to his feet. "Listen, I've got to go meet up with Hamilton and Dreyer. We'll talk later." He swiped his keys off the counter and headed for the front door.

Sara watched him leave with a bad feeling in her gut. She should've tried to talk him into staying home tonight. With that notorious temper of his, Garrett had never been able to hide from trouble. Somehow, someway, it always found him.

Two

Mike Andrews felt sick to his damn stomach. As he stood in the doorway of his childhood home, memories assaulted him like a swarm of bees, stinging him with their painful reminders.

The old man's dead.

He stepped into the living room and pushed the front door shut behind him. His nostrils flared in disgust. The house smelled the same as it always had. Well, at least since his mother had passed away nearly seventeen years ago, leaving Mike and his father to fend for themselves. The stench of stale beer mingled with the faint smell of cooked onions and the musty odor emanating from the basement.

His gaze settled on the old La-Z-Boy recliner that sat directly across from the twenty-five-inch console television his parents had received as a wedding present. The chair, originally a nice smoke blue, was now a dullish-gray, the upholstery worn and tattered, the seat cushion permanently stained with piss. The old man had passed out drunk in that chair almost every night since the day it was delivered to the house.

And according to the officer Mike had spoken to last night, he'd died in that chair. Suffered a massive heart attack while watching TV and sucking down a beer.

A truly fitting end for the old bastard. He deserved nothing better than to have died alone.

Bitterness welled up like bile in Mike's throat.

The shelves that held his mother's once prized possessions—porcelain figurines, framed photos of family and friends, the scented candles she'd loved so much—looked like they hadn't been dusted in—well, eight years. He'd box those things up and take them home with him once the house sold.

He moved through the living room into the kitchen, and the smell was even worse in there. *Damn.* What he wouldn't do for a can of air freshener. Hard to believe this room had been his sanctuary as a young boy. His mother had spent most of her time here, cooking and baking.

The only two things that hadn't pissed his father off.

Mike pulled a chair back from the table, flipped it around and straddled it. His eyes drifted around the room and came to rest on the cookie jar he'd bought for his mother when he was ten years old, a huge ceramic strawberry that had usually been filled with chocolate chip cookies. His favorite. Though, every once in a while she'd make peanut butter, and he'd loved those almost as much.

He folded his arms atop the back of the chair and rested his chin on them. His chest ached in a way he hadn't felt in years.

His mother had died of breast cancer two weeks before his thirteenth birthday. It had happened so fast that most people hadn't even known she was sick by the time she died. His father had known, though, and hadn't much cared. Mike didn't have a single memory of the old bastard helping her in any way. It hadn't mattered how sick she was, dinner had to be on the table by six o'clock or he'd bitch and gripe all night. If she was lucky. If not, he'd backhand her, yank her around by the hair. Sometimes, he'd shove her so hard she'd fall to her knees.

Mike squeezed his eyes shut, as if he could somehow block out the memories. But he knew he couldn't.

He'd been trying for years and had never been successful.

Mike rose to his feet, flipped the chair back around and moved to stand next to the sink. Reclining back against the counter, he crossed his feet at the ankles and rubbed his eyes.

Damn, he hadn't been this tired in a long time. He'd gotten precious little sleep the night before, and since he'd already tossed his bags in the truck, he'd taken off straight from the station. The only stop he'd made was for a couple of burgers to eat on the way. Maneuvering through rush hour traffic while choking down a burger had been quite a trick, but once he'd gotten past Milwaukee, traffic had thinned out, so he'd turned on the radio and tried to relax. The drive from Chicago had seemed a whole lot longer than he remembered.

Probably because he'd been so reluctant to make the trip.

After retrieving his bags from the truck, he made his way down the hall to his old bedroom. He paused on the threshold, wondering if his father had cleared out his room after he'd left. No, he decided, the old man had been much too lazy to have bothered. Mike turned the knob and opened the door.

And felt like he'd been punched in the gut. The room looked as if it hadn't been touched at all. Rock posters covered the wall to his left, bubbled and faded. His little league trophies still sat on the shelf above his dresser, each sporting half an inch of dust. Some of his old clothes were strewn across the room, most of them from the last time he'd been here and packed up his belongings in a rage.

Hell, there's even a glass still sitting on the nightstand.

He set his bags on the floor, walked over to the bed and stripped off the comforter and sheets in one quick pull. He grabbed the pillow cases as well and gathered all the bedding in his arms. Praying the old man had bought some detergent in the last few years, he strode down the hall to the laundry room. To his surprise, an unopened bottle sat on the shelf above the sink. He stuffed everything inside the washing machine, pressed the start button and poured a stream of detergent in a circle over the bedding. A quick search turned up no fabric softener, but hey, beggars couldn't be choosers. He shut the lid and headed back to his room.

He sat down on the edge of the mattress, and his eyes settled on the framed picture sitting on his dresser.

Sara.

So damn beautiful it hurt just to look at her. She'd turned sixteen shortly before that picture had been taken, and he remembered the day like it was yesterday.

Some of their friends had talked them into taking a ride down to Six Flags Great America, just over the border into Illinois. They'd had a blast, too, riding every roller coaster in the park, plus several water rides, and the double-decker merry-go-round. Her idea, not his, he remembered with a reluctant grin.

He leaned forward and snatched the photo off the dresser. Swiping the dust away with his thumb, he stared hard at the face that had haunted his dreams for the past eight years. What would she look like now? The vindictive part of him hoped the years hadn't been kind, although somehow he knew that wouldn't be the case.

She'd been a tiny slip of a thing, standing five-feet-two, a hundred and five pounds, if that. Her long, thick hair, the color of a shiny penny—not red, but a rich copper—had glowed like fire under the sun. Her eyes, Sara's best feature in his opinion, were chocolate brown and huge, turning up slightly at the corners. He remembered the first time he'd met her, how all he could do was stare into those beautiful eyes.

Mike tossed her picture back on the dresser and knelt down to pick up some of his old clothes off the floor. His thoughts drifted to Sara's brother, Nicky. He'd missed his old friend and had been tempted to call him many times over the years. But there was no way in hell Nicky would've sided with anyone—even him—over his own family.

And exactly why he'd been so drawn to the Jamisons in the first place. They were a close-knit bunch who loved one another fiercely. Eventually, Mike had started to consider himself one of the family, imagining he and Sara would marry one day, have kids of their own.

Cursing, he carried his old clothes into the laundry room and tossed them into the cracked, plastic yellow basket in the corner. The load of bedding hadn't reached the rinse cycle yet, so he decided to head out for something to eat. Starving, Mike knew he'd never get anything accomplished tonight if he didn't put some food in his stomach.

He flipped on the radio as he backed out of the driveway. Searching through the stations, he wracked his brain to remember which one he used to listen to. When an old Aerosmith tune blasted through his speakers, he cranked it up and smiled with genuine pleasure.

Mike had driven for maybe ten minutes before a familiar neon sign appeared up ahead on the right. His smile widened. *Krupp's*, he remembered, served up the best fried perch dinner in town. He parked his truck in the closest space he could find, noting the lot was pretty well packed.

As soon as he pulled open the door, the distinctive twang of country music spilled out, as did the tantalizing aroma of deep-fried chicken and fish. Making his way through the crowd, Mike sent up a silent prayer of thanks when he spotted an empty booth against the back wall.

He slid in and had just reached for the old, stained menu when one of the waitresses approached, her smile flirtatious. He read the name tag pinned to the baby doll T-shirt she wore, which bore the tavern's name.

"Hey, Mandy. Could I trouble you for a bottle of Bud and a fried perch basket?"

She tucked a stray wisp of shoulder-length, auburn hair behind her ear. "You want fries or onion rings with the basket?"

"Fries. And bring me some ketchup with that, if you don't mind."

"I don't mind at all," she assured him before strolling off with his order.

Mike's lips puckered into a silent whistle of masculine appreciation as he watched her swish away in one of the tightest pairs of jeans he'd ever seen. He leaned back in the booth, his free arm draped comfortably over the top of the seat. A minute later, an ice-cold bottle of beer was placed on the table in front of him.

"It'll just be a few minutes on the food." She flashed him what he assumed to be an 'I'm interested' smile before sauntering off to take care of some other customers.

Pretty though she was, Mike just wasn't interested. Her hair wasn't quite the right color, and her eyes were a few shades too light.

Scowling at the direction of his thoughts, he gulped down a large swallow of beer.

His gaze traveled around the room. It had been nearly a decade since he'd been here, and even then just for some carry-out food, but he was pretty sure the place hadn't changed much. Fairly large, it boasted roughly twenty tables and just as many booths. The bar was a good thirty stools long, and the walls were covered with the expected collection of beer signs, lighted mirrors and other beer paraphernalia. The jukebox stood against the far right wall between a couple of dartboards, and an old, unlit pinball machine sat in the corner next to the Men's room.

His gaze skimmed over the pool tables. Four were set up in a large square, and all were occupied.

Mike tilted the bottle to his lips and drained about a third of it in one long pull. His stomach rumbled when he spotted the waitress heading his way with a steaming basket and bottle of ketchup.

"Nice and hot. Enjoy," she said. "And just give me a holler when you're ready for another beer."

"I'll do that, thanks."

Mmmm, he hadn't had a good perch dinner in years. He picked up one of the batter-fried fillets and dunked it into the small bowl of tartar sauce.

"Hey, Mandy. We're ready for another round here."

Mike's hand stopped halfway to his mouth. Dammit, he knew that voice. Eight years had passed since he'd heard it, but there was no mistaking that deep baritone. He turned his head, and his gaze landed on the last person he'd have ever wanted to run into here in Green Bay.

Garrett Jamison.

"Ah, shit."

As luck would have it, Sara's oldest brother spotted Mike at almost the exact same moment. The guy muttered something he couldn't hear, then tossed his cue stick down on the pool table and strode toward him.

Great. Just what he needed—a confrontation with this hot-headed asshole.

Garrett came to a halt not two feet in front of Mike's booth. "What the hell are you doing here, Andrews? You're on the wrong side of town."

He took a careless swig of his beer. "Good to see you, too, Jamison."

One of Garrett's buddies reached his side. Mike couldn't help but notice the guy bore a striking resemblance to Al Pacino—only taller.

The Pacino look-alike slapped a hand on Jamison's shoulder. "Hey, man, I don't know what this is about, but you need to calm the hell down."

Sara's brother shrugged off his friend's hand, those dark eyes never leaving Mike's face.

Ignoring them both, he bit into the tartar sauce-coated piece of fish.

Quick as a whip, Garrett swiped the basket onto the floor.

A muscle in Mike's jaw started to tic. He tossed the half-eaten piece of fish down on the table and rose to his feet.

Most of the tavern's patrons had gone silent, as had the jukebox, which someone must have unplugged. All he could hear were a few hushed whispers.

Another guy appeared at Jamison's side. "What the

hell's going on?"

"Your friend here can't hold his liquor any better than he could a decade ago," Mike said. "Maybe you boys should—"

"You prick!" Garrett roared and took a swing at him.

He ducked out of the way, causing the drunken idiot to stumble. Jamison righted himself almost immediately and swung again. Mike easily dodged the second punch as well before tackling the guy onto the table. The beer bottle went flying and crashed against the wall.

If this asshole wanted a fight, Mike was happy to oblige. He leaned back and swung, aiming for his jaw. But Garrett brought his shoulder up, and Mike's fist cracked the table instead. Cursing, he shook his stinging knuckles, and a surprisingly hard shove sent him stumbling back. Jamison pounced, pinning him against the pool table, the smell of beer hitting him so strong he wrinkled his nose in disgust.

The crowd of people moved with them, and Garrett's buddies finally attempted to break up the fight. They got knocked on their asses for their trouble, though, as Mike sent the arrogant prick flying with a thrust of his legs, taking both of them with him.

Jamison's breath came out in ragged pants as he climbed to his feet.

Mike jumped off the pool table, keeping his eyes centered on his opponent. He was tired, hungry, and growing more pissed off by the minute. All he'd wanted was a beer and a little supper before heading back to the house, but hell no. He had to run into Sara and Nicky's obnoxious oldest brother. Who, as it turned out, was one hell of a grudge holder. And the most infuriating thing of all? *Mike* was the one who'd been wronged!

"Look, man. This is stupid," he insisted. "It's been eight years. Let it go."

"Let it go? As if I could ever forget what you did, you lowlife sonofabitch!" Face mottled red with rage and alcohol, Garrett's hands fisted, and he took a threatening step forward.

His buddies rushed up behind him and each grabbed an arm.

What I did? What the hell is he talking about?

"Garrett, the owner wants you both to leave. If we have to take you out in cuffs, we will," the Pacino look-alike warned.

Jamison swallowed hard and nodded. His buddies eyed him with suspicion, but slowly released him. It was a mistake. Without warning, the asshole swung, hitting Mike square in the jaw and sending him crashing into one of the tables, spilling food and drinks all over the damn place.

He gingerly fingered his jaw as he climbed slowly to his feet. Ketchup-coated fries stuck to his shirt, and he brushed them off with angry swipes.

Garrett's buddies tackled him to the floor, and even managed to pull his arms behind his back to cuff him. But then, he didn't seem to put up much resistance. He'd gotten in one good shot, and Mike figured if the satisfied gleam in his eye was any indication, it had been enough.

Mike gave him a cocky salute as they hauled the big boy to his feet. "It's been a pleasure, Jamison. Hope you get a good night's sleep on your cot."

The Pacino look-alike pushed Garrett down onto a chair before crooking a finger at Mike. He had another set of cuffs in his hand. Jamison let out a snort of laughter.

With a weary sigh, Mike held out his wrists.

"This is bullshit, you know. He started it."

"I finished it, too," Garrett boasted, rising to his feet.

"You sucker-punched m—" Mike's eyes were drawn to the badge hanging from Garrett's belt. "Christ, you're a cop?"

For some reason, that struck him as funny. Maybe because he was hungry, sore and tired as hell, but suddenly, he couldn't stop laughing.

THREE

Sara had just nodded off when the phone rang. She reached across the bed with a groan and snatched it up on the second ring. "Hello?"

"Sara? It's Hank Hamilton. Sorry to call so late but—"

"Hank? Wha—? Oh my God, it's Garrett, isn't it?" Alarmed, she sat straight up. "I just knew something bad was going to happen. He—"

"Sara, calm down. Garrett's fine, I promise. He just got into a little scuffle tonight at *Krupp's*."

She leaned back against the headboard and closed her eyes. Her shoulders slumped in relief. "I was afraid something like this might happen. So, where is he? And why didn't he call me himself?"

"Unfortunately, we had to arrest 'im."

"*What?* But Hank, you just said it was only a little scuffle."

"Actually, it was a little more than that. When Garrett started sucking down beers faster than usual, Dreyer and I knew something was wrong. But he told us it was nothing and to mind our own business. You know how he gets."

She sighed. "Yeah, I know."

"Anyway, I left to go take a—er, use the washroom—and the next thing I know some guy comes running in jabbering about how "that big cop" was about to kick some guy's a—uh, butt."

"Hank, tell Garrett I'll be there as soon as I can. I'll wake up Nicky or Uncle Luke to come with me."

"Uh, Sara, that's just it. Garrett made me promise not to call you. Said he'd just sleep it off 'til morning and explain when he got home."

"Well, that's ridiculous. I'm not going to let him sleep in a jail cell all night."

"I agree. That's why I decided to risk my neck and call. But maybe you could send one of the boys to spring 'im? He was real adamant about you not coming down here."

Sara sat straight up again, her mind reeling. *Good lord, it couldn't be.* "Hank, would you happen to know the name of the guy he got into a fight with?"

"Yeah, got it right here. It's Andrews. Michael Andrews. Why, you know 'im?"

She closed her eyes again and took a deep, calming breath. "I know him. Was he arrested, too?"

"Yep. But don't worry. We've got 'em in separate cells."

"Thanks, Hank. I'll send someone down to get him as soon as possible."

She hung up the phone and realized her hand was shaking. Squeezing her eyes shut for a brief moment to gather herself, she then tossed the covers back and slipped out of bed. As she threw some clothes on, she tried to decide who to take with her to the police station.

Because she *was* going. She didn't give a damn what Garrett wanted. She wasn't sure why, or what she expected to happen, but she knew she had to see Mike this one last time. It would probably be the last chance she'd ever have to look him in the eye and—*and what?*

She slumped down on the edge of the bed and took a deep, shuddering breath. Maybe Garrett was right. What good would it do? What purpose would it serve for her to see him? It's not as if she could slap him across the face through the bars.

And she certainly couldn't risk him finding out about Ethan. That would be a total disaster. Because if Mike decided to fight her for custody, Ethan's safety could be in jeopardy. And no way in hell would she let that happen.

Her choice made, Sara headed into the kitchen to put on a pot of coffee. She decided Nicky would be the best choice to send to the station, so she flipped on the coffee maker and padded down to his room.

A quick rap on his door received no response, so she inched it open and whispered, "Nicky? Nicky, wake up. We have a problem."

She heard a deep, masculine groan, then movement. "Sara? What's going on?"

"I just got a call from Hank down at the station." She slipped into his room and sat on the edge of his bed. "Garrett's been arrested, and I need you to go bail him out."

"What the hell did he do?"

"He got drunk and started a fight down at *Krupp's*."

Nicky cursed and swung his legs over the side of the bed. "We have to get that idiot into an anger management class before he does something really stupid and loses his badge." He reached down and pulled on the crumpled pair of jeans he'd worn that day.

Sara stood. "I know, believe me. Sometimes I worry about him so much I can't sleep." She returned to the kitchen, and Nicky slowly plodded in a minute later rubbing his eyes.

"Ah, coffee." He stuffed his wallet in his back pocket, then sat down to pull on his boots.

She set a steaming cup in front of him. "Nicky, there's something I haven't told you yet."

"Jesus, he *did* lose his badge, didn't he?"

"No," she hurried to assure him. "Hank would've said something if that were the case." She took the seat across from him. "What I haven't told you is *who* Garrett started the fight with."

Nicky watched her expectantly. Then his eyes widened as it dawned on him. "No way. Mike?"

She nodded. "And they were both arrested, so there's a good chance you'll see him."

Her brother closed his eyes and gave his head an almost imperceptible shake before raking his fingers through his hair. He was tired, but Sara knew it was more than that. He and Mike had once been as close as brothers, and Nicky had taken it almost as hard as she had when her ex left town.

He took one last swallow of his coffee, and then rose to his feet. "Well, I'd better go bail Captain Hothead out of jail."

Garrett lay sprawled on his back, one knee up, the other leg hanging off the side of the cot. One arm flung over his face, the other hand tucked into the waistband of his jeans. Loud snores poured from his open mouth.

Mike rolled his eyes. *Goddamn figures*. He sat back on his own cot, leaning against the cold concrete wall, and exhaled a deep sigh of disgust.

Voices reached him before the heavy clip of heels on

the cement steps announced someone's arrival. He watched with bated breath, mentally preparing himself for whoever was about to step around the corner. Since nobody would be coming for him, he knew it had to be a Jamison coming to bail out the poster boy for anger management.

When Nicky strode into view, Mike's chest tightened and a wave of relief washed over him. He'd missed his old friend and regretted...well, he regretted a lot of things. But he couldn't change history, so here they were, eight years later.

Hands on hips, Nicky faced Garrett's cell. He shook his head, his faced screwed up with disgust. He glanced up, his expression sobering when he recognized Mike. Slowly, his friend turned to face him.

"Hey, Nicky. Long time, no see."

The person he used to trust most in the world dropped his arms and nodded a curt greeting. "Mike." He took a few steps toward his cell. "I'm sorry about your father."

"I'm not. He's burning in hell, exactly where he ought to be."

"Kind of harsh, don't you think?"

Leaning forward, Mike rested his elbows on his knees and linked his hands together. "Hell, you know better than anybody what an evil bastard my old man was. You were standing right there when he whipped a plumber's wrench at my head. I'd be dead or crippled if I hadn't ducked in time."

Nicky's face hardened, and Mike knew his old friend remembered that day all too well.

"He was a mean SOB, that's for sure. But he was still your father."

Mike laughed bitterly and shook his head in

astonishment. "You're a good man. It's nice to see life hasn't jaded both of us."

It seemed as if the guy wanted to say something. Instead, he gave an almost imperceptible shake of his head and turned back toward Garrett's cell. "Take care of yourself, Mike."

"Nicky?"

He stopped, but didn't turn back around. "Yeah?"

Don't ask, just let him go. "How's Sara?" *Dammit.*

"Are you nuts?" Nicky demanded as he spun around. "You have the balls to say her name after what you did?"

Taken aback, Mike could only stare at him. *After what I did?* "I'd love to know how I became the bad guy when *I'm* the one who got screwed. Even Garrett made a comment tonight that made no damn sense. She must've told you guys some whopper of a tale."

"And I suppose it was her fault you were sleeping with her best friend? No wonder Garrett tried to take your head off. I only wish he'd succeeded, you asshole."

Mike surged to his feet and crossed the cell. He clutched onto the bars. "What the hell are you talking about? Sara was the one sleeping around, not me. I saw the proof with my own eyes!"

"Saw what? Man, you're an idiot. Sara was so in love with you there's no way she could've been with anyone else. And I can prove it. Sara—"

"Nicky, shut the fuck up!"

They both whipped around as Garrett's thunderous voice echoed off the walls.

Nicky cast Mike an odd glance before walking over to his brother's cell. "Man, you look like hell."

The eldest Jamison rubbed his eyes hard with his thumb and forefinger. "Christ, I told Hank not to call. Just wait till I get my hands on him." He sat up with a drawn-out groan and added, "Please tell me Sara doesn't know."

"'Fraid so. She's the one who answered the phone."

"She knows about *him*?" Garrett jerked his head in Mike's direction.

"Yep." Nicky lowered his voice. "I think she planned to come along, too, because she got dressed and made coffee. But something changed her mind."

"Yeah," Mike chimed in, exasperated. "She knew she'd finally have to tell you boys the truth about who screwed who." With that, he dragged his tired ass back to the cot and resumed his position against the wall.

Garrett slowly climbed to his feet. "You say one more derogatory word about my sister, and you'll be joining your old man in hell."

Mike leaned his head back against the concrete wall and closed his eyes. "Don't worry, I'm through defending myself. Sara knows what she did, and so do I. Besides, it was another lifetime ago and I really don't give a damn anymore."

Watching her older brothers make their way up the driveway, Sara's anger dissipated as a great wave of relief washed over her.

She held the front door open, and her brow knit with concern when she got a good look at Garrett's face. She shut and locked the door before following them into the kitchen.

"You look like you could use a cup of coffee. Nicky, how about you?"

"Hell no. I'm crawling back in bed and sleeping 'til

noon." He kissed her on the top of the head, then disappeared down the hall without so much as a backward glance.

Garrett took a seat at the table, crossed his arms on the placemat and laid his head down. "I'll take a pass on the coffee, too. It's late, and I definitely need a few more hours sleep if I'm going to make it to Shelly's birthday party."

Sara sat down next to him and let out a frustrated sigh. "You're not going to tell me what happened, are you?"

"Not much to tell. I drank a few beers way too fast, and they hit me like a ton of bricks. You know how stupid I can get."

"Garrett, I meant about Mike. How did he just happen to show up where you and your buddies were hanging out? And why, in God's name, did you pick a fight with him? I thought the whole idea was to avoid him."

He cracked an eye open. "Ah, hell, I don't know. I saw him sitting there all smug, as if he didn't have a care in the world. Then I remembered the look on your face the day you told me you were pregnant, and I guess I lost it."

She didn't say anything for a moment, just spun the Lazy Susan around a few times as she fought an inner argument with herself. Finally, she decided she had to know. "Did he ask about me?"

Garrett lifted his head and stared at her with mild surprise. Then his gaze turned compassionate. "Honey, I don't want to hurt you."

"So he didn't even...ask?"

He blew out a deep breath and reached across the table to grasp her fingers. "Let's just say he didn't have anything nice to say and leave it at that."

She frowned, opening and closing her mouth in

surprise. Eight years ago, Mike had accused her of sleeping around when he'd been the unfaithful one, leaving her pregnant and alone. And *he* didn't have anything nice to say? She would've laughed if her heart didn't feel like it was breaking all over again. And she knew she was being ridiculous. Their relationship, if one could call it that, had ended years ago.

When, for the love of God, would she finally be able to exorcise the man from her head?

She gave her big brother's hand a squeeze before rising to her feet. "Well, I think I'll crawl back into bed myself. If I'm lucky, Ethan won't wake me up for another four hours. 'Night, Garrett."

"You're okay, right?" He held onto her fingers a second longer.

She met his gaze with a reassuring smile. "Don't worry, I'll live. And if I never lay eyes on Mike Andrews again, it'll be too soon for me."

Four

"Sara, thank God!" Amanda Burnett, one of her part-time employees, rushed out from behind the bakery counter to meet her. "I tried everything I could think of to fix it, but I was afraid I'd make it worse."

With a reassuring smile, Sara walked past her directly to the ornery coffee machine in question. She silently scolded herself for not replacing the thing at the first sign of trouble.

"You did exactly the right thing by calling me." Sara set her purse beneath the counter and turned to face the girl. "I meant to leave a note for you, but...I got distracted."

Amanda's shoulders slumped, her relief evident. "I thought I broke it."

"No. It's been acting up for a while. I'll replace it next week. Why don't you go clean the windows and door outside while I deal with this disagreeable piece of crap."

With a grateful nod, the perky brunette grabbed the blue bottle of cleaner, a roll of paper towels, and headed out the door.

Sara blew out a frustrated breath as she faced the troublesome machine. "Couldn't have waited 'til Monday, could you? Rotten appliance."

Ten minutes later, she smiled with triumphant satisfaction as the sweet aroma of vanilla coffee filled the bakery. First thing Monday morning, she'd call the dealer and ask when they could deliver a new machine.

The bell above the door chimed. "See, Amanda. You just have to show this devil who's bos..." The words died on her lips.

Legs braced apart, a disdainful scowl curling his lip, Mike stood just inside the door. Her heart lurched and her breath caught.

This isn't happening, this isn't happening, this isn't happening—

"You sound just like that arrogant brother of yours."

Deep breath, compose yourself. "I'll take that as a compliment." She narrowed her eyes. "Now get the hell out."

"You need to work on your people skills, lady." He strode forward and stopped in front of the display case, looking around in obvious astonishment. "Well, I'll be dipped. When I saw the *Sara's Bakery* sign, I said to myself, no friggin' way. But morbid curiosity got the better of me. So a bakery, huh? Not much of a surprise, really—"

"What do you want, Mike?"

He turned toward her and she finally got a good look at the side of his face. *My God, had Garrett done that?* She couldn't help feeling a measure of satisfaction. Oh, who was she kidding? She hoped it hurt like hell.

He must have realized where her gaze rested because he reached up and fingered his jaw. "Don't get too excited, he sucker-punched me." He leaned over and tapped the glass above her jumbo chocolate muffins. "I'll take one of those and a large coffee. Regular, not that flavored crap."

With an angry huff, she stalked over to pour him a cup. Why did he have to look so damn good? Was it too much to ask for a receding hairline and a donut around the middle?

He wore his thick, blue-black hair shorter than he used to, which only made the resemblance between him and Ethan more pronounced. He'd put on a good twenty-five to thirty pounds of solid muscle as the black T-shirt stretched tautly over his chest could attest to. And those eyes—cobalt and incredible—had continued to haunt her over the years.

Ethan's were the exact same color.

Closing her own eyes for a brief moment, she prayed for strength. She turned around and set his coffee on the counter. She felt like she should say something about his father. "Sorry to hear about your dad."

"Don't be, I'm not. I hope the bastard suffered."

Her gaze flew to his. "My God, you're cold." She shook her head, surprised by his callous words despite...everything.

"My old man deserved a lot worse than what he got, and you know it. Or maybe you think I deserved what *I* got...?"

She gasped. "I can't believe you'd even say that to me." No child should have to go through what Mike had. Parents are supposed to love and protect their children, not abuse them. Unfortunately, it seemed Mike had inherited his father's cruel streak. A chill ran up her spine at the thought of him putting his hands on Ethan in such a way. She'd die before allowing that to happen.

Using a sheet of waxed paper, she snatched a muffin off the tray and stuffed it into a bag. "It's on the house."

She dropped the bag next to his coffee. "*Now*, get the hell out."

Mike flipped a folded five-dollar-bill on the counter. "Something tells me you can't afford to give out freebies. Not with the way you treat your customers."

That got her hackles up. *Jackass*. She flicked the bill off the counter using her thumb and middle finger.

His jaw worked back and forth. He didn't bother to pick up the money.

"Look, I'm on my way out," she finally said. "So if there's a reason for this visit other than to ruin my weekend, get the hell to it."

He glared at her for what seemed like forever. "You sure fed your brothers a line of bullshit, didn't you?"

"What in the world are you talking—" Before she could finish, the bell above the door chimed and Amanda walked in, humming softly.

Mike shot an impatient glance over his shoulder.

"You did a beautiful job, Amanda. Thank you."

The young woman walked behind the counter and stuck the bottle of cleaner and paper towels back under the register. When she straightened, she gestured toward the coffee machine. "Fixed it?"

Sara nodded. "If it gives you any trouble, though, just turn it off and clean it up."

"I will. So how come Ethan didn't come with you?"

Sara's breath caught. The inquisitive teenager couldn't have known the inner turmoil she'd just caused. She flicked her gaze Mike's way before replying, "He was still in bed when I left."

"Ah. Well, I still need to package those pies. Thanks again, Sara." Amanda gave Mike a curious once-over before disappearing through the swinging door.

"Who's Ethan?" he asked as soon as the door swung shut.

Sara met his gaze dead on. "He's the love of my life."

Mike's eyes hardened. "Hope you and this idiot are happy together." He snatched up his bag and cup and strode out the door.

Sara's knees buckled the moment the door closed behind him. She slapped her palms on the counter for support and let out a deep, calming breath. After all these years with no phone call, no letter, no *nothing*, he decided to just stroll into her shop and act as if—as if a whole eight years hadn't gone by since he'd slunk out of her life? *Since he'd betrayed me with that slut Rachel Montgomery?* Since he'd accused her of sleeping with Rachel's brother, Carl, then beaten Carl to within an inch of his life?

"You sure fed your brothers a line of bullshit, didn't you?"

What could he have possibly meant by that? Everything she'd told her brothers was the gospel truth, and he knew it.

Forget it. Forget him.

She let out a disgusted sigh.

Easier said than done.

Mike stalked into the kitchen and pitched his keys and the bag on the table. Why the hell couldn't he have just kept on driving when he'd spotted that *Sara's Bakery* sign on Velp Avenue? He took a sip of his coffee, and then scowled at the cup. Of course, she had to make a great friggin' cup of coffee, too. Why couldn't it have tasted like tar so he wouldn't have a bullshit reason to stop in again?

Like tomorrow. *Damn her.*

He wished he could reverse time and walk through the door of her bakery again. So he could do what he should've done in the first place—tell her to go straight to hell.

Or take her straight to bed. Mike wasn't sure which he'd rather do.

Okay, so he wasn't completely over her, even after all these years. He could admit that to himself—it wasn't as if he'd ever give her the satisfaction of knowing it.

But damn, he'd really thought if he came face-to-face with her again, whatever mysterious reason there was for this lingering attraction would disappear as soon as he laid eyes on her.

He'd never been more wrong.

She was as beautiful as she'd been at eighteen. And she certainly had more fire. Sara had been a bit on the shy side as a teenager, but she'd obviously gotten over that. Standing there, shooting flames at him from those gorgeous brown eyes, she'd been breathtaking.

He couldn't remember the last time he'd been that turned on.

Until she'd brought up his father.

Mike dropped onto the chair, set his coffee down and massaged his temples with both hands. Damn, why'd he come back here? He should've told them to pitch the old bastard in the city dump and donated the house to charity.

But then he'd come face-to-face with Sara, and knew exactly why he'd been drawn back. Closure. He needed it like a death row inmate needs absolution. He'd been living in limbo for eight years, and the thought of finally having that closure had been too great a temptation to resist.

"He's the love of my life."

With a frustrated sigh, Mike shook off the unwanted thought, reached for the bag, and pulled out the humongous chocolate muffin. Since it'd now been close to twenty-four hours since he'd eaten anything substantial, he polished it off in four bites. And damn if it wasn't as good as the coffee, loaded with chunks of white and milk chocolate. He wished he'd bought two.

You can always go back for another.

He crushed the bag and pitched it toward the garbage can.

It took some effort, but he managed to push thoughts of Sara aside—only to have memories of the night before flood his mind. He closed his eyes, wishing he could forget last night had ever happened; only he had the throbbing jaw to prove it had. What a cosmic joke that he should end up at the same place, same time, as Garrett Jamison, the last person on earth he'd have ever wanted to run into.

"As if I could ever forget what you did!"

"And I suppose it was her fault you were sleeping with her best friend?"

It seemed as if Sara had gone to a lot of trouble to convince her brothers she'd been totally devastated over their breakup. But why? Why had it been so important to her that everyone believe the worst in him? Especially when *she'd* been the one screwing around? Had she hated him so much that breaking his heart and making a fool of him hadn't been enough? She'd had to sic her brothers on him as well?

It just didn't make any damn sense. He'd never treated her badly—he'd never hurt her in any way. Plain and simple, he'd adored her. They'd been so absurdly happy that everyone used to comment on what a perfect couple they were.

The rational part of his brain said it was pointless to spend even another second thinking about Sara, Nicky, or the rest of them. But his cop's instincts were driving him hard to figure out exactly what the hell he was missing. It'd been so long he shouldn't even care anymore. But he did.

Lord help him, he still cared.

Despite the damn video.

He reached up to knead the back of his neck. When Rachel had showed him the footage—Sara in bed with Rachel's older brother, Carl—Mike had been devastated. Like a knife plunging through his young heart, the pain had been unimaginable, worse than anything he'd ever experienced before, including the many lumps and bruises his old man had doled out over the years.

So he ran.

Funny thing is, he would have run long before then if not for Sara. And Nicky. They'd made him feel like part of their family, and Mike had soaked up that feeling like a sponge.

Maybe that's why Sara's betrayal had hit him so hard.

He tapped his knuckles against the tabletop as he tried to recall those few seconds of video. It'd been shot from the doorway of Carl's bedroom. They'd both been under the covers, Carl on top, Sara's flaming hair spread out across the pillow.

Carl moving over her. Humping her.

"As if I could ever forget what you did!"

"And I suppose it was her fault you were sleeping with her best friend?"

A bad feeling mushroomed in his gut. Something was staring him right in the face, but he'd be damned if he knew what it was.

Pinching the bridge of his nose, he tried again to remember something—anything—he might have been too young and emotional to catch at the time. As a trained detective, he now knew that just one detail, no matter how small, could open up a world of possibilities.

He recalled he'd only been able to see Sara's head and hair because the covers had been pulled up to their necks, and Carl had been moving in a rhythm that seemed...hell, he wasn't sure. Like he'd been doing the *worm* instead of the jerky, unsure movements of a teenager having sex.

Almost as if he thought he was starring in a porno flick or something.

The hand holding the coffee cup paused halfway to his mouth. *No.* No fucking way had his life been ripped apart by a *staged* video.

He set the cup down with more force than necessary, sloshing coffee onto the table. Rachel had started flirting with him from the moment they'd met, though Sara insisted her friend was like that with everyone. And Carl's interest in Sara had been obvious the way he'd constantly hovered around them. Mike hadn't been too concerned at the time, figuring the guy's crush would eventually fizzle out. But...

Could those two spoiled, entitled, rich brats have set that whole scenario up? But how? They would've had to...*Jesus*. They would have had to drug Sara to pull off something like that. The thought sent a shockwave of fury through him. It seemed so inconceivable he almost dismissed the idea as crazy.

And he was arrogant enough to want to believe that no

way could someone have gotten one over on him like that. But he'd only been nineteen at the time, and to say his heart had overruled his head back then would've been the understatement of the century.

He pushed back from the table and shot to his feet. Pacing the house like a caged lion, he became angrier by the second. Because the more he thought about it, the more it made sense. Sara had never shown even the slightest interest in Carl. Hell, most of the time, she'd just seemed uncomfortable around him, although, after seeing the footage he'd assumed it had been an act—or a guilty conscience.

"*Sonofabitch!*" He slammed his fist through the wooden louvered doors that housed the furnace and water heater. Oblivious to the gashes across his knuckles, he stalked down the hallway to his old bedroom.

He swiped Sara's picture off the dresser, clutched it in both hands and slumped down on the edge of the bed. He stared at it, hard, his mouth drawn with a combination of rage and longing, anguish and regret.

Mostly regret.

He'd spent the past eight years believing the worst in her. Now, he couldn't think of a single reason for having doubted her, regardless of that damned video.

Or was he merely grasping at straws because, after seeing her again, he wanted it to be true?

Head throbbing, he stood and set the picture back down on the dresser. It wasn't until he flexed his right hand that he realized it stung like hell.

He had busted up knuckles, a swollen jaw, and no idea what to believe anymore. Had Sara betrayed him, or had they been set up?

One thing was for certain, he wasn't leaving town until

he uncovered the truth. Something he should have done eight years ago.

But first, he had to face his father one last time.

Five

"You're a doll, Sara. I really appreciate this," Nancy said as she stretched the neck of a particularly uncooperative balloon. "I thought for sure I'd have the decorations hung before you got here. I swear, next time I throw a party, I'm having it catered."

"I offered to make a few dishes for you," Sara reminded her.

"I know, but you have your hands full as it is." Nancy pointed to her husband, Dwayne, who was busy unloading a huge keg. "Besides, we'll have plenty of beer."

Sara laughed softly and shook her head. As if beer was the answer to everything. Her smile faded as her thoughts turned to Garrett, and she wondered whether or not he'd be drinking again today. God, she hoped not.

"Man, I can barely blow these suckers up," Nancy complained, as she stuck the balloon back in her mouth and blew hard.

Her friend's face turned red and her cheeks puffed out like a chipmunk. Grinning, Sara stuck another in her mouth and blew it up with no problem at all.

"You're hired!" Dwayne called out, doing his Groucho Marx cigar-tapping imitation.

Nancy rolled her eyes, and they both started laughing.

Once the yard, deck, and outside of the house were completely covered in streamers and balloons of every color imaginable, they carried out the non-perishable food items while Dwayne filled three large coolers with ice, bottled water and every flavor of soda imaginable. Sara would help Nancy bring out the rest of the food once the majority of their guests arrived, setting it up buffet-style on the tables lined up along the back of the house.

Nancy kept her busy for hours, and she couldn't have been happier. It left her absolutely no time to think about a certain blue-eyed jackass.

Well, *hell*. Almost.

The first of the guests arrived at five-to-eleven. Sara strolled around, chatting with one person after another, checking every fifteen minutes or so on the children to make sure everybody was getting along. When she noticed her friend carrying the food out, she made her way into the house to give her a hand.

Nancy flashed her a grateful smile. "I wasn't about to ask you for more help. You've gone above and beyond as it is."

Sara made an 'oh, pooh' gesture with her hand before picking up a bowl of pasta salad. "You'd do the same for me."

Ten minutes later, the proud momma waved her arm over her head and raised her voice to announce, "Time to eat, everybody!" She grabbed Sara's arm and grinned. "Come on. Let's get out of the way before Dwayne's family mows us down."

Sara wasn't all that hungry, but once traffic at the buffet tables died down, she decided to fix herself a small plate. She smiled when she spotted Danny and her uncle heading in the same direction.

"I was starting to wonder if you two would ever show up."

Her younger brother handed them each a foam plate. "You know me. Last minute shopper. Uncle Luke came along and helped me pick out Shelly's gift."

They made their way down the long tables with both men salivating as they filled their plates to overflowing. Sara shook her head. It never ceased to amaze her just how much food these guys could eat. She laughed, however, when Danny leaned over to smell a spoonful of what she knew to be tuna dip, wrinkled his nose, and dropped the spoon back into the bowl.

She led them over to an umbrella-covered table near the fence.

"Hell, I forgot to grab a beer," Danny said. "Uncle Luke, you want one?" He started to rise.

Sara waved him back down. "I'll get them. I was just about to go grab myself a soda anyway."

Halfway back, she saw that Nicky had arrived. He sat in her seat, picking at her food. She set the drinks down and playfully rolled her eyes. "I guess I'll go fix myself another plate."

"Hey, sorry I'm late. There was an emergency at the office with one of the programs I'm working on." He stood. "I'll go say hello to Nancy and Dwayne, and then fix my own plate." He patted her on the arm as he strode away.

She chatted with Uncle Luke and Danny until Nicky returned, a plate in one hand and a bottle of water in the other. The four of them ate and talked until, finally, Ethan ran up to the table.

He grabbed Sara's soda and slurped off it before announcing, "Mom, I want a trampoline for my birthday."

She raised a brow and reached out to rub a smudge of dirt from his cheek. "We'll see. In the meantime, why don't you sit down and have something to eat with us? I'll go get you a hotdog."

"Okay." He hopped up on her chair.

Nancy had just started to put the food away when Sara reached the buffet tables. "I'm just going to fix Ethan a hotdog, then I'll come back and give you a hand."

"You most certainly will not. You've done more than enough already. Besides, my sister-in-law is going to help me as soon as she's done eating."

"You sure?" Sara squeezed little dots of ketchup down the hotdog, just the way Ethan liked. "You know I don't mind."

"I'm sure. You go sit down and relax. Don't think I didn't see you yawning your head off earlier," Nancy added with a sidelong glance.

"You got me. I am a little tired," Sara admitted. "I'll definitely be crawling into bed early tonight."

"Good. Oh, and we'll be opening presents in about half an hour. Shelly's climbing the walls with excitement."

Sara glanced over to where a literal mountain of brightly colored gifts were piled on yet another table. "Can you blame her? I've never seen so many presents."

"Tell me about it. This is the biggest birthday party we've ever thrown for her."

Sara had to suppress a smile. At this rate, Shelly's sweet sixteen would have to be held at Lambeau Field.

Nancy picked up the untouched bowl of tuna dip and grimaced. "Not one of my better ideas, huh?" With a shrug, she headed for the house.

Sara returned to the table and set the plate down in front of Ethan. "Eat, sweetheart." She looked over at the men. "Shelly'll be opening her gifts soon, and Garrett isn't here yet. Am I the only one who's concerned about that?"

"He'll be here, don't worry," Danny assured her.

"Hey, look Mom, there he is!" Ethan shouted, pointing toward the patio doors.

Sara spun around in relief. He was talking to Dwayne, and from the looks of it, turning down the offer of a beer. Another weight lifted off her shoulders. She wouldn't have to worry about him going off half-cocked when she told him about Mike showing up at the bakery.

Garrett knelt down and gently tugged one of Shelly's pigtails before producing a pink and purple wrapped package from behind his back. The little sweetie squealed with delight and ran off to place it with the others. Her brother stood back up and scanned the crowd—an easy feat from his lofty height.

She began waving at the same time Ethan jumped off the chair and made a beeline for his favorite uncle. Garrett waved back, then bent down to scoop his nephew up in his arms. Sara knew her son loved to be held up high like that, where he could look down and declare, "Hey, I'm taller than you," to everyone who walked by.

"I was starting to worry," she said, when they reached the table. And for the first time, Sara realized Garrett wasn't alone. Standing beside him was a man she'd never met before.

And with a face like that, she damn sure would've remembered.

Grinning broadly, big brother winked at her.

She nibbled suspiciously on her bottom lip. *Garrett playing matchmaker?*

"Jason, I'd like you to meet my family," he said. "Uncle Luke, my brothers, Danny and Nicky, my sister,

Sara. And this guy here"—he ruffled Ethan's hair—"my nephew, Ethan. Sara's boy. Everybody, this is Officer Jason Thomas."

Officer Thomas nodded and shook hands with the men, even Ethan, much to his delight. But when he took her hand, he raised it to his lips for a gentle kiss. "Sara."

Good lord, the man was gorgeous. She glanced over at Garrett, who looked pleased as punch by her reaction.

Danny took a swallow of his beer and asked, "So, you new to Green Bay?"

"Yep. Relocated here about a month ago from St. Louis."

When Jason crossed his arms over his chest, Sara noticed how muscular they were. Not huge like Garrett's, but long and lean, and lightly covered with golden hair. The guy was tall, at least six-feet, had medium blond hair with lighter, sun-kissed highlights, and kept it trimmed, not buzzed, which Sara preferred. His eyes were on the smaller side, but still nice. They were an unusual color, like gunmetal, and framed by long, golden lashes. He was clean-shaven, too, which Sara also preferred.

What a package.

"Can I get you something to drink?" She tucked a stray wisp of hair behind her ear.

"I'd love a soda, if you don't mind."

"Not at all. Any preference?"

"No, whatever you grab is fine."

As she headed toward the coolers, she realized Nancy was waving at her furiously. She glanced back to make sure no one was watching, then made a beeline over to her friend.

Nancy grabbed her elbow and asked in a hushed voice, "Who's the stud muffin?"

Sara giggled, and the sound surprised her. "He is gorgeous, isn't he? He's a friend of Garrett's. Officer Jason Thomas."

Nancy's eyes widened in a feigned dramatic fashion. "Ooh, *Officer*, huh? Maybe if you're real nice, he'll frisk you later."

Sara cast a quick glance back at the table. "I could tell by the look on Garrett's face he's trying his hand at matchmaking."

"Judging by the look on *your* face, I'd say he's hit the jackpot."

Sara gnawed on her bottom lip. She glanced at the table again, then back at Nancy. "Maybe, but... I don't know." Gorgeous blue eyes suddenly appeared in her mind in all their unwelcome glory.

Dammit, Mike, get out of my head!

Nancy rolled her eyes. "Sara, you've been taking care of those men for years. And you haven't been out on a single date since I've known you. It's your turn, girl, take it."

"You only moved here about a year ago," Sara pointed out.

"A year is like forever for a single young woman not to have been out on a date."

She sighed. "Well, it's not like he's asked, and for all we know, he may not even be interested."

Strawberry blonde curls bounced as her friend cocked her head to the side. "Have you glanced in a mirror lately? There isn't a man on earth who wouldn't be interested. Hell, even Dwayne says he can't believe you're still single."

"Great," Sara grumbled. "Now I feel like some kind of freak."

"Don't be silly, it was a compliment." Nancy gave her a gentle shove. "Now, get back to that table and start batting those eyelashes."

Sara shook her head, unable to hold back a grin. She'd never met anyone like Nancy before, and that was a fact.

She made her way to the coolers and dug out a can of cola for Jason. Most people liked cola, so she figured it was a pretty safe bet.

Her legs slowed when she realized Jason had settled in the chair right next to hers, and he looked totally engrossed in whatever Danny was saying. Ethan sat on Garrett's lap playing with his badge, while Nicky and Uncle Luke watched some of the guests throw horseshoes.

Jason looked up when she approached and flashed those pearly whites. Sara handed him the can and sat back down in her chair.

"Thanks."

She watched as he pulled the top back and tilted the can to his lips. Her eyes were drawn to his tanned throat as he swallowed, and she silently berated herself for staring.

He leaned back more comfortably in the chair. "So, Garrett tells me you own your own business."

"I do, a bakery here in town."

"That's amazing. To own your own business at such a young age."

With one elbow resting on the table, she twirled a lock of hair around her finger. "I actually have Garrett to thank for that. He pushed me to follow my dream."

He smiled. "Your family seems to be pretty close."

"We are. There isn't anything we wouldn't do for each other." She quit playing with her hair and started drumming her fingers on the table.

Jason reached out and grasped her restless hand. Her

gaze was drawn up to his as if by a magnet. The thought popped into her mind that his eyes weren't quite the right color—not blue enough—and she silently cursed herself for allowing Mike to steal into her thoughts yet again.

"You have beautiful hands," he said, gently stroking her fingers.

The feel of his hand moving over hers in a soft caress caused her nipples to tighten. The erotic sensation surprised her so much she jerked her hand from his.

Because the face swimming before her mind's eye wasn't Jason's.

Damn you, Mike.

"I'm sorry. I didn't mean to be so forward." He leaned back and crossed his arms, his smile fading.

"No, I'm the one who's sorry." She glanced at Garrett who stared at her with raised brows. "I've been on edge the last couple of days."

Jason's smile returned. "Then how about you let me take you out tonight to relieve some of that stress? We can go see a movie. Nothing heavy, just a couple of new friends getting to know each other better over a tub of popcorn. Wha'd'ya think?"

She was tempted. "To tell you the truth, it sounds like heaven, but—"

"But nothing," Garrett chimed in, his smile so big he could hardly contain it. "Ethan and I are gonna go check out that new arcade tonight, so there's no sense you sitting home alone, is there?"

"Yeah, Mom. Go see a movie." Her son turned to Jason. "See a scary one. They're the best."

The guy leaned over in a conspiratorial manner. "I agree. But you know how girls are. What if she gets scared?"

Ethan grinned and shook his head. "Not my mom. She saw *Paranormal Activity* like five times."

"Five times?" Jason raised his eyebrows in mock astonishment. "She's a pretty tough chick, huh?"

His little chest puffed up with pride. "Yep. And she's not afraid of snakes, either. She caught one for me just the other day."

At that, Officer Thomas looked genuinely impressed. "No kidding. Well, I'll keep that in mind."

His gaze met hers and she couldn't help but blush.

"So, do I have myself a date tonight or what?"

Sara glanced first to Garrett and then Ethan. They were both nodding furiously. Laughing, she confirmed, "It's a date."

Staring down at the man who'd given him life, only to make it the most miserable existence any young person should have to live through, Mike felt as cold inside as his father's lifeless body.

He was alone in the funeral parlor, as he knew he'd be. John Andrews had had no friends or family. Basically, not a soul in the world would mourn his passing. It'd be sad if it were anybody else lying in that coffin. But his father hadn't given a damn about anyone, and there wasn't anyone who gave a damn about him.

Most especially his own son.

The funeral director murmured a few words as he shook his hand. While Mike made a genuine effort to at least appear to be grieving, the truth was, he couldn't have squeezed out a tear to save his life.

The rotten old man in that casket had never shown him

even the smallest amount of affection. He'd never ruffled his hair or patted him on the back. He'd never shaken his hand or said, "Good job, Mikey!" when he'd brought home yet another Little League trophy. And he'd certainly never heard the words, "I love you," come out of his father's mouth.

Mike stretched his neck from side to side, trying to ease some of the tension. He'd given up long ago trying to understand how a man could hate his own kid. Mike knew that if he ever had children of his own, he'd show them in every way possible how much he loved them.

He checked his watch before lowering his tired limbs onto the cream-colored arm chair in the farthest corner of the funeral parlor. Three o'clock. In another half-hour, his lone car would follow the hearse carrying his father's casket to the cemetery, not bothering to stop at the church for even a short service.

Mike had lost his faith a long time ago.

Hands folded in his lap, his mind drifted to thoughts of Sara. It had only been a few hours since he'd come to believe the two of them may very well have been set up all those years ago. The problem was, he had no idea what to do about it. Or if it was even true. He could confront her...

Shit, who am I kidding?

It'd be a miracle if she didn't spit in his face, let alone sit and listen while he explained what a moron he'd been. And what did it matter to her anyway? Nearly a decade had gone by. And she'd obviously moved on with that Ethan character.

"He's the love of my life."

With a silent curse, Mike popped a couple of antacids in his mouth and started crunching.

He was on his way back to the house when his cell phone rang. A quick glance down revealed the number of his superior officer, Lieutenant Kenneth Stoddard. Mike blew out a hard breath and answered the call.

"What can I do for you, Lieutenant?"

"Mike, I didn't catch you at a bad time, did I? I'd just finished dialing when I, uh, remembered what day it was."

"No, it's perfect timing. I'm on my way back to the house as we speak."

Lieutenant Stoddard cleared his throat. "I'm sorry to bother you today of all days, but there's something important I need to speak to you about."

Mike made a right onto Highway 29. "Don't worry, sir, I'm fine. What's up?"

"There's a particular case that's come to my attention, and since you're already in the area, I thought I'd see if you were interested."

Mike's curiosity was peaked. "I might be. What's going on?"

"This started down in Arkansas a couple years ago. There's an officer who's suspected of 'moving and providing protection' in the city of Little Rock. But no charges were ever filed, and he transferred to St. Louis where he became the model officer. A month ago, he transferred again, this time up to Green Bay."

"Lieutenant, forgive me for stating the obvious, but shouldn't DCI be handling this?" The last thing Mike wanted to do was step on anyone's toes. The Division of Criminal Investigations wouldn't take kindly to an out-of-state detective sticking his nose into one of their cases. Especially when one of their own was under investigation for helping drug dealers move narcotics.

"It was a friend of mine up in Madison who filled me in on the case. All you'd be doing is some under the table surveillance work. Just to give DCI a lead so this dirty bastard can be caught and brought to justice."

"Surveillance, huh? Would I be reporting to you, or directly to DCI?" Mike turned into the driveway of his parents' house.

"Does that mean you'll take the case?"

Mike killed the engine and leaned back against the headrest. He breathed deep and let it out on a silent breath. "It's gonna take a little while to get this house ready to sell, so I might as well have something else to do to break the monotony."

Not to mention this gave him a valid reason to stay in town and, hopefully, figure out exactly what happened that night so long ago.

"Excellent," Lieutenant Stoddard said. "And you'll be reporting directly to me, for the time being."

"What's this scumbag's name?" Mike finally asked.

"Officer Jason Thomas."

Six

"So, how do I look?" Sara pirouetted for Ethan, Garrett and Danny, who'd all just gathered in her room.

Ethan crinkled up his nose as he eyed her from head to toe. "You look pretty," he finally announced, without much enthusiasm.

"But...?"

He shrugged. "I don't know."

"Of course you do. Now, come on. Tell me what's wrong with what I'm wearing."

"I just don't want you to scare him away. Jason's cool."

Sara's brows rose. She glanced over at her brothers. "That bad?"

Garrett laughed. "That good. Jason will have a hard time keeping his eyes on the road."

"Literally," Danny said. "Which is why you're going to change into a sweat suit. Right now."

She rolled her eyes. "Danny, it's June. And by the way, I'm a little past the age of being told what I can and can't wear."

His little face screwed up in distress, Ethan said, "Mom, your...*you-know-what's* are showing. Jason's a boy, he don't wanna see that kind of stuff."

Garrett burst out laughing, and even Danny couldn't keep a straight face.

"Listen, Ethan," Garrett began, "I promise Jason will love what your mother is wearing. You see, big boys don't mind as much as little boys when a woman's—"

"Garrett!"

This time, Ethan joined his uncles in a chuckle, although Sara knew he had no idea what he was laughing about. She gave her head an exasperated shake, then turned back to the mirror to examine her reflection.

She'd chosen a simple, cotton summer dress that fit her to perfection, with spaghetti straps and a built-in pushup bra. The sweetheart neckline, although flattering, was a tad lower than she normally liked considering she was a full C-cup. But the color, a light shade of amethyst, matched beautifully with her coppery-red hair. Two-inch gold hoops hung from her ears, and her long hair was held back from her face by two gold barrettes. Wispy curls framed her face.

Her toes got painted for the first time in months, while a pair of white wedge slides added a couple extra inches to her petite frame.

Sara knew this was just a casual date, but she desperately wanted to look nice. It had been so long since she'd felt feminine and pretty.

Leaning in close, she examined her make-up. She didn't like to wear much, just some lip gloss, a couple strokes of blush, and mascara. She turned her face left, right, then shrugged. *It'll have to do.*

"I promise he'll be lucky if his knees hold up when he sees you."

Sara met Garrett's gaze in the mirror. "I hope you're right. My son here seems to be quite taken with him."

Nicky and Uncle Luke came in to take a peek at her. With all five of them exchanging glances and grins, her stomach did a little flip, and she suddenly grew self-conscious. "That's it, I'm cancelling. Garrett, give me Jason's number."

"Don't be silly," Nicky said. "We're just not used to seeing you look so...sexy." The uncomfortable look on his face made her laugh.

"You look beautiful, sweetheart."

"Thanks, Uncle Luke. I'm just a little nervous, you guys." She fiddled with one of her earrings. Good lord, she felt as if she were getting ready for her very first date.

Which had been with Mike.

He'd taken her out to dinner, and she was so nervous she'd actually launched a pork chop off her plate while attempting to cut into it. She'd never been more embarrassed, but they'd laughed the entire ride home.

Oh, no you don't. You are not going to think about that man tonight.

Her little man bounced off the bed and grabbed her hand. "Don't worry, Mom. If Uncle Garrett says Jason will like the way you look, I believe him. But if he don't..." He shrugged matter-of-factly. "Then he's a butthead."

She sighed. "Ethan James."

Everyone followed them into the living room. Ethan led her straight to the front door. "Stay right here. I'll go get your purse."

Sara laughed. "My goodness, he's not even here yet. Besides, I can't appear to be too eager."

"But you always make me wait by the door when Kyle and his mom come pick me up."

"This is different, kid." Danny leaned against the wall

with his arms crossed. "You see, girls like to play mind games with us guys. It gives them power if we don't know whether they like us as much as we like them."

Sara rolled her eyes. "Great, Danny. Sour my son against women at an early age."

"Hey, us guys have to stick together." Danny grinned at her, and then headed into the kitchen. "Have a good time," he called over his shoulder.

Ethan climbed up on the couch and grabbed his handheld game off the table.

Sara retrieved the little purple handbag she'd bought to go with the dress and checked inside to make sure she hadn't forgotten anything. Wallet, lip gloss, keys, and cell phone. Everything she should need and about all that would fit inside the tiny purse. Her hand froze. She'd forgotten something all right—to tell Garrett about Mike. She snapped the purse shut.

"Garrett, I had a visitor today at the bakery."

It took a moment, but his expression hardened as understanding dawned. He glanced at Ethan. "Hey, sport, would you do me a favor and go grab my keys off my dresser?"

"Sure."

They waited until he was out of earshot, then Garrett asked in a near whisper, "How the hell did he find you?"

"Dumb luck, or so he said. He was driving by and saw the sign. Said 'morbid curiosity' drew him in." She flicked her gaze down the hall. "There's something else. Amanda asked where Ethan was right in front of him—"

"Sonofabitch."

"—but I think I covered pretty well, and I didn't even have to lie. Told him he's the love of my life."

"Listen, I don't want you to worry about this. We'll

file a harassment charge against him, and if he shows up again, I'll have his ass arrested."

They both fell silent as Ethan returned to the living room, playing catch with Garrett's keys.

"You about ready to hit the road, sport? Jason should be here any minute, and we'll take off when they do."

"Wait, I gotta pee!" Ethan tossed his uncle the keys and ran back down the hall.

Not even two seconds later, Sara heard a vehicle pull into the driveway. She took a deep breath and let it out slowly.

Garrett walked past her and teased, "I'll get it. Wouldn't want you to 'appear too eager' now, would we?"

"Funny."

He opened the door before Jason even had a chance to knock. "Hey, Jason. Right on time." They shook hands. "Come on in. Sara's ready."

"She's ready? Holy cow, I just might have to marry this one."

Garrett laughed and thumped him on the back. "She's the best, didn't I tell you?"

Jason didn't reply, and when Sara met his gaze, she realized she was the reason.

"Wow." His eyes raked over her. "You look beautiful."

"Thank you. You look pretty awesome yourself." He wore a great pair of jeans, and a blue, short-sleeved shirt that fit him like a glove and sort of resembled a Polo without the collar. A pair of black boots completed the look.

Nope, she hadn't imagined it; the man was gorgeous.

"So, have you decided what movie you want to see?" he asked as Garrett motioned him toward the sofa.

"That new thriller looks good, unless you had something else in mind." Sara remained standing even though Mr. Obvious tried to motion for her to sit next to Jason. She resisted the urge to laugh. Subtlety had never been Garrett's strong suit.

"Sounds good to me."

Ethan flew into the living room and skidded to a halt in front of her. "Hi, Jason!"

This time Sara couldn't help but laugh. She'd never seen her son this excited over anybody other than Garrett.

"Hey, Ethan. How's it going? You and your uncle still going to go shoot some miniature golf?"

"Yeah, and skeeball, too. Ever play skeeball? It's an old-time game so you probably heard of it."

Sara put her hand over her mouth to stifle a giggle, but Garrett just outright laughed.

"You know, I think I may have heard of that one," Jason replied with a grin.

"Well..." She glanced at the clock. "We'd better get going. The movie starts in half an hour. Ethan, you be good for your uncle. When he says it's time to go home, no arguments, you hear me?" She reached down to kiss him on the forehead, but he surprised her by offering his puckered lips.

"Don't worry, Mom. I'll be good." Standing with his hands on his hips, Ethan looked very much like Garrett at that moment. "And remember what Uncle Luke told you about no hanky-panky on the first date."

Sara almost choked. Her uncle had been teasing when he'd said that, but of course Ethan couldn't have known. She cast a quick glance at Garrett who was having a hard time keeping a straight face.

But Jason simply knelt down in front of Ethan and

shook his hand. "You have my word as a gentleman, no hanky-panky."

"All right, let's get going," Garrett said, herding Ethan toward the front door. He raised his voice and called out, "We're out of here!"

Outside, Sara watched Garrett buckle Ethan into the back seat of his new Dodge Ram. When she looked up, Jason stood next to the passenger-side door of his own pick-up truck, which also looked fairly new.

And about the ugliest shade of yellow she'd ever seen.

Jason reached out to help her into the truck, his fingers lingering a little longer than necessary on her waist.

"Thank you."

He climbed in behind the wheel and turned to her with that great smile. "Like I said, I'm a gentleman."

Mike shook his head in disgust as he pulled away from the curb to follow along.

Sara was dating a suspected drug dealer. *Friggin' perfect.* They couldn't have been dating for long since Thomas had only been in town a few weeks, but that was cold comfort considering he had no idea how dangerous the guy could be.

And so much for that Ethan guy being the love of her life. *Poor schmuck.*

Mike had never seen her wear a sexy little dress like that before, either. Sara had been a jeans and T-shirt kind of girl back in the day.

An emotion he hadn't felt in a very long time gripped him—jealousy. Gut-wrenching, want-to-put-his-fist-through-the-goddamned-windshield jealousy. A bitter laugh escaped him. *Guess Ethan's not the only poor schmuck.*

He'd been tailing Thomas from the moment he'd left his apartment. When he pulled up in front of the Jamisons' house, Mike couldn't believe his lousy luck. Thomas and Garrett were buddies; maybe even partners. Christ, just what he needed.

But fifteen minutes later, Mike watched Garrett and some kid get into one truck, while Thomas handed Sara up into his own. *And what a waste of a truck*, he thought. Canary yellow? A man's truck should be black, or silver, or hunter green. Even a nice metallic or midnight blue would look sharp. But yellow? He shook his head in disgust.

They made a right onto Holmgren Way, then a left onto Willard Drive. He groaned as he watched them pull into the parking lot of the theater at Bay Park Square Mall. Damn, was he going to have to sit behind them in a darkened movie theater and watch as that son of a bitch put the moves on his Sara?

My Sara?

Mike knew he had no right thinking of her that way. Thanks to his own insecurities, Sara hadn't been 'his' for a very long time.

He parked his truck a couple of rows over from the yellow monstrosity, and followed them in, careful to keep far enough back so he wasn't discovered.

Although, since he'd seen her just that morning, he had the perfect cover. He'd simply claim to be a jealous ex-lover. And it was partially true. Mike certainly didn't need to go into the movie theater with them. In fact, if Thomas were out with any other woman, Mike wouldn't have even bothered. He'd have ducked into the tavern across the street and nursed a beer until the movie ended. Or simply waited in his truck. But the scumbag wasn't out with just any woman—he was out with Sara.

Mike's jaw clenched when he realized they were buying tickets to see that new thriller. Sara loved scary movies. He remembered how she'd sprawl across his lap and hide her face against his chest during the scary parts. He remembered the tickle of her hair against his chin, the playful way she'd nip at his chest, or draw lazy circles on his stomach—

Shit, he'd better keep his thoughts PG, or the next hour-and-a-half would be mighty uncomfortable.

They stopped at the concession for soda and popcorn before heading into the theater. Deciding what the hell, Mike peered down into the glass case and bought himself a big box of Junior Mints. He walked through the doors into the darkened theater just in time to see them take their seats. Finding a seat several rows behind, Mike settled in to watch the show.

Sara took a sip of her soda and tried to relax. An uneasy feeling bloomed in her stomach, but she couldn't pinpoint why for the life of her. Jason had been a perfect gentleman so far, just as he'd said he would. In fact, he seemed like a really great guy.

Yeah, she was pretty sure her uneasy feeling had nothing to do with Jason and everything to do with Mike. Why couldn't she get that jerk out of her mind?

She reached over and grabbed a small handful of popcorn. The lights in the theater dimmed down, signaling the start of the previews.

Jason leaned in and whispered, "You know, I haven't been in a movie theater since I was a kid."

She glanced at him, surprised. "Really? Where do you normally take your dates?"

He shrugged. "The girls I usually date prefer nightclubs. But I'm a little tired of that whole scene, know what I mean?"

"Honestly, I haven't been in too many," she said. "Between the bakery and Ethan, I'm lucky if I have time to soak in a bubble bath once a week."

Jason's gaze remained on her face, making her feel slightly uncomfortable.

"What?"

He licked his lips and cleared his throat, looking strangely guilty. "I'm sorry, but the visual you just gave me..."

Sara's eyes widened, then she laughed softly. "You're going to make me blush."

He reached up and gently smoothed his knuckles down her cheek; his gaze dropped to her lips. Her eyelids started to lower in anticipation—

"What the—" Jason slapped a hand to his cheek and spun around. "Something just hit me in the face. Damn kids."

Not knowing him well enough to predict what he might do, Sara grasped his arm. "Please, let it go. The movie's about to start. They'll settle down once it does."

He turned back to look at her, brow raised in surprise. "Heck, I was just going to flash my badge at them." He shook the large tub of popcorn. "You're going to help me eat this, aren't you?"

Relieved, Sara smiled and reached in for another handful.

Mike headed for the exit as soon as the credits started rolling, not wanting to take a chance on being seen by Sara. He'd had one close call when she'd gotten up to, he assumed, run to the ladies' room. Luckily, she never even glanced his way as she passed by.

But he found it quite interesting that as soon as she was out of earshot, Thomas had pulled out his cell phone and made a quick call. And from the furtive way he'd glanced around beforehand, Mike was confident the call had something to do with his suspected 'side' job.

Mike was safely behind the wheel by the time Sara and Thomas walked out of the theater. He waited until they turned onto Holmgren Way before pulling out of the parking lot to follow. He hoped the jerk would just take her home. But as they drove right past the turnoff that led to Sara's neighborhood, Mike gritted his teeth in annoyance.

Five minutes later, they made a right into the parking lot of a place called *Shady's* that looked like some sort of sports bar.

Shit, Mike thought, as he drove past the first entrance and turned into the second. The lighting inside *Shady's*, although probably dim, would certainly be brighter than inside the movie theater. Which made the likelihood of his being spotted too big a risk to take. He would just have to sit in his truck and pray they weren't inclined to stay too long.

And he'd also have to resist the urge to call a tow truck and have that yellow eyesore dragged to the nearest body shop.

Mike watched Thomas escort Sara across the parking

lot, his hand practically riding her ass.

He let out a heartfelt sigh and leaned back, his booted foot going up onto the dash. Damn, it was going to be a long night.

Mike sat up with interest when Thomas exited the place with his cell phone plastered to his ear, and no Sara. He crossed the parking lot, swung his truck door open and climbed behind the wheel.

Mike pulled a pair of binoculars from his glove compartment, wishing he could read lips as he brought the lenses into focus. Thomas looked downright pissed. He smacked the phone against the steering wheel and then pitched it onto the dash.

Leaning back, Mike set the binoculars on the seat. If DCI was correct, and his instincts told him they were, that exchange more than likely meant one of two things. Either something had gone wrong with the shipment, or they required his assistance and wanted him to cut his date short.

He hoped it was the latter, and not only because of Sara. If Thomas was indeed a drug-peddling, disgrace to law enforcement, he needed to be stopped now, before he had a chance to distribute any more poison to the citizens of Green Bay—or anywhere else.

Massaging the bridge of his nose, Mike caught sight of Sara heading toward Thomas's truck. He wanted to run out there, toss her over his shoulder and steal her away.

Blowing out a frustrated breath, he watched Officer Scumbag help her into the truck.

He followed them back down the highway and

breathed a sigh of relief when they turned into the Jamison's neighborhood. With any luck, he'd have Thomas in a jail cell before the end of the night, and he'd never have to worry about him putting his hands on Sara again.

From halfway down the block, Mike peered through binoculars as Thomas walked her to the front door. She turned around to face the guy, and Mike's jaw hardened as the scumbag took her hands and brought them to his lips.

"You don't want to kiss that jerk," he whispered, clutching the binoculars in a death grip.

Thomas leaned in for a kiss, but much to his delight, Sara turned and presented him with her cheek.

Mike wanted to stick his head out the truck with a taunting laugh and flip him the bird.

He settled for flipping the guy off as he hopped back in his truck.

Twenty minutes later and two small towns over, Thomas pulled into the parking lot of some little dive called *T&R's Place*. Mike purposely drove past the entrance, then made a U-turn a couple of blocks down the road. Thomas was just entering the bar when he pulled into the parking lot.

No longer concerned about being recognized since Thomas had no idea who he was, Mike followed him inside.

The place was small, dimly lit, and reeked of beer and mold. Not a pleasant combination by any means. He hung back while Thomas paid for his beer, and then continued on to the end of the bar where a man sat cracking peanut shells with his teeth.

There was something oddly familiar about the guy, but Mike couldn't quite place him.

Mildly frustrated, he ordered a bottle of Bud.

Thomas reached peanut guy and smacked him on the side of the head. He spun around and scowled at Thomas, who perched on the barstool beside him.

Mike stopped dead in his tracks. *Carl Montgomery.*

The sonofabitch who ruined his goddamn life.

Seven

Regaining his composure, Mike swiped his beer off the bar and continued on toward the empty table just behind and to the right of them. He took a swig of his beer and leaned forward in an effort to hear their conversation.

"...don't give a damn what they said," Thomas growled, his voice barely above a whisper. "I'm the one running this thing...You tell them they have until Friday or...what kind of shit are they trying to pull? The price is non-fucking-negotiable..."

Okay, so nothing would be happening until next Friday. In the meantime, Mike wasn't sure what the hell to do about Montgomery. If he confronted him, and Carl mentioned the exchange to Thomas, there was a small chance Thomas would do a background check on Mike and discover he's a cop. Which would be reason enough for the scumbag to pull up stakes and move on to the next city or state.

And Mike wanted to bust the son-of-a-bitch himself. Not only for Sara's sake, but for Billy Hahn.

A few years back, before he'd made detective, he had befriended a few of the kids in his neighborhood. And they were good kids, for the most part. He'd caught them partying a few times, drinking beer in the forest preserve, smoking a joint in their car. But he'd never had the heart to arrest them. He wished to God he had, though, because unbeknownst to Mike, Billy had been a meth addict. And two weeks after the last time he'd seen them, Billy's mom found her son dead in the bathroom from an overdose. The desolation in the woman's eyes was something that haunted Mike to this day.

Lost in the past, Mike nearly missed Thomas as he passed by on his way out. Torn, he stared at Carl's back, wanting nothing more than to confront the bastard. With a heavy sigh, he got up and followed Thomas.

Mike watched until the ugly yellow truck pulled out onto the street before hopping in his own truck to follow. When Thomas turned into the parking lot of his apartment complex, Mike kept on driving, relieved.

Another twenty minutes later, Mike walked back into *T&R's Place*, having decided to confront Carl after all.

He felt a moment's hesitation. In his present frame of mind, he was liable to beat the son-of-a-bitch to death if he confirmed Mike's suspicions. He'd come to the conclusion that Carl and his worthless sister *had* sabotaged his and Sara's relationship for their own selfish reasons. And there was a good chance they'd drugged Sara to do it. For that alone, he could kill them both with his bare hands.

Mike motioned to the bartender for another beer, then made his way to the end of the bar and took a seat on the stool Thomas had vacated. He shook his head, amazed by how badly Carl had aged. His hair had thinned considerably on the top, and he'd built up quite a beer gut over the years, making him look closer to forty than the thirty-years-old Mike knew him to be.

When Carl realized someone had taken the stool next

to him, he glanced over and did an amusing double-take, his eyes wide with apprehension. "Andrews? That you?"

Mike took a swig of his beer and set the bottle down on the bar. He turned and fixed Carl with a look meant to shrivel his nuts. "You remember me. I'm touched."

Carl's eyes darted around the bar, as if searching for allies in case things got ugly. Nobody paid them the slightest bit of attention.

His hand shook as he took a sip of his beer. "So, uh, what brings you back to Green Bay? I heard you moved away years ago."

"Yeah, I did. Eight years ago, to be exact. Come to think of it..." Mike swiveled in his seat, his left hand braced on his thigh, his right hand curled around his beer. "I left town the same day your sister showed me a video of you *fucking* my girlfriend."

The little prick swallowed, hard. He opened and closed his mouth a couple times before making a feeble attempt to laugh it off. "Man, I told you then, and I'll tell you now, I got no idea what you're talking about." Hand trembling, he took another sip of his beer.

"No, huh? Well, that's a shame. A real shame."

"W-why is that?"

"Because it means I'm going to have to drag your sorry ass out to the parking lot and beat you until your memory returns."

Carl swallowed again, his Adam's apple bobbing up and down convulsively. He quickly did another scan of the room, then eyed the exit door not five feet behind them.

Mike smiled.

"Holy shit. You're here to get revenge on something that happened eight years ago?"

"No, I'm here for the truth, not what you and your

bitch of a sister wanted me to believe was the truth."

"Man, I don't know what the hell you're talking about!" Carl insisted.

Mike knocked Carl off the barstool with one well-placed shove. He reached down, grabbed him by the collar of his shirt, and literally dragged him out the back exit. The putrid stench of garbage mingled oddly with the fresh scent of the pine trees that surrounded the building.

Another hard shove landed Carl on his hands and knees. He climbed to his feet and backed up, only to jump forward when he bumped into the dumpster behind him. He stood, breathing hard, eyes wild with fear.

Mike ignored the warnings of his professional inner voice as eight years' worth of built up rage gripped him. He wasn't leaving here without the truth, and by whatever means necessary.

Waiting a moment for effect, his cold gaze pinned Carl in place as if by physical force. Then, in one smooth motion, he pulled his Glock from the waistband of his jeans and pointed it at Montgomery's head.

A whimper reverberated in the little prick's throat.

Mike smiled with satisfaction.

"Now, Carl. I don't want to kill you, honest I don't. In fact, if you tell me everything I want to know, you'll walk back into that bar without a scratch." He pressed the barrel of the gun against the guy's temple. "That sounds fair, right?"

"M-more than fair."

Holding the gun steady, Mike nodded. "Good boy. Now, the first thing you're going to tell me is exactly what happened the night you and Rachel made that video. And don't leave *anything* out."

"Hell, it's been awhile, man. I'm gonna need a minute

to think."

Montgomery squeezed his eyes shut, quaking as if he were about to piss in his pants.

Mike had to resist the urge to roll his eyes. "Have I mentioned that I'm not a very patient man?" He nudged his temple with the gun.

"Okay, okay, I just don't want to get this shit mixed up. It's been a long time." Carl blew out a shaky breath. "Rachel wanted to split you and Sara up. She'd been trying to get you in bed so she could record the two of you having sex, but like I always told her, what guy would want her over Sara? I mean, it would've been like exchanging a porterhouse for Hamburger Helper."

His patience was wearing thin. "Stop editorializing and get the fuck on with it."

"Right. Let's see. Rachel had Sara spend the night, and then slipped a few sleeping pills in her soda. They were good ones, too. Prescription."

Mike's hand tightened imperceptibly on the gun. White-hot rage burned in his gut.

"When she passed out, I carried her into my room and, uh..."

Carl's words trailed off, and Mike knew he was scared shitless to admit the rest. "And...?" he prompted.

"I, uh, p-pretended to have sex with her, and Rachel recorded it."

Mike hadn't considered until just that moment Sara may have been raped as well. He went deathly still. "Pretended?"

"Yeah, man, pretended! We were dressed and everything! I never laid a hand on her...well, you know what I mean."

Slowly, deliberately, Mike slid the barrel of the gun

from Carl's temple to the middle of his forehead. "If I ever find out you're lying to me...that you put your filthy hands on her, there won't be enough left of you for an autopsy."

"Dude, I swear to God! I didn't do anything! I swear on my nuts!" The weasel's voice rose to a hysterical pitch on the last word.

The relief Mike felt was so intense his knees almost buckled. He had no doubt Carl had told him the truth. Only he wasn't through yet. He still needed one more detail before he could fully assess the damage that'd been done.

"What reason did Rachel give Sara for me leaving town?"

"Man, I've got no idea what Rachel told her—"

Mike gave him a quick smack on the head with the barrel of the gun. "What reason did Rachel give Sara for me leaving town?" he repeated through his teeth.

Montgomery's eye grew red; he looked close to tears. "All right! She told her you got her pregnant and..."

A red haze of blinding fury distorted his vision. Desperate to hold onto his composure, he blinked hard, a mere hair's-breadth away from losing what little self-control he had left. After what this lowlife prick and his sister had done, they both deserved to rot in hell.

"And *what?* I swear to God, Carl, you'd better tell me every damn thing I want to know, because right now your life means less than spit to me." Mike pressed the barrel of the gun into his temple, the urge to shoot the bastard so strong he had to force himself to ease off the trigger.

Carl squeezed his eyes shut and said in a rush, "That you beat her so bad she lost the baby!"

Mike couldn't move, couldn't think. He sucked in a ragged breath as his world spun on its axis. All these years, Sara thought him to be some kind of monster...

Like his father.

His stomach clenched, and he thought he might vomit. *Christ, she thinks I killed my own kid!*

Raw fury replaced his initial shock. His blood started pumping, fast and furious.

"That bitch!" He shoved Carl away and kicked the dumpster, the sound reverberating into the darkness like a gong. "I've never raised my hand to a woman, and I wouldn't have touched that slut with a ten-foot pole!"

He couldn't freakin' believe this. Garrett and Nicky's anger now made perfect sense. They thought he was lower than dirt, and rightly so.

And Christ, the way Sara had looked at him that morning...like the sight of him made her skin crawl. A sudden thought occurred to him. "Did that psycho sister of yours actually have you beat her up just to frame me?"

"No, you *did* give her a black eye. When you threw the camcorder at her."

"I didn't throw it at her, the lying witch. I smacked it out of her hand."

"Well, whatever you did, it hit her in the side of the face." Carl had the balls to grin. "Looked like someone popped her a good one."

Mike clicked the safety and stuck his pistol back in the waistband of his jeans.

Carl breathed an audible sigh of relief. "So, we're cool?"

He couldn't believe the little prick's audacity. "We're cool," he said. Then hauled off and smashed the creep's nose with a quick jab to the face. His knuckles still stung from earlier, but the pain of this hit had been so much more satisfying.

Montgomery screamed and grabbed his nose. Within seconds the front of his shirt was soaked with blood. "What the hell! You said you wouldn't hit me!"

"I said not a scratch, you fucking weasel. And you don't have a scratch, now do you?"

"I appreciate you coming out here to talk to me," Mike said as soon as Nicky opened the passenger side door of his truck. "Wasn't sure if you would."

After his confrontation with Montgomery, Mike had driven straight back to the Jamison's and parked out on the street. He sat in his truck for nearly twenty minutes before he finally worked up the nerve to give his old friend a call.

"Bullshit, you knew I'd come." Nicky climbed in, shut the door, and turned to face him.

"Okay, yeah, I figured you would," Mike conceded. "But knowing what I do, I wouldn't have blamed you if you hadn't."

"Look," Nicky said. "I'm too tired for riddles. Can you just say what you came to say?"

Mike reached into the front pocket of his jeans and pulled out his digital pocket recorder. "Christ, I don't even know where to begin."

He set the device on the dash, and Nicky eyed it curiously.

"Well, you've certainly got my attention."

Mike cleared his throat and tugged on his ear. "I know you think I left town because I got Rachel pregnant and...beat her so badly she lost the baby."

Nicky nodded. "I didn't want to believe it, but—"

"But what else could you think when I blew out of town the way I did?" Mike looked past Nicky toward the house he'd spent the best times of his life in, hoping to catch a glimpse of Sara walking past the big picture window. "Truth is, I left because *I* was led to believe Sara was sleeping with Carl."

"Yeah, Sara said you'd made some bullshit accusations." Nicky leaned back and propped his arm on the headrest. "How the hell could you have ever believed such a thing? I thought you knew Sara better than that."

Mike turned solemn. "Believe me, I'll never forgive myself for not questioning the source. But, the evidence was irrefutable. At least, I thought so at the time."

"Dammit, Mike. You and Sara were solid. How could you've taken someone else's word over hers?"

"The irrefutable proof was a video. I saw a recording of Sara in bed with Carl."

"No way," Nicky stated with complete conviction. "I know my sister, and there's no way in hell. I don't care what you saw."

"And if I'd only had your confidence back then, I could've saved Sara and me both a lot of heartache." He blew out a heavy breath. "I don't know, I guess some part of me couldn't help but believe it. I mean, I saw the proof with my own eyes. Even though my heart told me it wasn't possible, my head said it had to be true, because I was worthless. My old man had been telling me so for years."

His old friend stared at him for a moment in quiet contemplation, as if not quite sure what to say. "I wish you had called me."

"Believe me, it's one of my biggest regrets. Because you're right. The video and Rachel's 'pregnancy' were both staged, and I have Carl's confession on tape to prove it."

Nicky's brows shot up. "How the hell did you get that?"

"I, uh, ran into him tonight at a little dump called *T&R's Place*." Mike was quiet for a moment before adding, "Nicky, I never laid a hand on Rachel. Sexually or otherwise. I know what Sara and the rest of you were led to believe, but *none* of it's true. I loved your sister. I would've died before hurting her."

Nicky slowly shook his head. "I don't know what to say. This is all so frigging incredible."

Mike picked up the recorder. "I think it's time you heard the story straight from the asshole's mouth." He clicked the play button.

When the tape ended, Nicky stared at the recorder for a moment. "Where'd you hit him?"

"The nose. And he's lucky he got off that easy. I can't tell you how badly I wanted to pull the trigger. Scared the hell out of me."

"This is all so incredible," Nicky repeated, running his fingers through his hair. "I'll talk to Garrett first thing in the morning, let him decide the best way to handle this. She's going to be devastated, Mike."

"Actually, I'd like to explain things to Sara myself. My God, we have so much to talk about."

Nicky murmured something under his breath.

"Come again?"

His friend cleared his throat. "I said that's probably not a good idea. I understand you're anxious to talk to her, and you will. But the best way to handle this, at least for Sara's sake, is to let Garrett tell her. He's been her rock since the beginning."

Mike frowned. "I don't trust him. He's never liked me."

"I don't think it was you in particular," Nicky countered. "I doubt he would have liked anybody who was sleeping with his kid sister. Besides, you trust me, don't you?"

"Of course. Never trusted anyone more."

Nicky gave a half-smile. "Listen, it's late. Why don't you head home and get some sleep. I'll call you tomorrow afternoon and let you know what's going on."

Mike set his jaw, but nodded in agreement. "There's something else I need to talk to you about. Sara's date tonight, Officer Thomas."

"How do you know about Jason?"

"I followed him to your house. Long story short...he's a suspected drug dealer."

Nicky's brow beetled. He shot a quick look toward the house. "Jesus, are you sure? Garrett's going to hit the frigging roof when he hears—"

Mike gave his head an adamant shake. "No. Garrett can't know a thing about this. I shouldn't even be telling you, but I have no idea how dangerous he might be, and I don't want him anywhere near Sara."

"Shit." Nicky crossed his arms over his chest and leaned his head back. "I'm pretty sure she's planning on seeing him again. He called about an hour after he dropped her off. Sounded like they were making plans to take...a trip to the circus."

"The circus? That's an odd place to take a date. You'd think the smell of elephant shit would be a pretty big turn off."

They both chuckled.

"The circus is still two weeks away," Nicky said. "I'll

worry about it when the time comes. I have enough to think about tonight."

Mike angled back to lean against the driver's door. "So tell me, what've you been up to all these years? I assume you're not married since you still live at home."

"Never been married, no kids. I'm a computer programmer. Takes up most of my time. I guess you could say I'm married to my work."

Mike just stared at him for a moment, then they both burst out laughing. "Damn, man, that's pathetic. You do get laid once in a while, don't you?"

"Once in a while," Nicky admitted. "Although it *is* a little tough bringing a woman home to the bedroom I've had since I was a kid."

They both burst out laughing again.

"Nicky, I'm beat. I think I'll head back to my parents' house and try to get some sleep. I have a feeling tomorrow's going to be one of the longest days of my life."

Eight

Hurrying to beat the evening showers the weatherman had predicted, Sara finished weeding her garden in record time. She'd just put her hoe back in the tool shed when Danny stepped out the back door and waved her over. After a quick glance at her son, who was busy kicking and chasing a big rubber ball around the yard, she swiped the sweat from her brow with her forearm, and made her way up to the porch. "What is it?"

Danny cast Ethan an odd look, then said, "Garrett needs to talk to you."

"About...?"

He shrugged. "You'll have to ask him. I'll stay out here with Ethan."

Frowning, she walked past him into the house.

After scrubbing the dirt from her hands in the kitchen sink, she cast a quick glance over her shoulder. Garrett, Nicky, and Uncle Luke were all seated at the table, and all grim-faced.

Her stomach twisted like it had Friday morning when she'd found out Mike was back in town, and again when he'd walked into her shop.

She dried her hands on the dishtowel that hung from the refrigerator door. "Danny said you needed to talk to me about something, but from the looks on your faces, I'm afraid to ask what it is."

"Have a seat, Sara," Garrett said.

"Good lord, Garrett, I feel like I'm ten-years-old again. What in the world is this about?" She walked around the table and took the seat directly across from him.

"Nicky got a call from Mike last night."

Sara looked expectantly at Nicky. "Well? What did he want?" Suddenly, it dawned on her and her voice rose an octave. "Oh my God, he knows...doesn't he?"

"Sara, calm down. He doesn't know about Ethan," Nicky assured her. "At least, not yet."

"What the hell does that mean, 'not yet?'" She turned to her uncle. "Please, just tell me what's going on."

Uncle Luke reached over to grasp her hand, but it was Garrett who said, "Sara, the night Mike left town, it wasn't for the reasons you were led to believe by that so-called friend of yours. Rachel was never pregnant, and Mike *never* laid a hand on her."

An odd buzzing filled her ears. She turned to look at Ethan through the picture window that framed the backyard. Her hands went numb, and she absently rubbed her palms against her legs.

"Honey, are you all right?" Uncle Luke asked.

"But I saw her face," she said, unable to accept that everything she'd believed for the past eight years had been a lie. "Her cheek was bruised and swollen, and she had a black eye."

"Turns out that was an accident," Nicky explained. "She got hit in the face with her camcorder when Mike smacked it from her hand."

Sara frowned. "Her camcorder? What does that have to do with anything?"

Garrett cleared his throat. "Sara, there's more to the story, and...it has to do with the real reason Mike left town."

She scrubbed at her forehead as she flipped through the pages of her mind. "He'd accused me of sleeping with Rachel's brother. He was so angry..."

"He never would've hurt you," Nicky stated softly.

"Although it galls me to have to stick up for the idiot," Garrett said, earning a scowl from Nicky, "it turns out his anger was...somewhat understandable. The night before, you'd slept over at Rachel's house, do you remember that?"

"Vaguely. I spent the night there quite a bit. Why?"

"Rachel put sleeping pills in your drink. When you passed out, her brother carried you into his room, put you in his bed and..."

When Garrett's words trailed off, Sara gasped and clapped a hand to her chest. "A-Are you trying to tell me I was raped by Carl Montgomery?" Bile rose in her throat.

"No! My God, I'm sorry, I didn't mean for you to think that. It's just, as your brother, it's not easy telling you the rest."

Her pulse pounded in her ears, echoing the rapid beat of her heart, as one awful scenario after another cropped up in her mind. "Please, Garrett, just say it."

He blew out a deep breath, as if doing everything in his power to keep his anger in check. "They made a video. Carl pretended to have sex with you while Rachel recorded it. The next day, she showed the video to Mike. That's why he accused you of sleeping with Carl."

"He was devastated, Sara," Nicky added. "He loved you very much. I believe he still does."

Sara was in complete and utter shock. She could barely

catch her breath. "But…but how did he figure this all out? And why the hell did it take him so long?" She angrily swiped away a tear that had slipped from the corner of her eye.

"He's been beating himself up over that very question," Nicky said. "He couldn't understand why Garrett and I were so angry about something that happened eight years ago. Especially since, as far as Mike was concerned, *you'd* betrayed *him*. So when he ran into Carl last night, he took it as a sign of fate and forced a confession out of him, which he recorded."

"You've heard this confession?"

"Yes."

She glanced around the table, could see all three of them waiting for her reaction, probably afraid she would burst into tears, praying that she wouldn't. She knew they all loved her dearly, but she also knew they felt completely helpless whenever she was upset or emotional.

And this was so much bigger than PMS.

Sara's whole world shifted, and she thought she might faint from the dizziness of it. Rachel, that sick, twisted bitch, had drugged her and made a video of her in bed with Carl? She'd lied about Mike sleeping with her, *lied* about being pregnant. But worst of all? She'd accused Mike of something Sara should've instinctively known he was incapable of—raising his hand to a woman. Not after watching his mother suffer all those years.

Although Mike certainly wasn't blameless. He'd accused her of something *he* should've known *she* could never do, then ran out of town like a coward, without even giving her a chance to defend herself.

Sara pushed back from the table with more force than necessary and shot to her feet. "I need some time to think.

Figure out what I'm going to do."

"Sara, you have to tell him. He has a right—"

"Damn it, Nicky, don't you dare say it. Mike Andrews has no rights as far as Ethan is concerned. He's my son. *My* son. I raised him. I fed him. I clothed him. *I* love him. Mike did nothing."

"Look, I understand where you're coming from, but this isn't any more Mike's fault than it is yours. He was as much a victim as you were, and he's already missed out on more than seven years of Ethan's life. Isn't that punishment enough?"

"This isn't about punishing Mike," Garrett chimed in. "It's about doing what's best for Ethan. Period."

"And what's best for Ethan is getting to know his father," Nicky insisted. "Mike is a good man who'd make a great father if given the chance."

"You've always defended him," Sara accused, her eyes stinging.

"And now we know I was justified. Sara, please. Don't use Ethan to punish Mike."

She gasped, her brother's words like a knife in her chest. "How could you even think I'd do such a thing?" She stormed off for the sanctuary of her bedroom.

Sara sat on the bed, arms hugging her knees as tears spilled down her cheeks.

Angry as she was, her heart rejoiced over the revelation that Mike hadn't betrayed her. For so long she'd had to imagine him making love to another woman. And not just anyone, but her supposed best friend. She'd cried countless tears over him those first few months after he'd left, mostly in the middle of the night when she'd hoped no one could hear her. But she knew they could. She'd been able to see it on their faces the following morning.

The day Ethan was born, Sara decided she'd cried her last tear over Mike Andrews. She'd had her son to take care of, and he was all that mattered.

But as the months went by, fate seemed to mock her as that beautiful little face became more and more like his father's. He had Mike's nose, his full lips, his ears. He had the exact same cleft in his chin, the same thick, near-black hair. And those incredible blue eyes surrounded by absurdly thick, sooty lashes. He was Mike's spitting image, and it was only a matter of time before he saw him and figured it out for himself.

She had to tell him. She had to tell both of them. For years, she'd believed that even if Mike knew about Ethan, he wouldn't want anything to do with him. So she'd been able to justify, at least in her own mind, telling her son that his father was dead.

Because in her mind, he *was* dead. But now, knowing the truth, how could she deny Ethan his father? Or Mike his son? Nicky was right—they'd both already missed out on so much. She knew Ethan would be angry and confused, but it would only be a matter of time before he started following Mike around like a lost puppy, gazing up at him as if he'd hung the moon and stars.

Exactly the way he looked at his Uncle Garrett.

Garrett. This was going to be as hard on him as it would be Ethan. Garrett couldn't love Ethan more if he were his own son.

She sighed and swiped away her tears. Who knew, maybe this would be good for her big brother. She'd always worried the main reason he'd never become serious with anyone was because he felt responsible for her and Ethan. And Garrett was such a wonderful man. He deserved a good woman and children of his own.

Rolling to her side, she stretched out on the bed and tucked her hands beneath her cheek.

"He loved you very much. I believe he still does."

The thought that Mike still loved her excited her as much as angered her. On one hand, she wanted to smack him senseless for leaving without giving her a chance to defend herself. Dammit, if he'd just taken the time to cool off, they could've talked and avoided all of this!

She sat up and snatched the tattered, stuffed monkey off her dresser. Ethan's very first toy. She'd bought it when she was four-months pregnant and felt him kick for the first time. Tears welled in her eyes as she hugged it against her chest.

How dare Mike come back here now and tear her entire life apart!

Someone knocked on her bedroom door.

"Sara? Honey, can we come in?"

Uncle Luke.

She set the monkey aside, and used the edge of her shirt to mop up her tears. "Is Ethan still outside?"

"No, Danny took him downstairs to play video games. I'm opening the door, all right?" The door slowly swung open.

"It's okay, come in. I just didn't want him to see me like this." She leaned over to glance at her reflection in the mirror. Her eyes were slightly swollen and red, as was her nose, but overall, not too bad. Nothing a little cool water wouldn't fix.

Uncle Luke and Garrett both came in, each taking a seat beside her on the bed. Nicky followed them in and leaned against the corner of her dresser.

"You okay?" Garrett asked.

She nodded. "I just have a headache from trying to figure out how to tell my son his father's alive. And how to tell Mike about Ethan. I'm scared to death of what his reaction will be."

"He'll be shocked, and then thrilled," Nicky assured her. "You have nothing to worry about."

"Aren't you the least bit concerned about how he'll treat Ethan?" Garrett demanded. "I mean, let's be honest, because we've all thought about it. Mike's old man was an evil sonofabitch. What if it's hereditary? Because I'll say it again, if I even suspect he's put his hands on that boy, I'll break every bone in his goddamn body."

Sara's gaze flew to his face. Garrett was right—the thought *had* crossed her mind, though she'd hated herself for thinking it. "You don't really think he'd hurt Ethan...do you?"

It was Uncle Luke who answered. "I honestly don't think we have to worry about that. Mike was a good kid. I never saw any signs of violence from him."

"Tell that to Carl Montgomery," Garrett muttered under his breath.

Nicky shot Garrett a look before admitting, "I wondered about it, and just as quickly came to the same conclusion Uncle Luke did. Mike is nothing like his father. There's no way in hell he'd ever harm a hair on Ethan's head."

"I watched him attack Carl," Sara reminded them, her voice barely above a whisper. "I'd never seen him that angry before. Who knows what would have happened if they hadn't been broken up right away."

"Honey," Uncle Luke began, "I'm not condoning Mike's actions, and of course I wasn't there to see it. But jealousy can do ugly things to a man."

"He'd just seen a video of you and Carl in bed together," Nicky added. "I can only imagine how much that had to hurt. And you didn't exactly deny it, Sara."

"I never got a chance to!"

Garrett gave her shoulder a squeeze. "Calm down, you don't want Ethan to hear you."

Sara felt a fresh batch of tears threatening to spill and angrily shot to her feet. She took a few deep breaths and gazed out her bedroom window.

Uncle Luke cleared his throat. "Sara, why don't we invite Mike over for supper tonight? We'll eat, and when you feel comfortable enough, we'll give you two your privacy so you can talk. Ethan mentioned going to the movies with Hunter and his folks, so that'll be one less complication."

Sara thought about it for a moment. Even if she wanted to, she couldn't put it off for long. And the truth was, no matter how awkward it would be, she wanted to see him again. She wanted to force Mike to admit he was just as responsible as Rachel and Carl for missing out on the first seven years of their son's life.

Because he hadn't had faith in their love.

And no matter how much her heart still ached for him, that was the one thing she didn't know if she could ever get past.

"Nicky, tell him dinner's at five. I'll give Hunter's mom a call right now. It'll definitely ease my mind to have Ethan out of the house."

Garrett and Uncle Luke both rose from the bed. "Everything will work out fine, honey," her uncle assured her. "You'll see."

Nicky started to follow them from the room. He stopped in the doorway and turned back to face her, a rueful smile curved his lips. "Any chance you could whip up a cherry pie for dessert?"

"Pffft. Only if I can throw it at him."

He grinned. "In that case, make two."

NINE

Sara peeked in the oven to check on her lasagna. The cheese had melted, but needed to brown a bit yet. She'd already set the table, a still-warm loaf of Italian bread sat in a basket on the counter, and two cherry pies cooled right next to it.

She knew Nicky had asked her to bake a cherry pie because it was Mike's favorite, and at first, she'd considered being petty and making blueberry, which she knew he couldn't stand. But for some inexplicable reason, she was anxious to please him, though she'd die before admitting it.

Since she had a few minutes before the lasagna was ready, Sara ran back to her room and checked herself in the mirror for the thousandth time. She hadn't dressed up like she had for her date with Jason, but she still wanted to look her best.

She wore a pair of stone-washed, low-rise jeans and a violet, keyhole halter top that bared nearly her entire back. She'd applied very little makeup, though she did go a smidge heavy on the mascara. With her hair pulled up into a ponytail, just a few wispy curls framed her face. Also, she'd slipped on a pair of plain white slides with three-inch heels. Mike was almost as tall as Garrett, and she hated the feeling of being towered over.

Nicky stuck his head in and asked, "Hey, sis, need any help with supper?"

Still a little stung by his stalwart loyalty to Mike, she met his gaze in the mirror. But she loved her brother regardless of how big an idiot he could be. "Thanks, but I've got everything under control."

"As usual."

When he didn't leave, she asked, "Is there something else?"

He cleared his throat. "We're okay, you and I, aren't we? I mean, you know I only want what's best for you...right?"

Sighing, Sara walked over and wrapped her arms around his waist. "Yeah, we're fine." She felt him relax, and his arms went around her, too. "I know you only want what's best for all of us. Including Mike. You're still a loyal friend to him, even after all these years."

"He's a good man, Sara. He'll be a good father to Ethan. I'd bet my life on it." He gave her ponytail a gentle tug, and then headed toward the kitchen.

Would he be a good father? Because frankly, nothing else mattered.

She gave herself one last glance in the mirror before following in Nicky's wake.

Sara opened the oven door and pulled out both pans of lasagna to let them rest for a few minutes so the sauce and cheese didn't ooze out when she cut into them. She slid a pan lined with thick slices of garlic toast into the oven and turned the temperature up to four hundred degrees.

Nicky stood next to the counter, pouring a can of orange soda into an ice-filled glass. "Damn, that smells good. I bet Mike hasn't had a decent meal in years."

Sara grunted, wanting to say that it was his own darn fault, but decided to keep her opinion to herself. "Somehow, I doubt that. He's probably had plenty of women to cook for him over the years."

He looked up and met her gaze, his smile suspiciously knowing. "Even if that's the case, I'm sure none of them even compared to you."

"I'm not jealous, if that's what you're thinking, so you can wipe that smug look off your face right now."

His lips twitched, but he wisely kept his mouth shut.

Garrett and Danny came up from the basement arguing about the baseball game they'd been watching.

"He should be here any minute," Danny announced, heading into the living room.

Mike had always treated Danny like a little brother, and she suspected he might actually be looking forward to seeing him again.

Sara glanced at the table one last time before taking a deep, calming breath. Good lord, she had butterflies in her stomach. Which was absolutely ridiculous considering she'd seen him just yesterday. She pressed a hand to her stomach and looked at the clock, five-to-five. Boy, he really knew how to make an entrance, waiting until the clock struck the final minute before—

"He's here!" Uncle Luke shouted, coming in through the garage.

Garrett came up from behind and put his hands on her shoulders. He knew her so well.

"It'll be fine," he assured. "Don't worry. And I won't leave until you ask me to, all right?"

Sara nodded, grateful for his support.

Nicky opened the front door and went out to greet their guest.

She heard the two of them talking, their voices growing louder as they walked up the porch steps. The front door swung open, and Nicky strode in with Mike right behind him. Sara didn't realize her hands were clenched into fists until she felt the sting of her nails digging into her palms. She glanced down, surprised to see the red indentations her nails had made.

When she looked back up, Mike's eyes were fixed intently on her face. She froze. Having the full-force of those amazing blue eyes on her again was enough to steal her breath. Had it been just yesterday he'd walked into her bakery and back into her life?

She gave herself a mental pinch.

Dammit, she didn't want to feel breathless over him. She didn't want to feel anything for him at all!

Mike stopped less than two feet in front of Sara and held out the bouquet of red roses he'd bought on the way over. Judging by her scowl and the death grip her teeth had on her bottom lip, he half expected her to snatch them out of his hand and whap him over the head. He cleared his throat. "Hi."

She didn't respond or reach out for the roses, simply stared at him with borderline hostility.

He sighed and dropped his hand. Of course, he figured she wouldn't welcome him back into her life with open arms, but he'd hoped to see some sign that she wasn't completely indifferent to him.

Nicky thumped him on the back. "Did I mention Sara made cherry pie for dessert?"

He cleared his throat. "No, you didn't. Sounds great." His gaze flickered up to Garrett who stood over her like a sentinel dog.

Garrett gestured toward Mike's jaw. "Hope there's no

hard feelings."

Arrogant son-of-a-bitch. "Looks worse than it is. I bruise easily."

"Good to know."

"Uh, Sara, do you have something in the oven?" Danny asked.

She sniffed the air. "My garlic toast!"

Sara raced into the kitchen, Danny and Garrett right behind her.

Grinning, Nicky took the roses from him. "You knew she wouldn't make this easy on you, man, so buck up."

Yep, he'd known. And still, like a fool, he'd hoped to see a flare of...*something* in her eyes when their gazes locked.

Half tempted to run like hell out the front door, Mike took a deep breath and followed Nicky into the kitchen.

His friend pulled a vase from the cabinet above the sink and filled it with water. "Mike, why don't you have a seat on the end there." He stuffed the roses in the vase and set it in the middle of the table.

Danny and Nicky served the food while Sara poured the drinks. Everyone took their seats, and Mike had to hide a grin when she realized where she was expected to sit—right next to him. She shot her brother a nasty look. Nicky merely grinned.

Supper was mostly eaten in silence. Nicky attempted to start a conversation, but without much luck. Sara picked at her food, but Mike had no such trouble. He hadn't had a meal this delicious in years.

"I can't remember the last time I ate this good," he said, reaching for another slice of the warm bread.

"Hmph."

She never even glanced his way, and he blew out a

silent breath. Well, she hadn't dumped her plate over his head yet. That was something, he supposed.

When everybody had finished eating, Sara started to clear the table. Mike stood, intending to help, but without so much as looking at him she said, "I'll take care of it."

He dropped his hands to his sides and looked to Nicky who made a 'don't worry about it' face before motioning for him to join the men outside.

Danny sprawled out on the glider, Garrett plopped down on one of the chaise loungers, Uncle Luke and Nicky both took seats on either side of the umbrella-covered patio table, and Mike sat down on the swing.

"So, Mike, you made a pretty incredible discovery last night," Luke said. "We were all quite surprised, to say the least."

He nodded. "As was I, believe me. I just hope Sara will give me a chance to make up for my stupidity."

Garrett snorted. "Are you living in a fucking time warp? It's been *eight* years. You think she's just gonna fall back into your arms after all this time? Believe me, Sara has a better head on her shoulders than that."

Mike regarded him coldly. "She's also kind and forgiving. A couple of traits you certainly didn't inherit."

Slowly, Garrett sat forward. "I'd be happy to give you a matching shiner for the other side of your face, if that's what you're looking for."

"Well here, let me turn my back so you'll have the same advantage you had last time."

"Smart-mouthed son-of-a—"

"All right, that's enough," Luke announced. "This situation is hard enough without the two of you butting heads every five minutes."

Mike shot to his feet and started pacing, careful to

avoid eye contact with Garrett. After several passes, he turned to Nicky. "Look, I'm sorry, but I have to talk to her. I have to know where I stand, one way or the other." He strode purposefully toward the back door and pushed it open.

Sara glanced over her shoulder when the screen door opened. *Mike.*

"We need to talk."

The pan she'd been drying fell from her hands and clattered to the floor. "Where's Garrett?" she asked, attempting to peer around his broad shoulders while being careful not to make eye contact with him. As long as she didn't look him directly in the eye, she'd be able to maintain her composure.

"You've always put him on a goddamn pedestal."

She bent over to pick up the pan. "Don't you dare say anything unkind about him."

"He's a pain in the ass."

She shot up and faced him, despite her own self-warning. "He's certainly not alone."

A slow smile curved his lips. "Now, there's the Sara I know and love."

"Don't you dare throw that word around. If you'd loved me, we wouldn't be in this situation." A surge of emotion tightened her chest, and she silently cursed herself for letting him get to her.

Hands on his hips, Mike sighed. "Look, I know you have every reason to believe that, but it's just not true. I've loved you since the first moment I laid eyes on you."

She paused. God, how she wanted to believe him. But if he'd truly loved her as he claimed, he'd never have been able to stay away for so long.

She swallowed past the lump in her throat and reached

into the dish drainer for something else to dry.

"All right, I'm done playing. Come on, we're going for a ride." Mike reached out and grasped her elbow.

"I'm not going anywhere with you," she said, yanking her arm free. "If you want to talk, we'll talk, but we're doing it right here." She threw the towel down on the counter and crossed her arms over her chest to hide her shaking hands.

"You either follow me to my truck, or I'll toss you over my shoulder and carry you there. But one way or another, we're taking a ride."

She gasped. *Arrogant son of a...* "If you touch me, I'll scream bloody murder."

"Then I guess I'll have to gag you as well."

He took a step toward her. She took a step back.

"You stay the hell away from me." She took another step back and bumped into the table, quickly grasping it for support. Her pulse sped up, though she feared it was as much from excitement as anger. Damn him for making her...*feel* something.

"Not a chance. I made that mistake once, I won't make it again." He caught her around the waist and hoisted her up, but Sara had no intention of going easy. She kicked and pounded his back. He grunted as he flipped her over, and her supper revolted as her stomach slammed down on his shoulder.

"I'll give you one more chance to walk out of here on your own two feet. What's it going to be?"

"I hate you," she seethed, wiggling and bucking for all she was worth.

"What's it going to be?" he repeated, gripping her so tight she thought she might puke.

Wouldn't that be *just* what he deserved?

"I...don't want to be alone with you," she reluctantly admitted.

"Don't trust yourself, eh?"

"You're just so damn full of yourself," she muttered, trying to ignore the fact that he smelled incredible. Mike had never been one to wear cologne, so the spicy, masculine scent must be aftershave or—

He started toward the front door, and a wave of dizziness hit her as the linoleum floor sped past.

"Wait! Okay, I'll go with you. Just put me down or you'll be wearing my supper in about ten seconds."

Mike set her gently on her feet. "Fine. Let's go."

Danny stuck his head through the back door. "Uh, everything okay in here?"

"Your sister and I are going to take a little ride. We'll be back." Mike cupped her elbow and escorted her out the front door.

They drove in silence for several minutes. When it got to be too much, she reached over and turned on the radio. He immediately turned it off. She flashed him her most disapproving frown and turned it back on.

Mike turned it off again and said, "You're acting like a child."

"Because I want to listen to the radio?"

He made a left, and then a right at the next stop sign. Sara sat up a little straighter when it dawned on her where they were headed. *No.* He couldn't be that insensitive...could he?

"Because you're doing everything you can to avoid talking to me."

"Figured that out all by yourself, did you? Boy, you're some detective."

Mike shot her a quick look, and Sara resisted the urge

to stick her tongue out at him. Acting like a child indeed!

The partly cloudy skies darkened as the storm the weatherman had predicted that morning finally rolled in. The winds picked up and rain pelted the windshield, lightly at first, but turning into a downpour within minutes. Mike cursed softly as he flipped on the wipers.

He made a right turn just after the light and drove along the winding road until they reached the pavilion at the end. He pulled into the first parking space and killed the engine.

Sara sat speechless, unable to believe he'd brought her here, to Pamperin Park. This place held so many memories for them. They'd had their first kiss here, as well as their first fight. They'd picnicked here, fished in the creek that ran behind the pavilion…

And it was here she'd cried her heart out after discovering she was pregnant.

TEN

Mike turned and leaned back against the door to face Sara, who sat stiff as a board. He could count on one hand the number of times she'd made eye contact with him since he'd arrived at the house.

"Why won't you look at me?" he asked, his voice gentle.

She remained stubbornly silent.

"Sara?"

"You know why."

"You're afraid of what I'll see?"

She ignored him and continued to stare out the window.

He'd always been able to read her facial expressions, so he reached over and, using only his forefinger, tilted her face up. His heart wrenched when he realized tears were threatening to spill.

"God, Sara, please don't cry. I'm sorry. I'm sorry for everything."

She jerked her head and his hand fell away.

"You don't understand. The reason I'm upset..."

"Tell me. You can tell me anything, sweetheart."

"This is all your fault, you know. *You're* the one who left me. I had no idea where you were, or if you were ever coming back." She stopped and took a deep, shuddering breath. "This is all your fault."

Mike leaned forward and tried to take her into his arms. She shrunk away as if his touch burned.

"Damn it, Sara. I was a screwed up kid who had no reason to believe in anything back then. You have to understand, the reason it was so easy for me to believe you'd turned to Carl had nothing to do with you, and *everything* to do with *me*. I never thought I deserved you, and when I saw that video... Hell, Carl came from a wealthy family, and I came from the devil himself. Why *wouldn't* you have wanted him over me?"

Sara did look at him then—her eyes wide with shock. "You thought I was sleeping with Carl because of his family's money? *That's* how little you thought of me?"

He ran his fingers through his hair in frustration. "That's not what I meant, I—"

"You didn't even give me a chance to defend myself. You just threw some accusations around and attacked Carl. Later that night, when your father told me you'd packed your bags and left, I was devastated. When a week went by without hearing from you, I had no choice but to accept the truth. Or at least what Rachel told me was the truth."

His jaw clenched. She'd had so much faith in him; she'd even braved facing his old man. And there wasn't a damn thing he could say to make up for the fact he'd had zero faith in her.

He reached over to grasp her hand, and for the first time that day, she didn't fight him.

"Sara, if you've ever believed anything about me, please believe this—I love you. I always have, I swear it on my mother's soul."

It was obvious he'd managed to shock her again. Those luminous brown eyes widened and her cheeks grew flushed.

"I don't know what to believe anymore." She gave her head a small shake. "But there's something I have to tell you, and it's about the hardest thing I've ever had to do."

"I told you, you can tell me anything."

She stared down at their clasped hands for a few seconds before looking up to meet his gaze. "Two weeks after you left me... I found out I was pregnant."

Mike's gut clenched. His breath caught. It took all his concentration just to draw air into his lungs. "What?"

"I was pregnant," she repeated, tears spilling down her cheeks.

"Then...are you telling me...I'm a father?" Mike's head spun. He'd never been more grateful to be seated in his life.

"A father?" She tore her hand from his. "No, you're a sperm donor. There's a difference."

Mike was absolutely thunderstruck. He heard what she'd said, but the words barely registered. He gazed out the window, his mind trying to wrap itself around the incredible news she'd just given him. "I can't believe this. My God, I'm a father." He turned back to her, his heart pounding furiously. "Do I have a son or a daughter?"

"A son."

A flash of memory gave him pause. Could the little boy he'd seen getting into Garrett's truck have been...? "My God, I have a son." Jesus, his hands were shaking.

"No, *I* have a son! I don't recall seeing you in the delivery room where I labored for thirty of the longest hours of my life. And I certainly don't recall you changing a diaper, or rushing him to the doctor when he spiked a fever after his six-month immunizations. *I'm* the one who taught him how to walk, talk, go potty on the toilet. You didn't do a damn thing except leave us when we needed you most, so don't you dare call yourself his father!" With that, Sara threw the door open and jumped out of the truck.

Stunned, Mike bounded after her in hot pursuit. She slipped on the wet grass, and he caught up to her in no time.

He grabbed her by the upper arm and had to raise his voice to be heard above the whipping wind and driving rain. "Damn it, Sara, you can't just drop a bombshell like that and run off!"

She spun around to face him. "You're hurting me."

"I'm sorry." He let go of her arm. "Look, we have to talk about this. I mean, what did you think I'd say? 'Oh, I have a son, how nice' and walk away?"

She glared up at him, mascara running down her cheeks, wet hair plastered against her head. "Don't you mean walk away *again*? I was hoping."

Ignoring that last crack, he pulled her back toward the truck. "I want to meet him. Right now. Come on, let's go."

She dug in her heels. "Y-you can't!"

It was Mike's turn to glare. He picked her up in his arms and ran back to the truck. When they were both seated inside, he handed her a stack of fast food napkins and said, "Don't think for one minute I'm going to let you, or anybody else, keep me away from my own son. I've already missed the first seven years of his life. I don't plan on missing out on another second."

"It's not that. If I'd wanted to keep you from him, I wouldn't have told you about him in the first place." She dabbed at her eyes.

"Then why are you hiding him from me? Because he certainly wasn't at the dinner table tonight." Mike finger-combed his wet hair and wiped his face with the hem of his T-shirt, for all the good it did. He started the truck back up and cranked the heat full blast.

"He doesn't know anything about this. My God, I just found out this morning what Rachel and Carl did to us."

"Well, where the hell does he think I've been all this time? He must have asked about me at some point."

Sara's face crumbled.

Mike muttered a curse. He stared out the windshield for a moment while he regained his composure. Oddly enough, the ferocity of the storm soothed him. "Sweetheart, I know it must've been hell on you raising our son all these years without my help. But that's over now. I'm here for you, and I'm here for him. I realize it'll take some time for us to get to know each other again, and for...my God, I can't believe I forgot to ask you his name. What *is* our son's name?"

She went pale and a chill racked her body. Her nipples strained against the filmy material of her halter top, and he cursed silently as his body reacted. He reached behind his seat for the flannel shirt he kept there.

"Here, snuggle under this." He draped it over her, then adjusted the heat vents so they blew in her direction. The temperature had been in the mid-seventies when they'd left her house, but had dropped a good fifteen degrees once the storm blew in.

"Thanks," she mumbled, holding the shirt up to her neck.

"Sara, what's his name?"

She seemed reluctant to meet his gaze. "Ethan."

Mike froze. "Ethan? As in 'the love of your life'

Ethan?"

Her lips pursed as her expression grew fierce. "He *is* the love of my life."

"Dammit, Sara. You knew exactly what I thought when you told me—" Suddenly, the truth dawned on him. His heart hammered against his rib cage. "You wouldn't have told me," he said, his voice a near whisper. "You would've let me leave town without ever knowing I had a son." When she didn't respond, he growled, "Am I right?"

"Yes!" she cried, her face crumbling again. "I couldn't take the chance that...that you'd..."

When she looked away, his eyes widened in horror. "My God, you were afraid I'd...*hurt* my own son?" His stomach wrenched at the thought. She'd actually believed him capable of such a thing? Knowing what an abusive monster his own father had been?

She dabbed at her eyes with the wet lump of napkins. "I didn't want to. But after the way you attacked Carl...I'd never seen you hit anyone before."

"He deserved it."

"Maybe so, but I didn't know that until today. And Rachel said you'd...my God, Mike, her face was bruised, and she had a black eye. I didn't want to believe her, but the fact that I never saw or heard from you again only supported her story."

What the hell could he say to that? She was right. If he'd gone home and slept on it instead of packing his bags and taking off like a jealous idiot, none of this would've happened. They would've talked, compared notes, and confronted those two lowlifes. He would've been holding Sara's hand when she'd discovered she was pregnant, and they'd have gotten married.

And he wouldn't have missed out on the first seven

years of *his son's* life.

Mike leaned his head back against the seat and closed his eyes. Bitterness ate at his soul until all he could think about was revenge. If it was the last thing he ever did, Rachel and Carl would pay, and pay dearly.

"You asked me where Ethan thinks you've been all this time," Sara said with a sigh of resignation. "He thinks you're in Heaven. I told him you were killed in a car accident."

"*What?*" He shot up and glared at her. "Why the hell did you tell him that?"

"Because to me, you *were* dead." Sara set his flannel shirt on the seat and wrapped her arms around herself. She turned to gaze out the window. "How could you have ever believed I'd sleep with Carl?" she asked in a near whisper.

"The same way you believed me capable of hitting a woman. I saw the proof with my own eyes." He blew out a frustrated breath and finger-combed his damp hair again. "I was a kid, Sara. I wasn't equipped with the best decision-making abilities back then."

"And now?"

"Now, I'm a grown man who knows *exactly* what he wants." *And I want you, sweetheart. You and our son.*

She cast him a quick glance over her shoulder, but didn't say anything. What he wouldn't give to know exactly what was going through that gorgeous head of hers.

They'd been sitting in silence for a couple of minutes when she said, "I want you to promise me something."

"Anything."

She turned to face him. "Once Ethan learns the truth, and you become a part of his life, I want you to swear you'll never leave him again."

Again. So damn ironic. Until a few minutes ago, Mike had no idea he'd left him in the first place. "I want to be angry as hell at you for even suggesting I'd leave my own son."

"Mike, I didn't mean—"

"Sweetheart, I know I have no one to blame but myself. You and Ethan are the complete innocents in all of this."

His gaze dropped to her lips. He'd wanted to kiss her since the moment he'd laid eyes on her yesterday in the bakery. He looked up. Her cheeks were flushed and her eyes heavy-lidded. He knew that look—whether she was aware of it or not, she wanted him to kiss her.

And Mike had never been able to deny Sara anything.

He leaned forward, cupped her face with both hands, and rested his forehead against hers. "I've missed you so much," he whispered, as overwhelmed by emotion as by the intoxicating sweet scent that was uniquely hers.

With a groan full of eight years-worth of longing, Mike slanted his mouth across hers in a fierce, urgent kiss. He coaxed her lips with the tip of his tongue, just the way he used to, praying for a response. When she opened to him, he triumphantly deepened the kiss, pulling her up against him with one hand while his other tangled in her hair, cupping the back of her head. A sexy little moan escaped her, and he wrapped his arms around her, crushing her against him.

Suddenly, her hands pushed against his chest and she tore her lips free.

"No, I don't want this," she said, lifting an unsteady hand to her mouth.

Mike kept his frustration in check. He leaned back against the seat and let out a silent breath. "If the way you responded to me just now was any indication, I'd say you're in denial."

"Get over yourself. It was just a reflex. Besides," she looked away as if hesitant to make eye contact. "I happen to be seeing someone."

Mike clenched his jaw. It took all his self-control not to tell her *exactly* what kind of sleazeball her 'someone' was.

Bringing the subject back to the original topic, he said, "When am I going to meet my son?"

"Garrett and I plan to sit him down tomorrow after supper. We'll explain everything to him the best we can and hope he understands. I have no idea how he's going to react, though, so it may be a few days before he agrees to meet you. You'll have to be patient," she finished, as if daring him to contest her authority where their son was concerned.

Mike had to grit his teeth, not because he might have to wait a few days to meet the boy, but because it was Garrett who held that power in his hands. Hell, if it were up to Garrett, Mike would never get to meet his son. And then Mike would end up looking like the bad guy when he did something desperate, like force the issue.

Deciding to play it safe, he said, "I've waited this long, a few more days won't kill me. Besides, I have a lot of work to do before I can put my parents' house on the market."

She peered up at him through her lashes. "I guess that means you won't be moving back to Green Bay?"

"Of course I'm moving back," he said, frowning. "I've lost enough time with my son. But there's no way in hell he'll ever set foot in *that* house. Besides," he watched her face carefully, "There's nothing keeping me in Illinois."

"Oh?" She fanned the front of her halter top as if trying

to dry it out. "I figured you'd have women lined up around the block just waiting for you to get back."

He grinned. "Well, I wouldn't want you to attack my already over-inflated ego, but that sounded a bit like jealousy to me."

She rolled her eyes. "Like I said, I'm seeing someone. He's a wonderful man." She continued to gaze out the window as she added, "And Ethan's crazy about him."

Mike clamped down on the inside of his cheek. The thought of that scumbag getting anywhere near Ethan made him want to smash his fist through the windshield. But he reminded himself that Sara had no idea who Jason really was, or that Mike did. So he reined in his temper and played up on the jealousy angle.

"You just keep this Mr. Wonderful away from my son. It's going to be hard enough trying to build a relationship with him without you confusing him with other men. Christ, I'm going to have enough trouble just keeping Garrett from undermining any progress I make." *Or any progress you and I make*, he thought, fighting the urge to lean over and kiss her again.

"Don't worry about Garrett. He may not care much for you, but he loves Ethan and would never do anything to hurt him."

He noticed she didn't respond to what he'd said about Jason, but decided to let it go. At least for now. Besides, if Mike had his way, Sara would be in *his* bed before the week was out, and Officer Thomas would be a moot point. And possibly sitting in a jail cell if DCI's suspicions proved true.

He started up the engine and flipped on the wipers with a rueful sigh. "Well, I'd better get you home before your brother sends the entire police force out to look for you.

The last thing I want is my son's first glimpse of me to be on the front page of the Press-Gazette, spread-eagled and face-down against a squad car."

Eleven

"Sara, there is one fine-looking man asking for you out in the store," Teresa said, sticking her head through the door.

Sara rubbed her forehead with the back of her hand. "I'll be right out."

She was in the process of decorating a sheet cake for twin girls who'd be celebrating their third birthday the following day. But it was Ethan and Mike who'd been monopolizing her thoughts all morning.

Later that afternoon, she planned to tell her son that not only was his father alive, but she and his Uncle Garrett had lied about him dying in a car crash. The thought of what Ethan's reaction might be had kept her stomach tied in knots all morning.

She wondered what had Mike searching her out so soon. He was anxious to meet Ethan, she knew, but she'd told him it'd probably be a few days before the time was right.

The sudden urge to check her reflection in the mirror overcame her as she passed the restroom. She cursed herself even as she peeked inside to make sure she didn't have pink icing on her face.

Not good, but not bad, she thought, hating herself for

caring. She stepped through the swinging door.

And came face-to-face with Jason.

"Hey, beautiful." He smiled at her, then glanced around, looking very much like a kid in a candy store. "Man, there ain't nothing like the smell of a bakery. Hope you don't mind me stopping by, but your brother's been bragging about your sweet rolls all morning. And I have to admit, it was the perfect excuse to come see you."

Sara silently cursed the disappointment she felt. "Of course I don't mind. And let me guess, Garrett wants you to bring back a couple dozen sweet rolls?"

Jason grinned. "You know him well."

"That I do." She plastered a smile on her face, folded up one of the large white boxes and slid open the doors of the display case. "Well, I know what everybody down at the station likes except you. What's your pleasure?"

He sent her an odd look before glancing down to peruse his choices. "What are those?"

"Apple fritters. Would you like to try one? They're the best in the city, even if I do say so myself."

"No, I believe you. They look damn good. Throw a couple in for me."

Sara smiled and started filling up the box.

After a minute, Jason cleared his throat. "I was wondering, if you don't have plans tonight, would you like to have dinner with me? There's an Italian restaurant around the corner from my apartment I've been meaning to try."

She looked up, uncomfortable with having to lie to this man. He'd been nothing but great to her and Ethan both. But she barely knew him, so what choice did she have? She simply didn't feel comfortable enough speaking to him about personal family matters.

Though her pulse pounded in her ears, she managed to give an Emmy performance when she said, "Oh, I'm sorry, but I have family business to take care of tonight."

"How about this weekend?"

"I'll definitely try. But like I said, I have some personal stuff going on, and I'm not sure if it'll be resolved by then."

"You know," he leaned a hip against the display case, "if you need someone to talk to, I'm a good listener."

She sighed. "Thank you, that's really sweet. But frankly, I don't know you that well and—"

He held his hand up. "Please, you don't need to explain. That was pretty presumptuous of me."

"Jason, I didn't mean it like that." Sara felt like a first-class witch. She gave her head a rueful shake. "I'm just wound really tight today. But I'd love to have dinner with you. How about Friday night?"

He beamed. "Friday it is. Pick you up at seven?"

She taped the box and held it up for him. "I'll be ready."

Sara watched him leave with an uncomfortable feeling gnawing at her gut. Though she'd purposely insinuated to Mike that there was more between her and Jason than there actually was, that, of course had only been to buy her some time and personal space. She'd always worn her heart on her sleeve and her emotions on her face, so when he'd kissed her... Good Lord, all those long-buried feelings came rushing back, and she'd panicked, plain and simple. She'd needed some way to make Mike back off and knew throwing another man in his face would do the trick.

And she still wasn't sure how she felt about Jason. He seemed like a really great guy. Yet when she'd walked out into the store a few minutes ago expecting to see Mike, the disappointment she felt said more than she cared to admit.

With a shake of her head, she headed back into the kitchen.

Mike set the phone in its cradle with a feeling of complete satisfaction. Today, he'd accomplished everything he'd wanted to and more. He'd originally planned to clean out his parents' house himself, as he'd been long overdue for some vacation time. But now that he had a reason to hurry, he'd decided to hire professionals. He wanted to find a home for his new family as soon as possible.

He had Goodwill coming within the hour to haul away as much as they could fit into their truck, with the exception of his mother's things, which he planned to pack up personally and take with him. Four women from a local cleaning service were due shortly after to clean the house from top to bottom. He also had a carpenter coming to repair the louvered door he'd busted, and a few other things that had been neglected over the years.

Wednesday, he had a crew coming to paint the entire inside of the house. They'd assured him the job would be done by Friday, Saturday at the latest. Then all there'd be left to do is put the house on the market.

The lawn and some other yard work he'd take care of himself. And since the house was solid brick, there wasn't much that needed to be done to the exterior except repair a couple of windows. Amazingly, his father had sprung for a new roof recently, so Mike didn't have to worry about that either.

His father. Mike had received a call from a lawyer earlier informing him that his father had a will, and that he needed Mike to come down to his office so he could go over it with him. Frankly, Mike had been shocked. He'd half expected to spend months in probate court before the house was legally declared his. But as it turns out, the old man had done one decent thing—he'd left Mike the house. And also, according to the lawyer, a considerable sum in his bank account.

Leaning back in the kitchen chair, he took a sip of his coffee as his thoughts drifted back to Sara and Ethan. He still couldn't believe he had a kid of his own, and was so damn happy it was all he could do not to run to *Toy's R Us* and buy out the entire store. *Sara probably wouldn't appreciate that*, he thought with a grin.

But once he found the perfect house, he was going to let Ethan buy anything his little heart desired. Mike had a lot of birthdays and holidays to make up for. And since he'd managed to save a good majority of his salary over the years, as well as make a few decent investments, he had the means to spoil his son rotten.

Once he'd hung up with the lawyer, Mike had placed a call to Lieutenant Stoddard. After briefing him on what little information he'd gotten so far on Thomas, he'd told him about Sara and Ethan, and also his intent to stay in Green Bay permanently.

Much to his relief, Lieutenant Stoddard had been completely understanding.

"No shit, huh? An instant family. Well, I'm thrilled for you, Mike, I truly am. Life's funny, isn't it?"

The phone rang, bringing Mike out of his reverie.

"Yeah, hello?"

"Mike? This is Leslie Morgan from A-1 Realtors.

You're not going to believe this, but I think I may have found exactly what you're looking for."

Sara had never been more scared in her life. In only a few short minutes, Garrett would pull into the driveway with Ethan, and they would sit him down and explain about his father the best they could.

She'd rather face down a grizzly bear than tell her son the two people he trusted most in this world had lied to him. Besides the fact his little heart would be broken, he had one hell of a temper. Much like his Uncle Garrett.

She stood and started pacing the kitchen. Her eyes were drawn to the fridge where Ethan's latest artwork hung. A mosaic made from little squares of colored tissue paper in the shape of their house. And as with most of his pictures, he'd drawn a big ol' dog sitting next to the huge blue spruce in the front yard.

A tear slipped down her cheek. She tore off a paper towel from the roll above the sink and dabbed gently at the corners of her eyes. Without thinking, she's applied mascara that morning, and didn't want to worry about telltale black smudges giving her away when Ethan walked through the door.

She glanced at the table where a plateful of his favorite chocolate chip cookies sat.

Her thoughts drifted, and she wondered what Mike was doing at that moment. She couldn't even imagine what he must be feeling, walking through that house, reliving all the pain and humiliation he'd endured at his father's hands.

Yet his mother had also lived there. Mike had only

spoken of her a few times, but Sara knew how much he'd loved her and regretted the horrors she'd had to deal with while battling cancer. Mike had been too young to be of any help to her, and that had eaten away at him for years. For all she knew, it may still be eating away at him.

Sara gave her head a mental shake. The last thing she wanted to do was start feeling sympathetic toward Mike. Because sympathy could lead to other feelings, and she needed to keep as much emotional distance between them as possible...didn't she?

She made her way to the back door and looked out toward her vegetable garden. So far, everything was looking good. By the end of next month she'd be canning green beans and making tons of zucchini bread, for both home and the bakery. That was the great thing about zucchini—it grew in such great abundance.

She wondered if Mike liked zucchini bread. He'd probably love the chocolate-chocolate chip zucchini bread she made so much of. She would have to remember to send him some...

No. She was not going to get into the habit of feeding him and taking care of him. It would be too easy to fall back into that familiar pattern. Things had changed. *She* had changed. She was a mother now, a successful businesswoman.

The problem was, she still wanted him. Even after all these years. And he knew it, too, the conceited jackass. But pride wouldn't allow her to just fall back into his arms—back into his bed—as if nothing had ever happened. He hadn't trusted in her love, and Sara was having a very hard time getting past that.

And maybe she wasn't supposed to. Maybe kismet had delivered Jason into her life at this exact time for a reason.

They had mutual attraction and chemistry, which was a great start. Ethan sure did seem to like the guy. Though who knew what would happen once his father became a part of his life...

She heard Garrett's truck pull into the driveway and nearly had heart failure. Good lord, she wasn't ready for this! Everything was moving way too fast and she wished for just one more day with her son before she had to rip his comfortable little world apart.

The front door flew open, and Ethan ran into the kitchen, his eyes immediately zeroing in on the cookies. He reached for one, then paused as if remembering his manners. "Can I have one? I already ate lunch at Hunter's."

Sara nodded and hoped her somber mood wasn't reflected in her eyes. "Of course, sweetie. As a matter of fact, I brought them home especially for you."

Ethan stuffed one in his mouth and took a huge bite. "Wheally? Dhey all for me? If Unca' Danny wants one, I ca' say no?"

She smiled. "They're all for you. You don't have to share them with anyone. Unless, of course, you want to."

He pondered that for a moment while he chewed and swallowed. "Well, you can have one since you brought 'em home for me. But just you. No one else."

"Not even me?" Garrett asked with feigned outrage as he strode into the kitchen.

Ethan rolled his eyes. "Fine. But don't tell Uncle Danny or he'll want one, too."

Sara took a deep breath and soundlessly expelled it. "Ethan, can you take a seat, please. Uncle Garrett and I need to talk to you."

With a shrug, he hopped onto one of the chairs and

took another bite of his cookie.

She poured him a glass of milk before taking the seat to his left. Garrett was already seated to his right, and for the first time, she realized how nervous her big brother seemed. He'd swiped his hand through his hair several times, and started finger-tapping the theme to *Bonanza* on the table—both telltale signs. This was going to be so hard on him.

After a quick throat-clearing, he looked up and gave an almost imperceptible nod, as if to say, 'I'm okay, no worries.'

Turning to her son, she said, "Ethan, what I have to tell you is incredible. You're going to be so happy...I can't even describe it to you."

"Then why do you look like you're gonna cry?" he asked, dunking his cookie in the milk.

Damn her expressive face. She forced a smile to her lips. "It's just that I'm so happy for you, and you know how mushy I get when I'm happy."

Ethan's eyes grew big as saucers. "I'm getting a puppy!" He looked to Garrett for confirmation.

"Sorry, sport, you're not getting a puppy. At least, not yet."

"I can't think of anything else that would make me happy." He took another bite of his cookie and chewed thoughtfully.

She and Garrett exchanged glances before she continued. "Ethan, do you remember a long time ago when you asked me about your dad?"

"Uh-huh."

"I told you that he'd passed away in a car accident and lived up in heaven?"

"Yep. And he's an angel watching over me." He

dunked his cookie again and popped the rest into his mouth.

She closed her eyes for a brief moment, just to gather enough to strength to get the words out. "Ethan, it wasn't true. Your father is very much alive."

He stared at her, his little brow creased, as if maybe he hadn't comprehended what she'd said. "Was it like, a mistake? They thought it was my dad who died, but it wasn't?"

"No, honey. It was a mistake all right, but it was my mistake. I told you that your father had died when I knew he hadn't. I lied to you, and I'm so sorry."

"But...why? I don't get it."

Garrett jumped in. "Sport, your mom—all of us—had a very hard decision to make, and we recently found out we may have made the wrong one. And for that, we're sorry."

Ethan propped his elbows on the table and cradled his face in his hands. He looked more thoughtful than upset, and Sara felt optimistic for the first time that day.

"Am I gonna get to see him?" he finally asked.

She smiled and smoothed her hand over the top of his head. "Of course, sweetheart. Your father is very excited about meeting you. But I told him it would be up to you when the two of you meet, okay? So you don't have to feel pressured or—"

"Let's go now. Can I see him now?" He stared at her expectantly.

"Ethan, don't you think we should talk about this? I mean, you must have more questions for us...don't you?"

He shook his head. "No. I just wanna see my dad."

Sara looked helplessly at Garrett. He shrugged, obviously having no more idea what was going on inside her son's head than she did.

"Sweetheart, I think maybe if we wait a few days—"

"I want to meet him right now," Ethan insisted as he jumped off the chair. His temper started to show as his little face screwed up, and he stomped his foot. "Why can't I meet him right now?"

Garrett stood and put his hand on his nephew's shoulder. "Listen, why don't you head downstairs and watch T.V. for a while. Your mother and I need to talk."

"No, I wanna go meet my dad, not watch stupid T.V.!"

"Ethan James," Garrett growled, "I said go downstairs, and I mean right this minute. Your mother will give your dad a call and set up a meeting. But right now, you do as you're told."

With a mutinous glare, Ethan snatched another cookie off the table and stormed from the room.

Sara stared after him, stunned. Of all the scenarios she'd played in her mind, this hadn't even come close. "I don't know what to think. I was afraid he wouldn't even want to meet Mike. At least, not right away. But I never expected," she gestured helplessly, "this kind of reaction."

"He's in shock, that's all. Why don't you give Mike a call and set up a meeting time. Maybe supper again tonight?"

Sara glanced at the refrigerator, looking for the scrap of paper Nicky had written Mike's cell phone number on. She spotted it under the Hershey's Kiss-shaped magnet.

"I know this has been difficult, but everything will work out, don't worry." Garrett reached over and ruffled her hair, much the way he would Ethan's.

She resisted the urge to roll her eyes.

"And once Ethan starts to spend more time with Mike, you'll have more time to yourself. Then maybe you and Jason can get something real going."

Jason... She couldn't even think about him right now.

Garrett rose to his feet. "I might as well head back to the station. Give me a call if you need anything."

After her brother left, she sat for a moment, trying to work up enough nerve to dial Mike's number. What if he wanted to come right over? All the guys were at work, and Sara wasn't sure she wanted to do this alone. What if something went wrong when he and Ethan came face-to-face? Boys that age were notoriously unpredictable.

Sara grabbed the phone and dialed the number that had been burned into her memory for years. After eight rings and no answer, she disconnected and grabbed his cell phone number off the fridge.

"Yeah, hello?"

She swallowed. Lord, he had the sexiest voice. "Mike, it's Sara."

"Hey...I didn't think I'd be hearing from you this soon. Is everything okay?"

She took a deep, calming breath. "How would you like to meet Ethan...tonight?"

"Really? Absolutely I would. So, he took the news well?"

"Pretty well." She twirled a lock of hair around her finger. "Much better than I'd expected."

"I can't tell you how relieved I am. And I have some news of my own. I may have bought a house today."

"What? Already?"

He chuckled. "The realtor found exactly what I was looking for. I took a tour of the place a few hours ago, and as soon as I stepped inside, I knew it was perfect. I made an offer right away."

"Wow." Conflicting emotions wreaked havoc with her senses. Tears welled up in her eyes as a bubble of laughter rumbled in her chest. Sara didn't know whether to laugh or cry.

"That's it? 'Wow?'"

"I don't know what to say. I'm happy for you. And Ethan. I imagine it'll be pretty exciting for him to suddenly have two homes, two bedrooms, two backyards. I suppose you'll buy him a puppy, too."

"Uh, only if it's okay with you."

"He's been asking for one for a while now. If you want to buy him a puppy, I won't stand in your way." She swiped a napkin out of the holder and dabbed at her eyes.

"Sara, you sound funny. Is everything all right?"

She nodded, but of course he couldn't see. "I'm fine. Just a little worried about Ethan."

"Are you sure you want to do this tonight? I mean, if you want to wait a day or two, I'll understand."

So considerate of her feelings. "No, Ethan's anxious to meet you." She walked over to the sink to rinse out the coffee pot. "Would you like to come for supper again? Nothing fancy, just meatloaf."

"Do you still make the one covered in mashed potatoes and cheese?"

Surprised he'd remembered, she couldn't hold back a smile. "Yep, that's the one."

"Sounds like heaven. Is there any chance there'll be some of that cherry pie left?"

"The guys polished off one, but the other's still intact." Her smile widened, but then she silently berated herself and swiped it away. Damn it, she didn't want him to be able to make her smile!

"Excellent. What time should I come?"

"We eat supper around six during the week."

"Sounds good, I'll see you then."

She disconnected the call and blew out a hard breath. Of course, she was happy for her son. Thanks to a twist of fate, he would finally get the chance to meet and know his father. But Mike's presence in her life after all these years? Utter confusion.

Sara dropped her forehead to the table with a groan of frustration.

TWELVE

"You're pulling my leg, right?" Nancy leaned halfway across the kitchen table in rapt attention. "After all these years, he just comes traipsing back into your life? And he never knew about Ethan?"

Sara shook her head as she mixed up a mountain of ground meat, bread crumbs, eggs, ketchup and spices. Being the only female in a household of five males could be difficult at times. And lonely. She'd been in desperate need of a woman to talk to, and thanked God her neighbor decided to stop by.

"I had no way of telling him. He left town, and no one knew where he'd gone. Eventually, we had to assume he wasn't coming back. And he hadn't, until last Thursday when his father died."

"And what about you?"

Sara looked up, confused. "What about me?"

"How do you feel about having him back in your life?"

"He's not back in my life. He's going to get to know his son, and that's it."

"Mmm-hmm." Nancy sat back and blew into her coffee cup. "And that's it, huh?"

Frowning, Sara added another squirt of ketchup to the ground meat mixture. What *did* she feel? Mostly frustrated. And scared. Vulnerable. Anger, excitement...*desire*.

"You see this guy, the love of your life, for the first time in years, and you don't feel a thing?" Nancy pressed.

"I didn't say that." Sara scooped half the mixture on one side of a large, foil-lined pan and started shaping it into a loaf. Oh, she felt something all right. Her nipples tightened just *thinking* about that amazing kiss in his truck. She chanced a quick glance up at her friend while shaping the remaining meat-mixture into a second loaf.

Nancy leaned forward again, her eyes narrowed perceptively. *Damn the woman and her mental x-ray vision.*

"I knew it! You've still got it bad for him, don't you? Well, how does he feel about you? How romantic to think he might've been pining for you all these years."

Sara rolled her eyes, though her friend's sharp observation was dead-on. She washed her hands, then opened the oven door and slid the meatloaves inside. "I doubt he's been 'pining' for me. But..."

"But what? Come on, sister, throw a girl a bone!"

Sara laughed and gave her head a disbelieving shake. "Woman, you are a nut."

"So I've been told. Now, quit stalling and tell me what you're so obviously dying to tell me."

She pulled the garbage can up to her chair, grabbed her potato peeler and hefted the ten-pound bag of red potatoes onto the table. Meeting her friend's gaze, struggling to keep her excitement from bubbling forth, she admitted, "He kissed me."

Nancy took a cautious sip of her hot coffee then looked up, eyes gleaming. "Did you sleep with him?"

Sara almost choked. "How do you get from a simple

kiss to sleeping with him?"

Those strawberry-blonde curls bounced as her friend shrugged. "I think it's a pretty natural assumption. I mean, you've been on, what, one date since I've known you? You have to be horny by now. Unless, of course, you slept with that cute cop the other night."

Her mouth dropped open in shock. *After one date?* "You're serious, aren't you?"

"Like a heart attack." Nancy took another sip of her coffee. Abruptly switching subjects, she asked, "Hey, you know that big old house on the corner? The one with the huge backyard and in-ground swimming pool?"

She sure did. Sara had dreams of buying that house for herself and Ethan one day, if it ever went up for sale. "Yeah, what about it?"

"I think someone might have bought it today."

Sara froze. "Are you sure?"

"Pretty sure. I saw a realtor showing the house to some guy this morning."

"I didn't even know it was up for sale." Sara's eyes narrowed with suspicion. No...couldn't be. "I don't suppose you could describe him for me?"

"Oh, honey, he was gorgeous. Tall, dark, and handsome...with eyes so blue you could see them from clear across the street. I figure he must be married, though, to be buying such a big house."

That weasel! He'd stolen her house. Tempted to cancel the dinner just to be petty, Sara grabbed a potato and her peeler, and took out her aggression in a less vindictive way.

Okay, so technically it wasn't his fault. Mike couldn't have known she'd had her sights set on that house for years. But, dammit, Green Bay was a big city. Why did he have to come looking for a house in *her* neighborhood?

"Well, I'd better get my butt back home." Nancy took one last sip of her coffee and rose to her feet. "I need to get supper started myself. I hope everything works out for you. Oh, and don't do anything I wouldn't do," she teased, unaware of Sara's mood change.

Or the blue-eyed cause.

"You mean there's actually something you won't do?" Sara grumbled. Knowing her friend didn't deserve her petty resentment, she forced a smile to her lips.

"On second thought, wear that long, turquoise sun dress you have, but skip the panties." Nancy gave her hips a playful wiggle and added, "Easy access, baby."

At precisely a quarter-to-six, Mike parked his truck on the street in front of the Jamison's house.

He leaned his head back against the headrest, sat for a moment, and realized he was scared to death. It'd just hit him all of a sudden. He was afraid to meet his own son. *Incredible*, he thought. Afraid of a tiny little boy.

Or maybe he was afraid of himself. Not like he had a great role model to draw fathering experience from. What if Ethan made him angry? Would he react the same way his own father had, with his fists instead of his words?

For a split second, Mike considered starting up the truck and driving straight back to Chicago—for his son's sake. But he could never do such a thing. Not to Ethan, not to himself, and certainly not to Sara.

The thought of meeting Ethan for the first time wasn't the only reason he felt...anxious. Sara, too, had him twisted up in knots. God, how he wanted her. It was a miracle he could stand erect whenever she was in sight.

Erect, he thought with a groan. Wrong word to use.

The passenger-side door swung open and Nicky climbed inside. "Hey, Mike."

"Nicky."

"About Ethan. I wanted to tell you about him, I swear I did, but it just wasn't my place. I hope you understand."

"You know I do. Don't worry about it." Mike sat forward and laced his fingers on the steering wheel. "Besides, you almost did tell me, didn't you? Friday night at the police station when Garrett practically bit your head off?"

His friend confirmed with a rueful nod. "I always regretted that you left town before finding out Sara was pregnant. But there wasn't a damn thing I could do about it. Nobody knew where the hell you were."

"I know. Believe me, I don't blame anybody but myself." He blew out a ragged breath and ran his fingers through his hair. "It was hard enough finding out I'd left behind the best thing that ever happened to me. But finding out I'd left behind a child...my own son? Christ, I have no idea what to say to him. I have no experience with little kids."

"You'll be fine, don't worry about it. Ethan's a great kid. You've seen a picture of him, right?"

"No, I haven't," Mike admitted, his brow hiking up in astonishment. "I guess I was so shocked yesterday I never even thought to ask."

Nicky cocked a brow. "There's like ten-thousand pictures of him throughout the house. You didn't see one?"

He laughed. "Man, I was so freakin' nervous about seeing Sara again, I barely glanced at anything else."

There was a tap on Mike's window. He turned to see Danny grinning at him.

"Hey, you two gonna chit-chat all night, or is Mike gonna come in and meet his son?"

His buddy thumped him on the shoulder. "Come on, he's right. It's time to meet the best thing you ever did."

Sara took a quick peek out the living room window, and saw Mike getting out of the truck. She raced back into the kitchen and checked on the meatloaves. The cheese hadn't melted yet, so she'd give them a few more minutes. She glanced at the table. Perfect.

"Ethan, are you ready? He's here!" she called out.

When she didn't get a reply, she hustled down the hall to his bedroom and rapped on the door. "Ethan?"

"Come in."

Surprised by his timid tone, Sara opened the door and saw him sitting on his bed, a Transformer action-figure clutched in his fist. He wore a brand-new pair of jeans and his favorite Spiderman T-shirt, and as he stared down at his lap, eyes suspiciously bright, her heart gave a little lurch.

She sat down beside him on the bed. "You have the same look on your face as when you're going to the dentist."

"I was just thinking," he said.

Sara waited for him to elaborate, but he didn't. *He's so much like Garrett*, she thought. "About...?"

He turned his head and gazed up at her. "What if my dad doesn't like me?"

"Oh, sweetheart!" She wrapped her arms around him

and gave him a reassuring squeeze. "Your daddy is going to think you're the best thing since chocolate chip cookies, I promise."

"But his dad didn't like him."

She frowned. "Where did you hear such a thing?"

He gave a one-shoulder shrug. "I heard Uncle Garrett and Uncle Nicky talking about it."

"You were eavesdropping? What did I tell you about that?" she gently chided him.

"Sorry. It's just that I wanted to know more about my dad, and I accidentally heard 'em talking. Then on purpose, I stayed and listened," he admitted.

"Ethan, when you're older, your father will probably tell you about his own father. But in the meantime, I promise, your daddy already loves you and can't wait to meet you."

"Really?"

He looked so hopeful Sara's heart swelled with love for this incredible little person that was her son.

"Really and truly, honest to God. Now," she got to her feet and motioned toward the door, "ready to go meet your father?"

Ethan slid off the bed and eyed the Transformer figure clutched in his hand as if trying to come to a decision. Finally, he set it down on the bed and said, "Okay, I'm ready."

The guys hadn't come in yet, so Sara had Ethan take a seat at the kitchen table while she pulled her meatloaves from the oven. She realized she hadn't seen Garrett in quite a while, but then remembered he'd headed downstairs to do a load of laundry. She suspected there was more to it than that, and her heart broke for him. Though she knew her brother was happy for his nephew, he'd been Ethan's whole world since birth, and it wouldn't be easy sharing him with the man he'd thought he was protecting him from all these years.

Uncle Luke came in from the backyard and went to the sink to wash his hands. "Garden looks good this year. Everything came up."

"I know. Miracle, hey?" Grateful for the distraction, she set the pan on top of the stove, then reached into the top cabinet and pulled out the serving platter. "I just wish I had more space. I'd love to plant some pumpkins for Ethan one of these years."

Before Uncle Luke could respond, they heard the men coming up the steps of the front porch. She glanced at Ethan and saw him sit up a little straighter in his chair. She felt the familiar swell of pride in her chest that almost always caused her to have to blink back tears. In just a few seconds, both of their lives would be changed forever, and Sara was finally starting to believe that maybe, just maybe, everything would work out.

She walked up and stood behind Ethan's chair—where they both had a perfect view of the front door.

First Nicky appeared, casting his nephew a reassuring wink. Danny came through the door next, grinning from ear-to-ear.

And then Mike walked in, larger than life. Sara put her hands on Ethan's small shoulders for support, just as Garrett had done for her the day before. Had it only been two days since Mike strode back into her life? The thought astonished her. And the look of wonder on his face as he gazed at his son for the first time warmed her heart. She could only imagine what he must be feeling.

Mike paused for just a moment before continuing toward Sara...and his son.

His chest expanded as he sucked air into his lungs, and he flexed his fingers as he stared down at the little boy who couldn't be anybody *but* his son. He hadn't expected the resemblance to be so...remarkable. He'd flipped through some old photo albums just that morning, and the face staring back at him had been on nearly every page. His spitting image, some would say.

And now he knew for certain; the little boy he'd seen with Garrett the other night had, in fact, been Ethan. Christ, if things had worked out differently, he may never have found out that *that* little boy had been his own son. The thought caused his throat to constrict.

My son.

Ethan stared up at him, mouth agape, and Mike couldn't hold back a smile. What he felt was so strong and indescribable, so *personal*, he wished like hell they didn't have an audience. But he knew Sara's brothers and uncle were a great source of comfort to her and Ethan both, so he'd just have to do his best to keep the myriad of emotions coursing through him in check.

He glanced up at Sara and his heart swelled even more. With her hands resting protectively on their son's shoulders, an unsure smile wavering on her lips, she had never looked more beautiful to him.

The enormity of what she'd gone through over the years, without his protection, his support, both emotionally and financially, hit him like a ton of bricks, and it was all he could to stand on his own two feet. All those years wasted, brooding, feeling sorry for himself; believing Sara had betrayed him when in reality, she'd been busy raising and nurturing their son.

Had a bigger jackass ever walked the face of the earth?

Sara made the introductions. "Mike, I'd like you to

meet your son, Ethan James. Ethan, this is your father, Michael William Andrews."

"We have different last names," Ethan told him.

Surprised, Mike glanced up at Sara. It never even occurred to him that Ethan wouldn't have his last name.

"I was told I couldn't put your name on the birth certificate without your signature, and honestly, I never looked into it any further."

Mike held her gaze, tempted to pursue the issue. But that particular conversation would have to wait for another day. Today was about getting to know his son. Period.

He took another step forward and held out his hand. "Hello, Ethan."

Eyes huge in his little face, Ethan slowly lifted his hand. "You're almost as big as Uncle Garrett."

Mike's lips twitched. "Almost. But nobody's as big as your Uncle Garrett." He could think of a few other choice things he'd like to say about his son's uncle, but wisely kept his opinions to himself. Besides, regardless of how he felt about the guy, Garrett had been the one taking care of Ethan all these years, helping Sara raise him, clothe him, feed him. He'd been there when Mike hadn't, and he knew he owed the man a lot for that.

Mike enclosed Ethan's small hand in his and gave it a gentle shake. Nicky and Danny both thumped him on the back as Luke came over and ruffled Ethan's hair.

"You kinda look like me," his son announced, causing an eruption of laughter from everyone.

Ethan glanced up at Sara and asked, "What am I supposed to call him?"

She met Mike's gaze, her eyes slightly widened in question.

"I'd like you to call me Dad," he told his son, smiling.

"But if you don't feel comfortable, you can just call me Mike." He placed a hand on his head.

The first real smile split Ethan's face. "I'll call you Dad."

Hearing the word from his son's lips, tears sprang to his eyes. Blinking, he glanced at Sara who quickly wiped away a tear. She sniffled, and he wished like hell he could wrap them both in his arms. But that would have to wait for another time.

"I hope everyone's hungry," she said, pushing their son's chair in. "Let's eat before supper gets cold."

Ethan gazed up at Mike. "You can sit by me. I mean, if you want to."

"There isn't anywhere else I'd rather sit."

"Something sure smells good."

Upon hearing his uncle's voice, Ethan spun around excitedly. "Uncle Garrett, look! This is my dad!"

Garrett, who'd come up from the basement, took the seat to Ethan's right. He cast Mike a quick look. "Yeah, I can see that. You must be pretty excited, sport. I'm happy for you."

Sara placed the platter of her amazing meatloaves in the center of the table, and Mike's mouth watered as the savory aroma drifted his way. Meatloaf and mashed potatoes covered in bubbly, melted cheese? Damn, he'd missed her cooking.

He was about to offer to help when Garrett stood and started carving the loaves into neat slices. Sara took care of everything else, placing a heaping basketful of tiny dinner rolls in front of Ethan, the buttered green beans between Danny and Nicky, and a bowl of creamy cucumber salad next to Uncle Luke.

Unable to take his eyes off her as she squeezed in next

to Garrett on the extra chair, Mike searched for something to say to break the sudden awkwardness. "You've really got that down pat. Impressive."

"I've had a lot of practice." Reaching for a slice of meatloaf, she met his gaze, her usually expressive eyes inscrutable. He barely suppressed a groan as she forked a small bite into her delectable mouth. So sexy, so incredibly beautiful.

As always, she looked amazing. She wore a long summery dress that showed off every curve on her petite frame. It was styled like a tank top, but with a short row of buttons in the front. And the color, a kaleidoscope of tie-dyed purples, looked incredible against her fiery hair.

But the fact that she was running around barefoot is what turned him on the most. Mike remembered how playful she used to be under the table, teasing him by seeing how far she could slide her delicate little foot up into the pant leg of his jeans...

He felt himself grow hard under the table. *Shit. Think about puppies, dammit, puppies!*

Someone spoke and a comfortable conversation was struck up, with Ethan chattering on in all his excited glory.

Luke, Nicky, and Garrett were talking about pulling up some bushes to plant pumpkins for next year when Mike caught Sara's attention. "I almost forgot. I got a call from the realtor a couple hours ago. The house is mine. And even better, the elderly gentleman who owns it moved out over a month ago, so his family said I could move in by the weekend. They just need to rent a moving van to clear out his things."

"No kidding? Saturday, huh. Good for you."

Was it just him, or did she seem oddly disinterested?

"There *is* one small detail I forgot to mention," he said,

gauging her reaction closely.

"Oh? And what's that?" She reached for the green beans and dumped some onto her plate.

"The place I bought is just down the block. It's the big one on the corner, with the huge lilac bush in the front yard."

"No shit? You bought old man Pankovich's house?" Danny said. "Hey, Sara, isn't that the house you've had your eye on for a while?"

She shot Danny a sidelong glance. "I've thought about it. But I had no idea Mr. Pankovich had moved out, or was interested in selling." Her annoyance was evident by the chill in her tone.

"You're gonna live in old man Pankovich's house?" Ethan asked, clearly excited.

Mike nodded, a little concerned by Sara's reaction. He'd expected her to be relieved their son's second home would be so close. "Sure am. And I was hoping once I move in, you'll want to come spend some time with me."

To Sara, he added, "I thought it might make things easier on all of us if I lived close by. That's why I asked the realtor to find me something in this neighborhood. I just never expected her to find me a house on your block."

Sara forked a few green beans into her mouth, her smile brittle.

"You mean, like a sleepover?" Ethan asked, oblivious to the fact his mother was less than ecstatic.

"Exactly like a sleepover. We'll rent movies, order pizza. Whatever you want to do."

"Hell, Sara, I think it's a perfect idea," Nicky said. "Won't it be comforting to know Ethan's only a few houses away when he's visiting Mike?"

"I agree," Garrett chimed in, surprising everyone,

including Mike. "This is going to be an adjustment for all of us, especially you and Ethan. Won't it ease your mind to know his second home is so close by?"

Sara shot Mike a look before glaring at her traitorous brothers. *Second home? This is Ethan's home!* "I suppose it will."

Mike cleared his throat. "You know, Sara. I was hoping you might give me a hand with the house. I can fix what needs to be fixed, paint, you name it. But I haven't the slightest idea how to decorate it."

Decorate it yourself, you house thief! "There's really not much to it. You just buy things you like."

"Oh, well, excellent then." He draped his arm across the back of Ethan's chair. "So if I want a green couch and red chairs in the living room, it'll look all right? And I was thinking of painting each room a different color and theme, you know? Like the living room would be orange with a southwestern flare, the kitchen navy blue with, like, a nautical theme. I was also thinking that wicker furniture would—"

She held up her hand, palm forward. "Stop, please, you're making me dizzy. Okay, I'll help you decorate. But on one condition."

"Name it."

"You can't help *at all*."

"Deal."

Everybody at the table burst out laughing.

Sara forced a smile when in truth she probably should've had her head examined. Her emotions were jumbled and all over the map, and all she wanted to do was crawl into bed and pull the covers over her head. Every minute spent in that man's company left her feeling even more vulnerable than the time before. If she wasn't careful, she just might fall back in love with the faithless jerk.

Would that be so bad?

Yep. She definitely needed to have her head examined.

Thirteen

Mike forked the last bite of cherry pie into his mouth and washed it down with the rest of his coffee. He was in heaven, plain and simple.

The Jamison men had all taken their dessert out onto the patio to give him and Ethan some time alone to bond, and he was grateful to finally have all of their support.

A week ago, he'd merely been existing in this world. He did his job, paid his bills, occasionally went out with his co-workers. But he'd been dead inside for so long, he'd completely forgotten what it felt like to live.

Now here he was, looking across the table at his son, while Sara poured him a cup of coffee. It was such a perfect scene, such an incredible feeling, Mike was afraid to blink for fear it would all disappear, and he'd be back in his one-room studio apartment, staring at the tube, eating a frozen pizza, and feeling sorry for himself.

"Want the rest of my pie?" Ethan asked, peering up at him. "Mom said cherry's your favorite."

Mike smiled. That seemed to be all he could do tonight. "That's awfully generous of you, but I'm stuffed. Honest."

His little boy shrugged and went back to eating his pie.

His boy. How Mike loved the sound of that.

He watched as Sara finished loading the dishwasher, then grabbed the broom and started sweeping up imaginary crumbs. Nervous energy, he figured as he watched her flutter around the kitchen.

It scared the hell out of him how attracted he still was to her. He didn't know what he'd do if she told him she didn't feel the same. The thought was inconceivable. He wanted her, damn it.

"Sara?"

She didn't look up. "Yeah?"

Mike glanced at Ethan and then back at her. "There's somewhere I'd like to take Ethan this week, unless, of course, you think it's too soon...?"

Ethan's head popped up, a glob of cherry pie filling clinging to his chin. "It's not too soon, right, Mom?"

"That depends," she said, looking uneasy. "Where exactly do you want to take him? Because I'm sorry, I won't allow you to take him all the way to Chicago, if that's where this is heading."

"That's not even close to what I have in mind. I was going to suggest we head over to that new indoor water park and resort that I've seen a million commercials for. We could splash around all day, have supper, then spend the night. You know, stay up watching movies and eating snacks out of the vending machines. Sound like a plan?"

Ethan bounced up and down on his chair. "Mom, can we? Pleeease?"

Sara realized Mike was new to this whole parenting thing, but she'd have to make it very clear to him that discussing things in front of their son was a no-no. "Honey, I'm sorry, but I think it's a bit too soon for that. My goodness, you've only just met each other."

"Then come with us," Mike said, with obvious purpose

to put her on the spot.

Gritting her teeth, she made a mental note to have a *very* long talk with him about the do's and don'ts of parenting.

"Yeah, Mom, come with us. It'll be great. And the three of us can have a sleepover!"

"We haven't had a sleepover in a long time," Mike mischievously pointed out.

"Mike—" she growled in warning.

"We'll have a great time," he rushed to add. "I promise. All fun, no pressure. And needless to say, everything is on me."

"Come on, Mom. It'll be awesome!" The little stinker clapped his hands together in a pleading gesture. "Please, please, please!"

Oh, how she'd like to crack the man over the head. The snake knew exactly what position he'd put her in by asking in front of their son. But they *did* have an awful lot of time to make up for. How could she possibly say no to what sounded like a great time for Ethan? And now she couldn't refuse, of course, unless she wanted to come off looking like the wicked witch of the west.

"All right, we'll do it. But," she cast Mike a meaningful look, "I insist on separate rooms."

"Spoilsport."

"But, Mom, I bet they have a bed big enough for all of us," Ethan said, his little brow screwed up.

Mike coughed.

She cast him a quelling glance before replying, "Sweetheart, it wouldn't be proper for us all to stay in the same bed. Or room, for that matter."

"Don't worry, *Mom*. I'll reserve two rooms." Mike looked back at Ethan and added, "They might even have rooms with balconies that open up over the water park."

Her little boy's eyes lit up. "We can jump into the pool from the balcony!"

Mike laughed. "Sorry, son, but there'll be no jumping from the balconies, period. Your mother will never let you leave the house again if you end up breaking bones on our very first outing."

Son. Sara could feel her eyes start to mist. *He's my son, dammit!* She knew she was being selfish, but she wasn't ready to share him yet. This was all happening way too fast.

Mike glanced at the clock. "Well, I should probably call it a night."

"You don't have to go yet! It's not bedtime, right, Mom?"

Before Sara could answer, Mike said, "I'm sorry, Ethan, but I have a lot to get done tomorrow, so I really should get to bed early. And I'd like to call that resort tonight. Which reminds me," he glanced back at Sara, "what night works best for our little excursion? Friday? Saturday?"

She took a deep breath, fighting to get her emotions back under control. "I have plans with Jason Friday, but Saturday would work."

Ok, so she'd purposely mentioned her date out of petty spite. Lord knew she wasn't perfect. And judging by the way his jaw clenched, her jab had hit home. So why did she suddenly regret throwing Jason in his face? A sudden thought occurred to her. Was she really keeping Mike at arm's length out of self-preservation...or as punishment because she blamed him for the past?

A twinge of remorse had her adding, "Or maybe even one night this week. Ethan is on summer break, and my work schedule is pretty flexible."

He cleared his throat. "Great. I'll let you know tomorrow which night I've reserved. Or maybe I could swing by after supper and take the two of you out for some ice cream?" he suggested with a hopeful look.

"Yay! We can go to Dairy Queen!" Ethan started bouncing up and down on his chair again.

Sara shook her head, her annoyance with the man flaring back to life. As if he didn't know exactly how the promise of ice cream would pan out. "You two had better not start ganging up on me every time you want your way."

They glanced at each other, then grinned at her, and she knew it was impossible for Ethan to look any more like his father than he did.

"Well, what do you think, *Mom*?" Mike persisted with that sexy grin of his. "Can I take the two of you out for ice cream tomorrow?"

"Come on, Mom!" her keen little man implored with his puppy-dog eyes.

"Fine," she conceded on a sigh.

"All right! Mom, you're the best!" He hopped off the chair and went to set his fork and plate on the counter.

"Thanks, Sara. I really appreciate you letting me spend time with him again so soon. Now that I'm a part of his life, I'd like to see him as often as I can."

Trying and failing to ignore the rush of compassion his words invoked, she glanced over at Ethan, who was now digging around in the refrigerator. "Summer break just started, so Ethan's going to have a lot of free time on his hands over the next few months. I suppose it'd be all right if he spent a few hours a day with you."

"I don't know what to say. You're being so great about

this." He rose to his feet and carried his own plate to the sink.

"I love my son more than anything in this world." She crinkled her brow. "*Our* son. This really is going to be an adjustment."

He turned to face her. "I'll make it as easy on you as possible, I swear it."

Sara could see the love shining in his eyes. For his son, of course, she knew. But had he meant it when he'd sworn to have always loved her?

Doesn't matter, she emphatically reminded herself. *You can't trust him with your heart... No way in hell will you be falling back into his arms*—or *his bed.*

"Well, I can honestly say this has been the best night of my life. Ethan?" Mike gestured for him to come stand before him, then knelt down and placed his hand on his son's shoulder. "I want you to know how sorry I am that I missed out on so much of your life. If I had known about you, nothing, and I mean *nothing,* could have kept me away. But I swear to you, from this day forward, you can count on me to be the kind of father you deserve. Understand?"

Her amazing little boy gazed at his father with something akin to hero worship. "Are we gonna live together? You can move in with us, if you want. You can have my bed, and I'll sleep on the floor in my sleeping bag."

Mike smiled. "That's incredibly generous of you, Ethan. But remember what we talked about earlier? That I bought a place of my own? It's just a few houses down, so we'll be neighbors. You can think of it as your home away from home. Hey, maybe one day this week we'll take a ride and see if we can find the perfect bedroom set for your new room."

"Can I get bunk beds? I really, really, really want bunk beds."

Mike glanced over at Sara. "Three 'really's,' huh?"

She forced a smile. Of course, Mike would simply buy Ethan every single thing his heart desired with zero regard for her feelings. A puppy, bunk beds...what would be next, a go-cart? Reminding herself that she was being petty again, and that Mike *was* brand new to parenting, she said, "His friend, Hunter, has bunk beds."

"'Cept *my* bunk beds will be way better than Hunter's. Right, Dad?"

Mike scooped Ethan up in his arms and squeezed the stuffing out of him. Tears sprang to her eyes. Ethan was as happy as she'd ever seen him.

"If bunk beds are what you want, bunk beds are what you'll get."

Ethan started laughing and wrapped his arms around Mike's neck. "I want one with a slide."

"They make bunk beds with slides?"

"Uh-huh." He leaned back and met his father's gaze. "They even have one that looks like a castle fort."

"No kidding? Well, when the time comes, you can pick out whichever one you want. How does that sound?"

"It sounds awesome!" He threw his arms back around Mike's neck for another quick hug and then wriggled to be free.

Mike laughed and released him. "Don't forget, we have a date for Dairy Queen tomorrow."

"I would never forget about Dairy Queen," Ethan informed him. Then he whirled around and took off down the hall.

"Well," Mike said with a tentative smile, once their son

disappeared into his room. "Guess I'd better hit the road. I'll see you tomorrow."

He gazed at her for a moment, brow slightly creased, as if he had something on his mind. But before she could ask, he spun on his heel and headed for the front door.

He'd just grasped the doorknob when, with a softly muttered curse, he paused and turned back to face her. Sara's pulse kicked into overdrive as he strode back through the living room, into the kitchen, not stopping until they were standing toe to toe.

He gazed down at her, those mesmerizing blue eyes as potent as ever. Her breath caught as her heart beat wildly against her ribs. He brought his hand up, as if to cup her face, then hesitated, curling his fingers and dropping his arm back to his side. "Sara, I know this is going to sound incredibly lame, but...thank you. Thank you for my son."

Her throat constricted, the sincerity in his voice unmistakable, and it was all she could do to keep the tears at bay. God, what *an emotional day*. She swallowed past the lump in her throat and took a half-step backward. At six-foot-three, the man towered over her, which, at the moment, was a bit unnerving. "I have no idea what to say. I guess I should be thanking you as well. I certainly didn't make him by myself."

"He's such a great kid, though. And we both know I didn't have a damn thing to do with it."

"You'll have the rest of your life to be his father," she said. "If you want to have a good relationship with him, you will. Because he's already crazy about you, I can tell you that much."

He raised his hand up again, but this time he did cup her cheek, his thumb stroking lovingly against her soft skin.

Sara grew warm in places that had lain dormant for a very long time. Her gaze moved slowly down to his lips.

He leaned forward, and she watched as if in a trance, her eyes closing in natural response. He was going to kiss her, and she wanted him to. Oh, how she wanted him to...

The back door flew open and Nicky strode in, empty dessert plates stacked in his hand.

She sprang back in surprise, and Mike gripped her shoulder as if to steady her.

Nicky came to a halt just inside the door. A broad grin spread across his face. "Did I interrupt something? Sorry about that."

Sara cleared her throat. "No, you didn't interrupt anything. Mike was just leaving, right?"

"Yeah, I was just on my way out the door. See you tomorrow night. Around...seven?"

Biting her bottom lip, she cast a quick look in her brother's direction. "Seven is fine."

Mike grinned down at her. "'Night, Sara. Sweet dreams." He gave Nicky a quick nod, and then headed for the front door.

When the door clicked shut behind him, Sara reached out to take the dirty dishes from her brother. Glancing up, she saw the smug look on his face and muttered, "Oh, go soak your head."

Mike watched with a bit of déjà vu as Jason made his way to the back of the bar and sat on a stool next to Carl. Only this time, his suspect sported a smile and gave Montgomery a jovial thump on the back.

When the bartender approached, Mike pulled a fin

from his pocket and ordered a Bud. Not that he had a taste for one, but it would certainly draw attention if he just sat there and stared toward the back of the room.

Folding his arms down on the bar, he kept an eye on the two of them through his peripheral vision. Their exchange seemed pretty tame compared to last time, and Mike wondered if something might be going down tonight. After maybe five minutes, they got up, polished off their beers and slipped out the back door.

With a softly muttered curse, he took a swig of his beer and weighed his options. He'd be foolish to follow them outside since he had no way of knowing what he'd be walking into. They could be standing right outside the door for all he knew. He'd have to leave through the front and hope to catch them pulling out of the parking lot so he could tail them.

Mike wasn't sure what kind of vehicle Carl drove, but if Thomas' Big Bird mobile was still in the lot, he'd know for certain *something* was going on behind the tavern.

When he pushed open the door, his eyes immediately landed on Thomas' truck. *Empty*.

Taking a deep breath, he pulled his pistol from its holster and stealthily made his way around to the back of the building. He heard voices. Carl's he recognized, others he didn't, and Mike became concerned with his odds. As badly as he wanted to bust the SOB, he couldn't make any rash decisions that might jeopardize the case.

Or his own neck. Up until a couple days ago, he wouldn't have given a rat's ass about his own safety. He'd have gone back there, gun drawn, and worried about the repercussions later.

But he had a family to think about now, and he certainly wanted to live long enough to enjoy them. And make up for all the time they'd lost thanks to his own insecurities.

Blowing out a frustrated breath, Mike stuck his pistol back in its holster and quietly made his way to his truck. He scanned the other vehicles in the lot—they all appeared to be empty.

He'd barely climbed inside when Jason and Carl appeared from around the back of the building. He rolled his eyes when Carl opened the door of an old piece of shit, sky-blue Chevy Cavalier. *Guess his parents don't piss money away on him the way they used to*, he thought with a smirk.

Thomas made a left out of the parking lot, and Montgomery made a right. Mike chose to follow Thomas, who drove straight to his apartment. After nearly forty-five minutes of waiting, Mike figured it was doubtful anything would happen tonight, and headed back to his parents' house.

He'd had Carl's file downloaded Sunday morning and found nothing more than a handful of petty crimes, most of which had occurred before his twenty-first birthday. Surprisingly, his record had remained clean until last October, when he'd been picked up for a drunk-and-disorderly outside a bar over in Sobieski Corners.

Mike had also done a little digging on Rachel. She'd gotten married several years back to a podiatrist. She had three kids, a house, a Lexus, a picket fucking fence. Everything she'd deprived him and Sara of all these years. The injustice of it made him crazy.

He could only hope that, one day, the two of them got exactly what they deserved.

Fourteen

Sara held her breath as Mike hoisted Ethan up onto his shoulders and ran to his truck with their son laughing the entire way. She followed behind, nervously shaking her head.

"Please be careful!" she called out. "That's precious cargo you've got riding on your shoulders!"

No doubt just to be a smart-ass, Mike spun around and ran backwards. His exuberant little passenger laughed even harder.

Sara chewed on her thumbnail. *If he doesn't slow down*, she thought, *he's going to be wearing that huge ice cream cone my voracious little eater just wolfed down.*

But they managed to make it to the truck without incident, and Mike even had Ethan buckled in by the time she caught up to them. He held the door open for her and grinned.

"If you're jealous, I can give you a ride on my shoulders, too. Except…I'd prefer you facing the opposite way."

As understanding dawned, her cheeks flamed. She gave an inconspicuous nod toward the back seat and whispered, "Mike, you have to watch what you say."

"Come on, he's seven. What could he possibly know?"

He shut her door and headed around to the driver's side.

"More than you could imagine," she informed him as he slid behind the wheel.

He turned at the same time she did to peer at the little person seated between them.

"I know if she's facing the other way, you won't be able to see where you're going," Ethan patiently explained to his father.

Mike's face turned beet-red, and Sara bit the inside of her cheek to hold back a laugh.

He cleared his throat and stuck the key in the ignition. "Listen. I was thinking, since it's still so early, how would you two like to go check out some bunk beds?"

"Yeah! Can we, Mom?"

"I suppose. We can check out some different bedroom and living room sets while we're there. That's a big house you bought. You'll be amazed by how much furniture it's going to take to fill it. If I remember correctly, it's four bedrooms, right?"

Mike turned the key and the truck roared to life. "Yep. With a dining room, rec room and full basement."

She cast her ex a sidelong glance. He wore a smile from ear-to-ear as he pulled out onto the highway.

He looks happy and sounds eager, she thought, once again inundated by conflicting emotions. Like he can't wait to get started with his new life. But what about his life back in Chicago? She already knew he didn't have anyone special waiting for him, he'd made that clear the other night. But had he been seeing someone recently? Had he broken some woman's heart before heading back to Green Bay?

A twinge of jealousy tightened her chest, and she realized she didn't like the thought of Mike with anyone else. If life had worked out the way it was supposed to, they'd have gotten married right after she'd found out she was pregnant, and they'd be celebrating their eighth wedding anniversary this year. They'd feel comfortable and completely at ease with each other instead of awkward and unsure.

But that undeniable...*something* that had drawn them together in the first place was still there. Chemistry, she supposed. It crackled to life every time Mike looked at her—as if he wanted to devour her. And she couldn't deny, at least to herself, that she felt the same. Even as she hated herself for being so susceptible to him. But her lack of trust sat between them like a dividing wall, and no matter how hard she tried, she couldn't seem to work past it.

As he maneuvered the truck through traffic, she took the opportunity to study his profile. He'd shaved that morning, but already sported a five-o'clock shadow. She remembered as a teenager he could go days without shaving. Now, his skin was tanned and work-roughened. There was nothing boyish looking about Mike these days. He was one-hundred percent man.

She crossed and uncrossed her legs. Lord, just looking at him made her...hot. Maybe she was coming down with a fever. With a sigh of self-disgust, she redirected her gaze out the passenger-side window, wondering what kind of thoughts were running through his mind.

Consumed with fantasies involving Sara's legs wrapped around his neck, Mike could barely contain himself as he turned left onto Shawano Avenue. They'd been teenagers the first time they made love, and while exciting and emotional, the experience had also been incredibly awkward.

But that was eight years ago. They'd made love several times since the first, and both had several years of experience under their belts since then. So, why had she turned beet red when he'd made that joke in the parking lot of Dairy Queen?

They'd never actually performed oral sex on each other, although he'd tried—once. But Sara had nearly died of embarrassment, so Mike decided to wait awhile before trying again. Unfortunately, life ripped them apart before their love life had become more...interesting. Not that it hadn't been wonderful. Mike had never known a more loving, giving woman than Sara. In or out of bed.

Ah, hell, he was starting to get a woody. *Time to think about something else, anything else—*

"Hey, Dad? Are we gonna be able to swim in your pool this summer? Uncle Luke said it'll probably take a miracle to get it working again."

"As a matter of fact, I had someone take a look at it today. We think alike, kid." He ruffled Ethan's hair. "And yeah, it's going to take quite a bit of work, but I was promised the pool will be ready by the Fourth of July."

Sara glanced over at him. "Planning on throwing a party?"

"I'd like to. Nothing big, obviously, since my guest list would be pretty short. But I was hoping you, Ethan, and the rest of your clan would join me. And Nancy, her husband, and their little girl."

Sara's brows lifted. "You've already met Nancy and Dwayne?"

"Just Nancy. She came by earlier and introduced herself while I was waiting for the pool guy." He cleared his throat. "She said she'd have me gelded if I hurt you. I take it she's a friend of yours?"

Sara laughed softly. "Sorry about that. I, uh, explained the situation to her yesterday, and she's worried about me. And yes, she's a wonderful friend."

"I liked her."

A few minutes later, Mike pulled into the parking lot of the furniture store.

As soon as they walked through the doors, Ethan took off running.

"Ethan, slow down, please!" Sara called after him. She shook her head. "It's a miracle he doesn't trip over his own feet."

"You worry too much, honey. He's just a normal boy."

"Easy for you to say, you're still new at this. Just wait until the first time he draws blood. You'll be singing a different tune then. I guarantee it."

"Ethan, listen to your mother!"

Sara laughed, the tinkling sound music to Mike's ears. He knew she hadn't had much to smile about the last few days, and it killed him to know he was the main cause of all her anxiety. To suddenly have to share her son with a man she'd feared to be an abusive bastard? He could only imagine the stress she'd been under since finding out he was back in town.

Earning her trust again after all these years wouldn't be easy, and patience had never been his strong suit. But no one had ever been worth the effort more than his Sara. He loved her as much as he ever had—more, if that were possible. One way or another, he'd find a way to win her back.

And he wasn't above fighting dirty, if he had to.

By the time he and Sara caught up with him, Ethan had already climbed to the top of one of the many bunk beds on display. He started bouncing up and down like a ping pong ball.

"Ethan," his mother said in a warning tone. "No jumping. I'm sure it's against store policy."

His little face screwed up in defiance, but she crossed her arms, tilted her head, and narrowed her eyes—a look Mike found surprisingly sexy—which worked like a charm. The little shit stopped bouncing and refocused his attention, gazing around the humongous furniture store in wide-eyed wonder. Hell, you'd have thought he was at Great America.

"Man, isn't this awesome? They have everything here! See, Dad, I told you they have bunk beds with slides! And look," he pointed to his right, "that one has a castle fort, just like I said! I wonder if I could jump from here to there."

He looked about ready to find out, so Mike plucked him from the top of the bed and set him on his feet.

"Ethan, this is non-negotiable. No jumping on the beds, no jumping from one bed to another and...Well, no anything that could cause you bodily harm. Got it?"

With a slight pout, he insisted, "I would have made it, ya know."

Mike grinned. "You probably would have. You do have my long legs—"

Sara gave him a warning poke in the ribs before turning a meaningful glare on their son. "But we are not going to find out, young man. Is that clear?"

"Yes," Ethan sulkily replied.

Mike gave him a pat on the back. "Come on. Let's go find you the perfect set of bunk beds."

Nearly an hour-and-a-half later, Sara watched as Mike and the salesman filled out the necessary paperwork. She was mildly surprised when he paid for everything with his debit card rather than apply for store credit.

Ethan ended up choosing the bunk beds with an attached slide. Mike surprised her by picking out a king-sized bed with a gorgeous polished brass headboard that she would have chosen herself. They came across a great deal on a five-piece oak bedroom set, which he ended up buying for both guestrooms. She also found a steal on a cherry wood kitchen table and four chairs that he loved. They couldn't find a dining room or living room set either one of them liked, so he decided to save those purchases for another day.

It was nine o'clock by the time Mike parked his truck in front of their house.

"Do you wanna come in?" Ethan asked. "Mom brought a chocolate cake home today."

"I'd love to, Ethan, I really would. But I still have some business to take care of tonight. And don't forget, we'll have all day Thursday together."

Ethan's face fell, and Sara wondered exactly what kind of business one took care of at nine o'clock at night.

Mike chucked Ethan under the chin. "Hey, you're not gonna send me away with that look, are you?"

"I wanted to show you my collection of Yu-Gi-Oh! cards. Can I bring 'em with us to the water park?"

"Of course. I can't wait to see them." He cocked an eyebrow. "So, we're okay then?"

Ethan nodded, smiling. "Yeah. But if I can't save you a piece of cake, it's not 'cause I'm mad. With Uncle Danny, cake doesn't last long in our house."

Mike laughed. "Don't worry about it. I can wait until your mom brings home another one." He unbuckled Ethan's seat belt.

"Can I have a ride to the door?" he asked with a

hopeful grin.

His father lifted him up onto his shoulders and galloped to the front door.

Sara shook her head as she opened her door and climbed out of the truck. Two days and Ethan already had his dad wrapped around his finger. And she couldn't get over how good Mike was with their son. She knew he couldn't have much experience with kids...unless maybe he'd dated women with children. A scowl fought to chase her smile away. Dammit, she didn't like this feeling of jealousy one bit.

"Thanks for the ice cream," she said, stepping up onto the porch.

"Yeah, Dad, thanks for the ice cream," Ethan echoed as his father set him on the ground.

Mike opened the door for them; he patted his son on the back. "I'll see you Thursday, kiddo. Don't forget to pack your swim trunks and a nice change of clothes for the restaurant."

"And my Yu-Gi-Oh! cards?"

"And your Yu-Gi-Oh! cards," Mike agreed with a nod.

Ethan ran into the house, and as soon as he was out of earshot, Mike turned to her and said, "Quick question."

"You have no idea what Yu-Gi-Oh! Cards *are*, do you?"

"Not a clue," he admitted with a sheepish grin.

She laughed softly. "I only know the basics. It's a Japanese trading card game that, I believe, spun off from a television show about a little boy who loves to play games. Ethan can probably give you more details when he shows them to you."

He nodded, smiling. "Got it. And thanks for all your help tonight. I really appreciate it."

"No problem. I love shopping."

"I remember."

Sara thought he might be trying to hypnotize her with those smoldering baby blues of his. Her heart rate picked up speed as they lowered to her lips, and she wondered if he would try to kiss her. She remembered the kiss in his truck—the incredible feel of his lips on hers—and her eyes started to lower in anticipation. She'd pulled away then, terrified by the overwhelming surge of emotions that kiss had invoked. Tonight she wanted nothing more than for him to wrap her in his arms and—

"Hey, Mike? I was hoping I could have a word with you before you leave?"

Sara's eyes flew open. *Dammit, Nicky.* Disappointment settled like a brick in her belly.

Good lord, what was she thinking? Her brother had more than likely just saved her from making a complete fool of herself. The last thing she wanted to do was give Mike false hope.

He gazed down at her, those gorgeous eyes alight with promise. "I'll see you later," he said in a near whisper, then he looked up at her brother through the screen. "Sure thing. Sara, thanks again for your help."

"What help?" Nicky stepped through the screen door and held it open for her. She avoided his knowing look as she stepped past him into the house.

"We took a ride to WG&R after we finished our ice cream. Ethan found his dream bunk beds, and Sara and I picked out some furniture for the rest of the house."

"We still have the dining room and living room to take care of," she added, "but there's plenty of time for that."

"Maybe we could hit that furniture store in Pulaski this weekend? If they're still in business."

She turned to face him through the screen door. "They are, and that would be fine. Although I'd better warn you, they're a little pricey."

He shrugged. "Can't hurt to look."

"We'll talk about it Thursday. Good night." She gazed at him, suddenly regretting the missed opportunity to feel those lips on hers again.

"'Night." It took every bit of self-control Mike had not to yank the door open and pull Sara into his arms.

He turned his attention back to Nicky and the knowing smirk on his friend's face. "You have some piss-poor timing, you know that?"

"Sorry."

Mike shook his head, a reluctant smile curving his lips. "So? What's up?"

Nicky cast a quick glance over his shoulder. "I'll walk you to your truck." When they reached the sidewalk, he said, "I need to know when I can tell Garrett and the others about Jason. I don't like keeping this from them."

Mike let out a heavy sigh as he leaned against the side of his truck.

"Look, I know it's asking a lot having you keep this to yourself. But if my cover's blown, Thomas'll transfer to another precinct, probably in another state, keep his nose clean for a couple years like he's done in the past. And DCI will have to start from scratch yet again. Who knows how long it'll take to build another case against him. I'm sorry, but I can't let that happen."

"You make it sound personal or something."

Mike thought about Billy Hahn and his grief-stricken mother. "It's my job, Nicky. But I'll admit the fact that he's sniffing around your sister makes it personal. Especially now that I know Ethan's my son. I don't want that dirty cop anywhere near my kid. Or his mother. And let's face it, Garrett's a hothead. I can't take a chance on him screwing this case up until I have something concrete to report, one way or the other."

"Garrett's a damn good cop. I'm sure he'll be able to put his personal feelings aside—"

He snorted. "Are you kidding me? That idiot'll have Thomas strung up from the nearest tree before sun-up, and you know it. Besides, there's no reason to alarm anybody yet. As long as Sara keeps her distance—"

"But that's just it. She has a date with him Friday night. Garrett told us about it before you pulled up. He has it in his head that Sara and Jason are some perfect match."

Mike glared toward the house. He already knew about the date—which would happen over his dead body. "Your brother's been a thorn in my ass since the moment we met."

"Come on, this isn't Garrett's fault, and you know it. If you'd just let me tell him about Jason, he'd help you to bring him down. I know he would."

"Forget it. Please, man, I need you to keep quiet a little while longer. Something's going down soon. I'm sure of it."

Nicky tried and failed to hide a grin. "Well, at least you know it won't be Friday night, because he'll be busy wining and dining Sara."

Mike turned his glare on his smartass friend. "There's no way in hell I'm going to let that prick within a hundred feet of Sara—or Ethan—ever again. You can count on it."

Nicky shrugged. "If you say so."

"What the hell does that mean?"

"Just that my sister can be pretty stubborn, in case you've forgotten. Especially when someone tries to tell her what to do. If you tell her to stay away from Jason, you can bet your ass she'll go out with him just to spite you."

Frustrated by the prospect, Mike ran a hand through his hair. "Then I'll just have to make sure she has no desire to go out with him. And if that doesn't work, I'll handcuff her stubborn little ass inside the house until Thomas is behind bars."

Fifteen

Sara was grating cheese for tacos when she heard a truck pull into the driveway and glanced at the clock. *Garrett*, she thought. Uncle Luke and Nicky would be home soon as well.

Her oldest brother came through the front door and sniffed the air. "Damn, it smells good in here. Tacos?"

"Yep. Tacos, rice, and beans." She set a bowl of shredded lettuce and a smaller bowl of diced tomatoes on the table, then dug the salsa and sour cream out of the fridge.

Garrett disappeared down the hall, and returned a few minutes later in a well-worn pair of Levis and a Packers T-shirt that looked two sizes too small stretched over his massive arms and chest. He hefted the coffee carafe before pouring himself a cup. "Need any help?"

Sara stopped dead in her tracks, and then climbed up on one of the kitchen chairs closest to him. She placed her palm against his puzzled forehead. "You don't feel hot." She moved her palm to his cheek.

He chuckled and gave her a helping hand off the chair. "All right, so I don't offer to help often enough."

Sara snorted and went back to setting the table.

After a minute, he said, "Ethan's pretty excited about

your little family outing tomorrow."

"Yes, he is."

"Are you?"

Surprised by the question, she cast him a quick, sidelong glance. "'Excited' isn't the word I'd use to describe how I feel about tomorrow." She heard him move away from the counter and take a seat at the table.

"Yeah, I suppose. I mean, you're only going along because it's too soon to let Ethan go off with Mike alone." There was a short pause. "Right?"

She glanced back at him in surprise. What in the world was he getting at? "Of course. Why else would I be going?"

"No reason I can think of. I just wanted to make sure you're all right. I've been worried about you."

She set the pot of rice on the table before meeting his gaze. "I'm fine. Honest." She smiled for emphasis. "And so is Ethan. He and Mike are getting along great. Everything is working out as it should. No worries."

Garrett's smile didn't quite reach his eyes. Sara knew that look—he was having a hard time sharing Ethan with Mike. Her heart ached for her big brother, who had been more of a father figure in his nephew's life than an uncle. He loved her son like no other, and the feeling was absolutely mutual—Ethan simply adored his Uncle Garrett. Mike's sudden presence in their lives had been a huge adjustment for them all, but Garrett maybe most of all.

Tears stung her eyes, and she blinked rapidly to get herself under control. If her overprotective brother saw her distress, he'd no doubt assume Mike was the cause.

As if on cue, Ethan ran up the back stairs into the kitchen. His eyes lit up when they landed on his uncle.

"Uncle Garrett, I just made it to level five on my new game! Wanna see me beat that big robot, huh? Wanna?"

Garrett laughed and rose to his feet. "'Course I do. Heck, at this rate you're going to have that thing mastered by the weekend."

As he followed Ethan downstairs, Uncle Luke came in through the back door.

"Man, it smells good in here. Tacos? But we just had tacos last week." He set his keys on the counter and pulled a coffee cup out of the cabinet.

Sara set a bowl of seasoned meat in the center of the table. "I made Spanish rice, too."

He picked up the carafe and gave it a shake before pouring the rest in his cup. "Best part of the meal."

She was about to call everybody into the kitchen when Nicky walked through the front door.

"Hey, sis." He stopped and sniffed the air with suspicion; his eyes lit up. "Tacos? It can't be. We just had 'em last week."

"What can I say?" she teased, with a silent laugh. "I'm a Goddess."

Nicky set his briefcase on the floor beside the hall closet. "Can't argue with that. Tacos twice in less than two weeks," he said to himself, as if he couldn't quite believe it.

Sara smiled. When it came to certain things, men were such simple creatures.

They ate in silence for a while before Ethan said, "Just think, Mom, tomorrow we'll be racing down a water slide and floating around in those inner tubes. We're gonna have the best time ever."

She gave his little shoulder a squeeze. "You bet we are. And it's going to be a long day, so we should probably both get to bed early tonight for a good night's sleep."

"'K."

Sara glanced at Garrett, who ate his supper as if he hadn't had a morsel of food in days. She wanted to say something to ease his mind, but figured it might be best to just let things be.

"Don't forget to take plenty of pictures," Nicky said. "I'd pay anything to see Mike trying to float in one of those little inner tubes."

Uncle Luke chuckled. "Or going down one of those water slides. I can just see his big limbs getting caught."

Garrett made a noise that sounded suspiciously like a laugh. "Yeah, I wouldn't mind seeing *that* myself."

He cast a quick smile at Sara, and her heart felt lighter than it had in years. She'd been so worried her family would have a hard time accepting Mike back into their lives, even if only for Ethan's sake, when in fact, they'd been wonderful. Open and understanding, showering both her and Ethan with plenty of love and support. Even Garrett, though she knew it would be a long time before he let his guard down where Mike was concerned.

Sara realized she was suddenly looking forward to tomorrow's little family excursion.

"They should make these things a little wider," Mike grumbled to no one in particular as he struggled to squeeze his large frame down the smallest water slide in the park. He'd climbed up there behind Ethan, but hadn't realized how narrow the damn thing was until he'd reached the top.

Adding to his embarrassment, a line of kids had

formed behind him, huffing and complaining, while Ethan stood at the bottom laughing himself sick. The little shit.

And if that wasn't enough, Sara held her cell phone aimed directly at him, grinning while she snapped one picture after another. *Have your fun, woman*, he thought, silently promising retribution.

Finally admitting defeat, he told the kids to clear the ladder so he could climb down the way he came. Cheers and sullen rejoinders accompanied him, and a reluctant smile tugged his cheeks as he scanned the mob of tiny scowling faces.

Ethan ran up and grabbed his hand. "Come on, Dad, let's climb up on the pirate's ship!"

Mike allowed himself to be dragged along as he looked around in amazement. The place was massive, with five separate pools, each with its own water slide. An overhead maze of tubes and netting ran from one end of the park to the other, and if one weren't afraid of heights—or too big to fit—it was probably a blast to crawl through.

Ethan dropped his hand as they passed Captain Kidd's Buccaneer Blast, where kids could shoot foam balls at each other, race up and down the three-story fort complete with slides, swings, climbing ropes and a fountain that continually sprayed foam balls into the air. Kids soaked each other with waterblasters, and even some parents and grandparents joined in on the fun.

He spotted Ethan, who stood in front of a playfully spinning waterfall, shrieking with laughter as he tried to dodge the overhead deluge. Then he ran up to the top of the pirate's ship, grabbed ahold of a rope, and swung back and forth over the shallow pool.

Sara stood off to the side, smiling as she held her cell phone up, capturing every moment on video.

"Dad! Dad, look at me!"

Mike waved, his chest swelling with pride. Watching his son have so much fun, energetic and happy without a care in the world...that's the way every child should feel. Loved, safe, content.

"Man, this place is awesome!" Ethan announced as he ran past. "I'm gonna go down the Shiver-Me-Timbers slide."

Mike took a seat on one of the many benches for a quick break, while Sara followed behind their little bundle of energy, cell phone in hand. Personally, he'd rather have headed down to the Dells. He'd always dreamt of riding the Ducks as a kid, and he knew they'd built the area up over the years.

But Sara wouldn't have approved of an overnight excursion so far from home, and this place had other selling points—on top of being the largest waterpark in Northeast Wisconsin. A huge arcade with over a hundred different games where you earned tickets for prizes, an old-fashioned ice cream parlor, a gift-slash-coffee shop, not to mention three on-site restaurants. A sports lounge so you could watch a game with a beer and a monster-sized cheeseburger. An elegant French-style bistro for those in need of a romantic atmosphere. And a family restaurant that sounded perfect for their first official meal alone together as a family.

Now, if he and Sara were here by themselves, he would've opted for the French bistro. But the family restaurant had a television at every table. And this was, after all, Ethan's night.

At least until he falls asleep, Mike thought, a slow smile spreading across his face.

He thought back to when they'd first arrived and

changed into their swimsuits. The moment Sara had emerged from the bathroom, Mr. Happy nearly tore a hole through his swim trunks.

It never failed to amaze him just how beautiful she'd become. Not that she hadn't always been gorgeous. But standing there in a lavender-colored string-bikini, with one of those lacy sarongs wrapped around her slim hips, she was, without question, the sexiest woman he'd ever laid eyes on.

And she was his. After tonight, there would be no doubt about that either.

"Hey, Dad! Look what I can do!" Ethan shouted from somewhere up above him.

Mike looked up just in time to watch him swing over the pool, then splash into the water like he'd been doing it for years. He had a feeling that the smile on his face was as doting as it got. He got up and made his way over.

"That was awesome, kid!" he said when Ethan surfaced. "Have you ever taken swim classes?"

Sara aimed the cell phone back in his direction. "He's been taking classes at the 'Y' for the past few years."

"It shows." Mike slid into the pool and swung his son up onto his shoulders. They turned toward Sara, who still held that damn cell phone in her hand. Mike tilted Ethan down so he could whisper in his ear, then started inching closer to the ledge where she stood.

She must have realized their intent, because she dodged out of the way, her face a mask of outrage.

"I can't believe you were going to pull me in! This phone cost me a small fortune!" She needlessly held it up for them to see.

"We weren't going to pull you in, were we, Ethan?"

"Nope. We were gonna splash you."

"And that's supposed to be better?"

"Well, sure. The phone would get ruined if we pulled you in. It'd just get a little wet if we splashed you," Ethan patiently explained.

Sara laughed. "Well, don't you splash me, either. I just bought this phone last month. I don't want to have to replace it already."

"Then toss the thing in your purse and join us," Mike said.

"Yeah, Mom. You haven't even got your hair wet yet."

Mike grinned at the look of mock horror on her face.

"Get my hair wet? Good lord, I can't do that. I spent almost an hour perfecting this 'do.'" She reached up and playfully patted her ponytail.

"Mom, who cares how your hair looks? We're swimming. Everyone's hair gets wet."

Sara's lips pursed as she appeared to think it over. "Well, I suppose I *could* put it in my bag for a little while so I can sit on the edge and get my feet wet."

"Get your feet wet? Mom, I want you to go down that slide with me." Ethan pointed up toward the highest and scariest looking water slide in the entire park.

Sara literally gulped. "Ethan, your father can—"

"Uh-uh, you have to face your fears. Right, Dad?"

Mike shrugged. "Sorry, but the boy's got a point. Besides, you'll be perfectly safe. The slide is a completely enclosed tube, so it's not as if you can fly off or anything. We can go down one after the other. I'll go first, you can be in the middle, and Ethan can bring up the rear. Sound good?"

"Nope."

Mike couldn't help but laugh. He'd almost forgotten how adorable she was when she pouted. "Okay, I have a better idea. You can sit between my legs, and Ethan can sit between yours. We'll go down as one."

"Yeah, Mom! It'll be great! Come on, don't be such a *girl*."

Hands on hips, Sara huffed, "I *am* a girl. And I'm still not going down that slide."

"I *could* just throw you over my shoulder and carry you up there."

Her eyes narrowed. "You'd have to catch me first. And I'd be long gone before you even got one foot out of the water."

"So you're saying I can't catch you?" Mike asked, very much wanting her to say yes.

She crossed her arms over her chest and scoffed, "Please. This place is so packed, there's no way. While I'm busy dodging under tables and between peoples legs, you'd be tripping over everything in sight."

"Now you're saying I'm clumsy?" He feigned outrage while choking back a laugh. God, how he'd missed this woman.

She shrugged. "If the big clumsy feet fit..."

He stared at her in silent challenge, giving her plenty of time to back down. Then Ethan whispered, "Go get her, Dad," a second before flipping himself into the water.

Heart racing with excitement, Mike sprang out of the pool with the swiftness of a cheetah. Sara shrieked and jumped back, then kicked off her sandals and ran like hell.

But she'd sadly miscalculated his abilities, and he caught her before she'd even reached the concession stand.

"Big talker," he said, flipping her over his shoulder.

"Mike, put me down!" she whispered furiously. "This is embarrassing!"

"What's that? I can't hear you over all these people."

"Man, I can't believe how fast you caught her," Ethan exclaimed as he ran up to meet them. His eyes glowed up at his father with such adoration, Sara's chest tightened with an emotion she was loath to identify. It seemed incredible to her that they'd only known each other for four days.

"Aw, she's just a big bragger. It was like chasing a toddler—Ow!"

She'd pinched his very nice ass. His own fault for leaving her staring at it for so long. "Okay, so you're not as slow as you look. I admit it. Can you *please* put me down now?"

Mike obliged, setting her gently on her feet. He pointed to her cell phone. "Why don't you go stick that thing in your bag so we can take a run down the slide."

"You're like a dog with a friggin' bone." She gave her head an exasperated shake.

"Come on, Mom. Dad caught you fair and square. You have to go down the slide now."

"Come on," Mike echoed, "you have to be a little tempted, even if you are afraid of heights."

She sighed. There was no hope for it. Obviously, they planned to nag her until she gave in. She smiled at her son. "All right, for you, I'll do it. I'll go down the stupid slide."

"Cool! This is going to be great, Mom, you'll see."

Somehow, she doubted that. But she'd promised, so she slipped her phone inside her bag and took it over to the desk clerk. When she turned around, Mike and a giggling Ethan each grabbed one of her arms.

She rolled her eyes. "I said I'd go, and I'm going. You don't have to escort me like a convict."

Mike grinned down at her. "Habit, sorry."

They made their way to the far end of the waterpark with Ethan chattering excitedly the entire way. At the entrance to the aptly named Devil's Mountain, Mike picked up one of the long inflatable rafts and tucked it under his arm. He turned and offered her a smile. "Ready?"

"No."

He chuckled. "You'll be fine, come on."

The climb to the top couldn't have been more nerve wracking. Sara's heart pounded with each step as she reminded herself over and over not to look down. Ethan, who thankfully didn't share her fear of heights, rushed on ahead, while Mike slipped a comforting arm around her waist.

"You okay?"

She blew out a hard breath and gave a sharp nod. "Peachy. Are we almost there?"

"One more flight; about eight steps."

"Come on, Mom, hurry up!"

Once they reached the top, Mike sat down on the back of the inflatable raft, gestured for Sara to slip between his legs, and then positioned Ethan between hers. Mike wrapped his long arms around both of them while she clutched her son tight. Feeling him squirm a bit, she loosened her grip and forced herself to relax, waiting with bated breath.

"Say a prayer and hold on tight," Mike advised a second before the attendant pushed them into the tunnel of rushing water.

Sara squealed the entire way down. The raft swung from side to side with dizzying speed, the ride seeming to last forever. Then, suddenly they were airborne for a split second before the raft landed in the pool with a jarring smack. She bounced off and went under water, panicking when she lost her grip on Ethan.

Clawing to the surface, she came up sputtering. As her feet found purchase on the bottom, she realized the pool was only a few feet deep and stood up, swiping her wet hair back off her face. Quickly spotting Mike, who held their son safely in his arms, she heaved a ragged sigh of relief.

As she waded over, she saw the two were laughing—at her. In fact, Mike laughed so hard it was a miracle he didn't choke. She wished he would, though, the jackass.

He set Ethan down, who immediately begged to go down the slide again.

"Why don't you go down a few more times while your mother and I catch our breath?"

"Really? Awesome!" Ethan climbed out of the shallow pool and took off like a shot.

Before she realized his intent, Mike slid one arm beneath her back, the other under her knees, and lifted her in his arms. Too tired to protest—and if she were being honest, a little turned on by the thoughtful gesture—she clung to his neck as he carried her out of the pool.

He settled her onto one of the chaise loungers, then plopped down beside her in an arm chair. "Well, that was fun, huh?"

Leaning back against the padded headrest, she said, "It was a blast until we hit the bottom. I've never been down a water slide before."

"Me neither."

Sara had to admit, she hadn't had this much fun in years. Little by little, her defenses were crumbling—and it scared the hell out of her. She realized how easy it would be to fall right back into his arms. And his bed. She wanted him as much as she ever had, and her reasons for keeping that emotional—as well as physical—distance were starting to dissipate like dandelion tufts into the wind.

She blew out a silent breath of frustration and turned to check him out. His rock-hard chest was covered with a light, T-shaped sprinkling of crisp black hair that traveled over his abdomen and disappeared into the waistband of his swim trunks. Sara wanted to press her lips to the hollow of his throat and trace a path down his tan flesh, following the line of curling hair over his stomach—

"Are you *trying* to give me a hard-on?"

"Don't be ridiculous," she scoffed, her face burning with mortification at having been caught ogling him. *Please, ground, open up and swallow me.* "I was just...admiring the pattern on the chair you're sitting on."

"That's the best you could come up with?" He snorted in disbelief.

"I'm not that great under pressure," she admitted with a reluctant grin.

Mike threw back his head and laughed, and Sara couldn't hold back a grin herself. She'd also just made a decision about later tonight.

If she didn't lose her nerve.

Sixteen

At five-to-seven, Mike proudly escorted Sara and their son down to the restaurant.

The atmosphere inside was perfect for a seven-year-old boy. Retro style television screens covered every inch of every wall, and it seemed as if each screen had a different cartoon, movie or sitcom playing. And the décor was reminiscent of a classic 50s diner, with shiny red vinyl booths, colorful neon signs, and a black and white tiled floor.

Sara and Ethan slid into the booth, and Mike sat down across from them. "I wonder if we get to choose what we watch."

"I hope so. I hate this show. It's for *girls*." Ethan started playing around with the television.

Sara opened her menu. "You thought it was the greatest show on earth last year," she pointed out, causing Ethan to roll his eyes.

Mike smiled, trying to remember the last time he'd felt this happy and content. He and Ethan were getting to know each other better every day. His son was nothing short of incredible. Funny, smart, outgoing. He had good manners, yet was impetuous enough to forget himself sometimes. A typical little boy. And even though he resembled Mike physically, he had a lot of his mother in him as well, especially his sense of humor. Sara used to be able to make Mike laugh harder than anyone. And he knew that once she started to open up more, her sense of humor would return full-force.

A waitress approached their table dressed in a traditional pink diner uniform with a white apron. She wore her curly blonde hair up in a loose bun, and couldn't have been more than twenty-years-old. "'Evening. Is everyone ready to order?"

"I want chicken and french fries," Ethan announced, grinning up at her.

The waitress smiled at him. "Fried chicken?"

"Yep. And soda."

"He'll have a large glass of milk," Sara told her, earning a scowl from Ethan. "And I'll have the breaded pork tenderloin, mashed potatoes and gravy, a side salad with Thousand Island dressing, and a large glass of skim milk, if you have it."

The waitress nodded. "We do. Sir?"

"I'll have the baked mostaccioli, a cup of minestrone, and let's make it unanimous, a large glass of milk."

The waitress smiled and took the menus from him. "I'll be right back with your drinks."

Forty minutes later, Mike and Ethan waited on their hot fudge sundaes, amusing themselves by watching Sara nibble at her food.

"It's like this wherever we go," Ethan said. "Uncle Garrett says she's the slowest eater on the planet."

"One of the few things your uncle and I agree on."

Sara forked a half-inch morsel of food into her mouth and looked up at them in what had to be mock surprise. "What? You two finished already? Well, excuse me, but I like to taste my food on the way down."

"We thought maybe you were throwing it a farewell party in your mouth," Mike teased, with a conspiratorial wink in Ethan's direction. "Heck, woman, I could have eaten the food on your plate three times by now."

Sara shrugged. She set her fork down, pushed the plate away and swallowed. "Whew, that's it. I couldn't eat another bite."

Ethan's eyes practically bugged out of his head. "What about dessert?"

"Not a chance. I'd explode, I swear."

The waitress approached the table and set the sundaes down in front of him and Ethan. "And what can I get you for dessert?" she asked as she picked up Sara's plate.

Sara held her hands up in front of her, as if to ward off any more food. "Nothing, thank you. I'm a stuffed pork chop."

The waitress laughed softly and pulled the bill from her pocket. She slid it onto Mike's side of the table and said, "You all have a good night then. Enjoy your sundae," she added, ruffling Ethan's hair.

Mike held a spoonful of ice cream, hot fudge and whipped cream in front of Sara's nose. "Come on, one bite. You have to taste this."

"Thanks, but I know what a hot fudge sundae tastes like."

He shrugged. "Suit yourself." He stuffed the spoon in his mouth and let out a loud moan of delight.

Ethan giggled and joined in on his silliness, the two of them drawing the attention of several diners.

Sara glanced around, clearly embarrassed. When Mike spooned up another bite, she surprised the hell out of him by leaning across the table and intercepting it. She closed her eyes, and let out a moan of ecstasy that put Mike's to shame and had Ethan howling with laughter.

"The connecting door is open," Mike told them when they reached their adjoining rooms. He slipped the card in the slot that unlocked his door. "Just come on in when you're ready."

"I want to get Ethan into his pajamas and have him brush his teeth," Sara said as she opened the door to her and Ethan's room. "Give us maybe fifteen minutes."

As Mike stepped inside the spacious hotel room, he silently prayed she didn't decide to change her own clothes as well. The turquoise dress she'd worn to dinner was one of the sexiest things he'd ever seen her in. It was long and fit her like a glove, with a slit up each side.

He ran into the bathroom to brush his own teeth and change into a plain white T-shirt and sweatpants—they were, after all, going to be lying on the bed watching a movie. Then he picked up the phone and placed an order to room service.

He was leaning against the headboard of the massive king-sized bed, hands linked behind his head, when the door flew open and Ethan ran into the room. He jumped on the bed and started bouncing like a Ping-Pong ball. Mike laughed. His son looked adorable in his superhero pajamas.

Watching with anticipation for Sara to enter the room, he had to remind himself to breathe. When she strolled in, he blew out a silent sigh of relief. She hadn't changed. He scooched over and patted the spot beside him.

"Hop up, *Mom*," he said. "There's plenty of room."

Sara moved around to the opposite side of the bed and slowly sat down on the edge of the mattress, barely making a crease in the boldly colored, mosaic-patterned bedspread. She cast an odd glance down at herself, then cleared her throat. "So, what are we going to watch?"

Mike picked up the remote and flipped on the pay-per-movie channel. He started naming off movies until Ethan shouted, "I wanna see *Wreck-It Ralph!*"

"*Wreck-It Ralph* it is then." Mike ordered the movie, then gave his son a hair ruffle.

Ethan sat Indian-style at the foot of the bed, bouncing softly from side to side. Mike glanced at Sara, who had her legs curled beneath her and gaze glued to the television screen. He could tell her nerves had gotten the best of her and was anxious for his room service order to arrive.

As if on cue, there was a knock at the door. *Perfect timing.*

"I thought we should have a celebratory drink," he said a moment later, shutting the door behind him. "I have a bottle of apple juice for Ethan and," he held a familiar, long-necked bottle up for her to see, "a couple of Coronas for us. A couple each, that is." He grinned. "I even remembered the lime slices."

He uncapped the bottle of apple juice and handed it to Ethan, then stuffed a slice of the lime into the neck of each bottle of Corona. He walked over and handed her one before clinking his own against hers. "To fate. And new beginnings."

He wasn't sure, but he thought he saw a gleam in her eye as she tilted the bottle back to her lips.

By the time the credits were rolling, Ethan's soft snores filled the room. The sound was music to Sara's ears.

Mike leaned forward to peer at their son, the love shining in his eyes nearly bringing her to her knees. How could she have ever thought this man would be anything less than a wonderful, loving father?

"If you don't mind, I'd like to carry him in to bed. I know it sounds silly, but I've never got to do it before."

Sara's heart swelled even more. "It's not silly. I love carrying him to bed. Though it's getting harder and harder for me to pick him up."

Mike gave an absent nod and rose to his feet. He came around to the foot of the bed, scooped Ethan into his arms, and cradled him against his chest, his eyes glued to their son's face. Sara walked ahead of him into the adjoining room.

She rubbed her arms and wondered aloud, "Is it me, or is it chilly in here?"

He laid Ethan on the bed and pulled the blanket up to his shoulders. "I've felt a little warm all night."

Her hands stilled and she met his gaze. "Maybe you have a fever."

Mike's eyes blazed with an emotion she'd been trying to keep in check all day.

Desire.

He broke the spell when he bent down to press a kiss to Ethan's forehead. "That's the first time I've ever kissed him."

"Yeah, they're a little easier to lay on him when he's dead to the world," she teased.

But Mike's mood had altered startlingly fast. He looked angry. Intense.

"I should've been here to kiss him every night since the day he was born. Instead, I was off feeling sorry for myself."

He looked up, and Sara almost flinched from the pain reflected in his eyes. "Maybe I am like my old man after all."

"How could you even think such a thing? My God, your father was a monster. *You* were a victim of someone else's hatred and jealousy. There's no comparison."

He looked back down at their sleeping son and seemed to shake off whatever funk had invaded his thoughts. Straightening, he said, his voice compellingly gentle, "I was hoping we could talk. There are so many things I need to say to you. And I have questions. I...hell, I don't even know his birthday, or anything about the day he was born."

"His birthday is December twenty-first. He was a month early and weighed seven pounds-ten ounces." She grinned. "They told me he would've been a nine, maybe ten-pound baby if he'd been full-term."

"Ouch."

Sara laughed softly. "Believe me, seven pounds-ten ounces was plenty 'ouch' enough."

Mike stared at her for a moment, then held out his hand. Sara took it and followed him into the other room, closing the door softly behind her.

He sat on the edge of the bed, and with a gentle tug, guided her until she was sitting beside him. He reached for her other hand and said nothing for a moment, just stared down at their clasped hands. The tenderness of his touch nearly brought her to tears. She swallowed hard, striving to keep her emotions at bay.

Finally, he looked up and met her gaze. "You know

how I feel about you, Sara. I've never stopped loving you. Wanting you. And I realize giving me a second chance would be one of the hardest things you've ever had to do. But if you feel even half of what I do, we can make it work. I know we can."

"Mike, I—"

"Please, just let me get it all out before you shoot me down," he said, bringing both of her hands up for a kiss. "You know this isn't only about Ethan, though I won't deny I'd like my son living under my own roof."

"Our son," she corrected.

"Our son," he repeated. "But what I want just as much is for your beautiful face to be the first thing I see every morning for the rest of my life. And what I want more than anything right now is you." His voice grew husky. "I need you, sweetheart. Please say you feel the same."

They gazed at each other for what seemed like forever.

Sara had never been more torn. She wanted him. *Ached* for him. Loved him desperately, even after all these years. But she wasn't ready to make any promises about the future. Truthfully, she didn't know if she'd ever be able to trust him again. And how could they build a relationship without trust?

But for tonight, she couldn't deny herself—she wouldn't.

"I do. I want you, too."

Mike let go of her hands and reached up to cup her face, pulling her close for the kiss she'd been dreaming about all week.

Unable to tamp down a soft cry of longing, Sara opened for him. Her hands stole around his neck as his arms wrapped around her waist, crushing her against him. Their kiss was searing—hot. Their mouths and tongues meshed while their hands and arms reacquainted themselves with each other.

Mike leaned back onto the bed, pulling her with and on top of him. He caressed her arms, her shoulders, her rib cage. He kneaded the soft flesh of her lower back, pressing her against his erection.

Sara rocked her hips, dragging another groan from him.

"Evil woman," he growled, playfully nipping at her lips.

She pulled back and gazed down at him, her eyelids growing heavy with desire. "Maybe you deserve to be tortured a bit." She leaned back until she was straddling his hips, his erection like an iron bar between them.

He let out a shaky breath. "Can't argue with that."

Sara stroked her hands down his muscled chest until she reached the edge of his shirt. She slipped her hands inside and flattened her palms against his hot flesh—he quivered in response. She glanced at him through her lashes, taken aback by the intense hunger darkening in his eyes. God, how she'd missed that look.

"Take off your shirt," she demanded, feeling rather uninhibited thanks to the beer she'd consumed.

She reclined back, watching as he crossed his arms and grabbed the hem of his shirt, peeling it off in record time.

Like magnets, her hands were drawn back to his chest. She leaned down and pressed her lips to the hollow of his throat. The arousing, masculine scent of his warm flesh combined with the faintest hint of musky aftershave was like an aphrodisiac—her skin tingled in response.

Mike reached up to run his fingers through her hair, tangling them in the long, silken strands. Another growl rumbled in his throat as she moved her lips slowly down the middle of his chest, using her tongue to trace a fiery path across his rock-hard stomach. She shimmied backwards, ending her exquisite torture at the button of his jeans.

He sucked in a breath.

Mike caught her around the waist, pulled her up, and flipped her onto her back.

"Sorry, sweetheart, but with you in charge, I'd have five seconds, tops."

His deep, husky voice was like a cool breeze over wet nipples—Sara shivered in response. And then he was on top of her again, kissing her breathless.

Mike trailed his lips down the curve of her neck, his right hand coming up to gently cup her breast. His fingers caressed softly, his thumb and forefinger finding her nipple through the fabric and squeezing ever so gently.

Sara moaned, her head turning into the pillow as she arched against his hand. It'd been so long since she'd felt his touch, and she silently cursed the fact that they still had so many clothes between them.

As if reading her mind, his hand slid down to her knee, then slowly inched its way up to where the hem of her dress bunched up around her thighs. He slipped beneath the gauzy fabric, continuing his path with slow precision. When his hand reached her hip, he pulled back and gazed down at her.

"You're not wearing any panties," he needlessly pointed out, his voice thick.

Sara's eyes were heavy-lidded with desire. She gazed up at him and shook her head.

He gave her hip a gentle squeeze. "You were planning on seducing *me*?"

She bit her lip and nodded, pleased by his reaction to

her little surprise.

"As if there was any doubt I wanted you."

"Mike?" She caressed little circles on his back with her index finger.

"Yeah?" He gently squeezed the back of her thigh.

"You're awfully chatty."

She felt a rumbling in his chest, then he leaned back down until his lips were barely an inch from her own.

"Don't worry, sweetheart. I'm done talking."

He rolled backwards and sat up, pulling her with him. He grasped the hem of her dress with both hands. Meeting his gaze, she lifted her arms. In one fluid motion, he pulled the dress up and over her head.

Sara had been feeling extremely self-confident up until now. But straddling his lap, completely naked, she suddenly felt vulnerable and unsure. It'd been so long since they'd made love—since he'd seen her body. She was eight years older, had given birth to their son. Would he still find her as attractive as he used to?

"You're even more beautiful than I remembered," he said, unknowingly soothing her fears. He reached up to cup the back of her head, caressing her cheek with his thumb while his other hand massaged the gentle curve of her back. "I've never wanted a woman more."

Sara closed her eyes and turned her face into his caress. "Mike," she whispered, silently cursing the tears that threatened to spill. He would, of course, think something was wrong, when in fact nothing had ever felt more right. She loved this man. Always had—no doubt always would. "I want you, too. *Please*. I can't wait another second."

He took her mouth in a near savage kiss and once again turned her onto her back. He peeled off his sweats and boxer-briefs in one smooth motion, tossing them onto the floor.

As their lips and tongues mated, she worked her hand between them and curled her fingers around his erection, squeezing gently.

Mike rocked back. "Slow down, sweetheart, or I'll never make it inside you."

Sara smiled, loving the feel of power that gave her. She ensnared him in her grasp again, moving her hand slowly, as he'd asked, stroking him up, circling the head with the pad of her thumb.

"Ah, hell," he muttered, reaching down to break her grip. He gathered both her wrists in one hand and pulled them up over head. With his other, he traced a fiery path down her stomach, through the triangle of soft red curls. His middle finger sought and found her clitoris—already wet and swollen—and stroked softly. He leaned in and sucked one of her nipples into his mouth.

She cried out, her back arching as her body came fully alive. So long…it had been so long since she'd felt this man's touch, and she squeezed her eyes shut as she hovered on the edge of sweet release.

"Calm down, honey. Relax," he whispered.

"I want you inside me, Mike. Now. *Please*."

He slowly worked his finger inside her. *Oh, God, oh, God, oh, God*…She cried out again as she came, hard and fast, her hips moving in desperate rhythm against his hand.

"Jesus…I didn't know you were so close," he rasped against her neck.

He withdrew his finger, and then suddenly his hard length slid inside her. She clenched her legs around him and urged him on as the most incredible orgasm continued to ripple through her. Mike pumped himself into her several times before joining her on the other side, his shout of satisfaction muffled against her throat.

The rhythmic cadence of their hips slowed and then stopped. Mike lay on top of her, his breathing heavy and ragged and…wonderful.

Eyes closed, her chest heaving as she fought to catch her breath, Sara smiled with lazy contentment. She held him tight, her arms clutched around his rib cage, her nails digging into the flesh of his back. Unclenching her hands, she realized she'd left marks. Her fingertips smoothed over the indentations her nails had left, as a whimper of distress escaped her throat.

"Don't worry," he murmured against her throat. "They'll go away."

"I'm sorry. Does it hurt?" she asked, trying to soothe away the pain with her fingertips.

"Not even a little bit."

"Good."

He lifted his head and gazed down at her. She smiled and pulled her knees up to cradle him between her thighs.

He immediately grew hard again inside her.

Satisfied, Sara grasped his face and pulled him down for a kiss while rocking her hips against him, urging him to move.

Mike tore his mouth from hers and gazed down.

"What's wrong?" she whispered, concerned.

"I want you to admit you love me, Sara. I want to hear the words."

Half amused, half frustrated she could only stare at him. Mike insecure? Such a hard thing to fathom. He'd come across so self-confident, arrogant even, since his return. "Isn't it usually the woman asking for declarations of love after sex?"

Mike didn't look amused. "Is that all it was to you? Sex?"

"Okay, now you're starting to worry me. What's the matter with you? I thought things were going," she gestured to the fact they were in bed together, "pretty good between us."

He sighed and rested his forehead against hers. "They are. I've never been happier. My son is safe and sound in the other room. And his mother, the woman I love, is lying naked beneath me."

She reached up with both hands to cup the back of his head as her calves wrapped around the backs of his thighs. Then she pulled his head down and kissed him soundly.

Mike growled low in his throat and slanted his mouth to deepen the kiss, his tongue delving inside as he braced his elbows on either side of her. He started moving his hips, slowly thrusting in and out. Sara followed his rhythm, her heels digging into his backside, urging him on, needing this man more than she needed air.

He broke off the kiss and leaned back, his thrusts coming harder and faster. Sara clutched at his back, his arms, his hips, relearning every inch of his body as he loved her thoroughly, like no other man ever could. She'd been without him for so long, and hadn't realized just how deeply she missed him until he'd walked into her bakery and back into her life.

The tension built as their bodies strained together in carnal harmony. Sara choked back a sob and grasped him tighter, her core throbbing with sweet anticipation as another orgasm was nearly within reach...

"Mike, oh my God, *Mike*..." She pulled him down and buried her face in the crook of his neck as her second climax hit her with the force of a freight train. *I love you. I love you so much.*

She bit gently into his neck and it was like a white-hot flame to dry kindling. His thrusts grew frenzied as she convulsed around him. He covered her mouth and swallowed their cries of satisfaction as he pumped himself inside her one final time.

Once the tremors subsided and their breathing returned to normal, Mike spooned her from behind and wrapped his arms around her. Sara snuggled against him, safe and warm within the circle of his arms.

"Sara?"

"Mmm."

"You're going to cancel your date with Jason tomorrow when we get home, right?"

Jason. A prickle of shame burned her cheeks. She hadn't thought about him even once today—or tonight. "Of course I plan to break things off with him. But I should probably tell him in person."

Mike's arm tightened slightly. He didn't respond for almost a full minute, then said, "Fine. Just...don't go off alone with him. Tell him at the house when he comes to pick you up."

Sara's brow creased. Jealousy? She laughed softly to break any tension and nestled her backside against his awakening erection. "You know, I'm trying to enjoy the moment here. Can we please not talk about him, or anyone else?"

She turned in his arms and made sure he didn't have the time—or inclination—to think about anyone but her for the rest of the night.

Mike ground his heavily aroused body against Sara's sweet little backside while gently kneading her breast. Even after three rounds of lovemaking, he couldn't get enough of her. Talk about making up for lost time.

She moaned and wiggled back and forth, teasing him. Then she stiffened. "Shit," she muttered, sitting straight up in bed, dislodging his hand from her breast.

He rolled to his back and threw his arm over his eyes. "What is it? What's wrong?"

Sara slid from the bed and reached for her dress. "The sun's up, which means Ethan should be running in here any minute." She slipped it over her head and then started finger-combing her hair.

"So?" Once he and Sara were married, they'd share a bed every night. Couldn't hurt for Ethan to get accustomed to that now.

She turned, the look on her face incredulous. "*So*, if Ethan had found us in bed together, they would've been the first words out of his mouth when we got home."

Mike's smile faltered. "So the hell what? We're consenting adults. You don't need anyone's permission to sleep with me." Suddenly, his eyes narrowed. "Wait a minute. I know what this is about. Son of a bitch." He threw the covers back and leapt off the bed. "This is about Garrett, isn't it? You probably assured him you wouldn't touch me with a ten-foot pole, and now you're afraid you'll have to admit you jumped in bed with me the first chance you got!"

Sara gasped. "You are the biggest asshole I've ever known," she said, enunciating every word.

Taken aback, Mike reached down and yanked on his sweatpants before closing the distance between them to take her into his arms.

"Don't you dare touch me," she spat, darting away from him.

Christ, what the hell was he thinking? They'd only just reconnected, and he acted as if she owed him loyalty over the brother who'd been by her side all these years.

The same brother who'd had a hate-on for him since the day they'd met.

"Look, you're right, I'm an asshole. What I said was inexcusable. It's just...I know what kind of influence Garrett has over you, and the thought that he might possibly have the power to keep us apart—"

"Do you even hear yourself? Garrett isn't a magician or a sorcerer. He's my brother, and he's been my rock for the past eight years. He held me when I cried my heart out over you. He was in the room when I gave birth to Ethan. He co-signed the loan so I could open my bakery. So don't you dare say another unkind word about him. If not for Garrett, we might not even have a son."

"What the hell does that mean?" Mike sat down on the edge of the bed and took a deep breath, his eyes never leaving her face. "Did something happen?"

"Nothing, forget it." She looked away. "I have to go wake up Ethan so we can get out of here."

"Sara, we're not leaving until you tell me what you meant by that. Did something happen to Ethan? Was he in the hospital? Was he sick?"

She reluctantly sat down beside him on the bed. "After I found out I was pregnant, I...made an appointment to have an abortion. Garrett found out and forbid me to go through with it. An hour after the scheduled appointment, I knew he was right. I cried all night, heartsick by what I'd almost done."

"Jesus." He wrapped his arms around her.

"I've never told that to anyone before. Garrett and I are the only ones who know how close Ethan came to...not existing." She said the last two words in a choked whisper, and Mike crushed her to him.

Not for the first time since returning to Green Bay, he found himself at a complete loss for words. Garrett, the man who'd been a thorn in his side since the moment they'd met, the man who despised him with a passion, was the sole reason Sara hadn't destroyed their child. His throat was so thick he knew he couldn't talk, even if he wanted to. Which he didn't. He just wanted to hold Sara in his arms for as long as he could.

"Omigod!" She stiffened and pulled away from him. Reaching across the bed, she picked up what looked like a three-ring binder.

"What? Sara, what the hell is it?"

"These," she flipped it open for him to see, "are Ethan's Yu-Gi-Oh! cards."

Ah. The kid must have woken up at some point and decided to show him the card collection he was so proud of. Mike fought to hide a grin. This wasn't exactly bad news in his estimation, but he knew Sara didn't want her family finding out about them like this. Being blurted out by a curious little boy who had no way of knowing he'd be starting WWIII between his father and his favorite uncle.

"Maybe he couldn't see anything in the dark, so he just set the book down and headed back to bed?"

"Yeah, or maybe his Yu-Gi-Oh! cards floated in here all by themselves."

Mike scowled. "Smart ass."

"Mom? Mom, where are you?"

At the sound of their son's voice, Sara's eyes widened

in dismay. She jumped off the bed and called out, "I'm coming, baby!"

Mike snatched his shirt off the lampshade and pulled it over his head. "I'm coming with you."

Ethan was sitting up in bed with the covers thrown back, rubbing his eyes. He smiled when he saw them. "'Morning. I'm hungry."

Sara sat on the edge of the bed and patted his leg. "How about if I fix you a great big breakfast as soon as we get home?"

He looked up at Mike. "Dad, too?"

"Dad, too. I'll make pancakes and bacon, how does that sound?"

"Awesome!" Ethan slid off the bed. "Let's go!"

Sara laughed. "Um, Ethan, don't you think you should get dressed first?"

He glanced down at his Hulk pajamas. "Oh, yeah."

"Listen, I'm gonna go get dressed myself and gather up my things," Mike said. "You two come on in when you're ready, and we'll head back to your place for that pancake breakfast."

"Okay!" Ethan grabbed his backpack and raced into the bathroom.

Mike came up behind Sara and wrapped his arms around her. Seemed as if maybe they'd both overreacted. Ethan didn't seem at all confused or concerned about finding his parents in bed together. "Try not to worry so much. Everything will work itself out, you'll see."

Seventeen

Sara sat at the kitchen table brooding over a cup of coffee. She'd decided she had no choice but to keep her dinner date with Jason that night. But only because she owed the man an explanation. Mike wouldn't be happy, but he would just have to trust her. She'd considered asking Garrett to break things off with him for her, but knew that was the cowardly way out.

And she wasn't a coward.

An idiot, perhaps, for even considering giving Mike another chance to break her heart, but she wasn't a coward.

Taking a sip of her coffee, she glanced at her watch. Three o'clock? It seemed as if she'd just finished cleaning up after breakfast. Amazing how fast time flew by when one was brooding.

She got up and poured the rest of her coffee down the sink, then headed down to her bedroom to get dressed. It was a bit early to start getting ready for her 'date,' but she had nothing else to do since the guys planned on ordering pizza for supper.

She opened her closet and searched for something...less than flattering, sliding over hanger after hanger until a big brown turtleneck sweater caught her eye. She giggled. Hell, that would be too obvious considering it was the first week of June and nearly eighty degrees outside. Though she knew Mike would certainly approve.

Mike. My God, they'd definitely made up for lost time last night. Her skin warmed just thinking about all the wonderfully delicious things they'd done in that big comfy bed. How hard it would be to sleep in her own bed tonight—alone.

Blowing out a hard breath, she finally decided on a pair of white slacks and an olive green blouse she'd almost forgotten she owned. Once dressed, she sat in front of her mirror, brushed her hair, and put on a light application of make-up—blush, a little lip gloss, and a few strokes of mascara. If for no other reason than she hoped to see Mike again later in the evening.

Needing to keep herself busy lest her nerves get the better of her, she headed back into the kitchen and put on a fresh pot of coffee. The guys would be home soon, and usually the first thing any of them did was give the coffee carafe a shake.

Ethan came bounding up the stairs just as she finished.

"Mom, I'm hungry. Can I have a toaster pastry?"

She glanced at the clock. "Uncle Garrett will be ordering pizza in less than an hour. Can't you wait?"

"*Nooo*," he whined in perfect seven-year-old fashion. "I'm starving. I'll eat my supper, too. I promise."

"Fine," she relented with a sigh.

He was sitting at the table squeezing the icing over his pastry when he asked, "Are we gonna go live with my dad when his new house is ready?"

Taken aback by the question, she took a seat beside him and carefully explained, "You can certainly spend as much time at your father's house as you like. But *this* is our home, Ethan. At least for the time being."

"But you slept in my dad's bed last night at the hotel. Doesn't that mean we should go live with him?"

"You *what*?"

Startled, she spun around. Garrett stood in the doorway, hands on hips, his expression thunderous.

How hadn't she heard him pull up? She swallowed and tried to make light of the situation. "We watched movies all night, and wouldn't you know it, I fell asleep."

"Dammit, Sara. What the hell were you thinking? You have a date with Jason tonight, for chrissake." He stormed into the kitchen and pitched his keys on the table, then over to the counter and gave the carafe a shake.

"I just put another pot on," she said, hoping to distract him from a conversation she had no desire to have.

"Ethan, go downstairs, please. I need to speak to your mother alone."

"But I'm not done with my toaster pastry yet."

Garrett shot him a look. "Take it with you."

Scowling, Ethan did as he was told.

Sara sat down and propped her elbows on the table. She didn't care for the tone he'd taken with her son, but decided to let it go since she knew how hard this whole situation has been on him. She also knew few people loved him more than his Uncle Garrett.

Her brother poured a fresh cup of coffee from the pot brewing, carried it to the table, and took the seat across from her. "I don't get it. You said there was nothing between you and Andrews, yet you jump in bed with him the first chance you get?"

Damn, did he have to use the exact words Mike had? "I was horny; it'd been awhile," she flippantly replied.

"Real nice, Sara." He ran his fingers through his hair, never breaking eye contact with her. "Where does this leave Jason? He's crazy about you. And he thinks you feel the same."

With a sigh, she got up and poured the fresh coffee into the carafe. Over her shoulder, she admitted, "I was planning on breaking things off with him tonight."

"That's just great. Let the guy buy you dinner, then dump him."

She spun around, exasperated. "Would you rather I give him a call and 'dump him' over the phone? Because believe me, I'd rather do that. We've been on *one* date, Garrett. He's not going to die of a broken heart over this, and you know it. And this isn't about Jason anyway. It's about Mike. Admit it."

He set his cup down with more force than necessary. "You're damn right it is! He ran out on you, Sara. He ran out on you and Ethan both. How could you forget that? Is he so good in the sack you're willing to sacrifice your pride just to lay under him?"

Sara stood frozen in shock. She couldn't believe Garrett had spoken to her that way. He was letting his jealousy over Mike's relationship with Ethan turn him into someone she didn't recognize.

Through gritted teeth she said, "Don't you dare say another word to me until you're ready to apologize. I'm a grown woman, Garrett Jamison, and nobody, I mean *nobody*, tells me who I can or can't spend time with. Maybe if you had a life of your own, you wouldn't feel the need to stick your nose in mine!"

With that parting shot, she stormed from the kitchen.

Staring down into his coffee a short time later, Garrett didn't even look up when Danny and Uncle Luke came in through the back door. They both offered a greeting, but he was so miserable he barely grunted a reply. Miserable because he'd let his anger get the better of him and said some incredibly hurtful things to the sister he loved dearly.

And miserable because she was right. Garrett needed a life of his own. He'd avoided serious relationships because he'd become so wrapped up in Ethan and Sara's lives. If he were to fall in love and get married, where would that have left them?

But now with Andrews back in the picture, Sara and Ethan didn't need him anymore, and it felt like a betrayal. Because he'd given up so much for them, yet they were doing just fine without him. And though he knew he was being ridiculous, the jealousy gnawed at his gut.

Somebody patted him on the shoulder. "You all right, son? You don't look so good."

Uncle Luke. The older man came around and took a seat at the table beside him.

Garrett nodded and even managed a rueful grin. "Yeah, I'm fine. Except I dug myself a deep one with Sara. She's as pissed at me as she's ever been."

"What the hell did you do?" Danny poured a cup of coffee, then took the seat across from him.

"Sara and Mike have...rekindled their relationship. When I found out about it, I said some pretty...inexcusable things to her."

Danny's brows shot up. "How'd you find out? There's no way she would've told you."

He eyed his youngest brother as he propped an elbow on the table and rubbed absently at his forehead. "I overheard Ethan asking her a pointed question about last night."

"You don't have to tell us, if you don't want to," Uncle Luke was quick to say.

"Aw, come on, I wanna know," Danny insisted with a laugh.

Garrett dragged his hand down the lower half of his face, then shot up and strode over to the counter to pour a head on his coffee. "He asked if he and Sara were going to go live with Mike since she'd slept in his bed last night at the hotel."

Uncle Luke let out a low whistle. "He didn't, uh, catch them in the act, did he?"

"I don't think so or Sara would've been a lot more upset about it."

"Are you going to tell us what you said to make her so upset?" Danny asked as he snatched the take-out menu off the Lazy Susan and skimmed it over.

"No."

"Hey, isn't she supposed to go out with Jason tonight?" his brother persisted, grinning. "I guess that date's been cancelled."

"Actually, she plans on telling him over supper."

"She's gonna let him buy her dinner, and then dump his ass?" Danny's grin widened.

"I think you're enjoying this a little too much." Garrett frowned and leaned back against the counter. "Don't forget, I have to work with the guy. And Jason's a decent sort. I hate that he's going to get his heart broken."

His brother arched a brow, his expression sobering. "They've been out on *one* date, Garrett. He'll live."

Deciding it best to let the subject drop, he took the menu from Danny and flipped it open. He'd make things right with Sara later, after she'd had a chance to cool down. "Let's get an order together so I can phone it in. I'm starving."

The three of them were all sitting at the table eating supper when Garrett realized one special little person was missing. "Hey, sport! Time for supper!" he called out, getting up to pour his nephew a glass of milk.

Ethan came up from the basement and took his usual seat at the table. He cast a quick, nervous glance his way before sliding a slice of pizza onto his plate.

Garrett felt as if he'd been sucker-punched. His face burned with shame, and it was all he could do to hold his head up. He'd acted like a bully and complete ass earlier, and now the little guy who meant more to him than anyone was afraid to look him in the eye. He set his pizza down and propped his elbows on the table, clasping his hands.

He gazed at his nephew's bent head and said, his voice gentle, "Ethan, you heard your mom and I yelling at each other, didn't you?"

Ethan looked up and nodded. A spark of anger lit his eyes. "You yelled at her about my dad. Why don't you like my dad?"

Good God, where to begin? "Sport, your father and I have a history of not getting along so well."

"Why?"

One little word, yet it asked so much. "You know, it's just a lot of silly adult stuff that would be pretty hard to explain. But the good news is, starting right this moment, I'm done being a cranky butt."

"And you're gonna like my dad?" Ethan demanded.

Damn, the kid drove a hard bargain. "Sure. For you, anything." Hell, he'd even give Mike a big wet one if it would put a smile back on the little guy's face.

He mentally shivered in revulsion.

"Cool." Ethan smiled up at him, and it felt as if the weight of the world had been lifted off his shoulders. The kid picked up his pizza and started wolfing it down.

Garrett looked up and caught Uncle Luke staring at him. The older man smiled and nodded his approval. Suddenly, he felt better than he had in days.

Sara was lying on the bed, flipping through a magazine when Mr. Judgmental showed up at her bedroom door. She squeezed her eyes shut for a brief moment, unsure if she was ready to have this particular confrontation.

"Can I come in?"

Without waiting for a response, he stepped inside and shut the door behind him. Sara didn't bother to look up.

"Now how can I apologize if you won't even look at me?"

She licked her finger and turned another page.

"I know I've been acting like a jerk lately, but as your oldest brother, I'm ordering you to forgive me."

Her lips twitched.

"I saw that."

She let out a heartfelt sigh and rolled over to face him. "Look, I'm not even sure if things are going to work out between Mike and me. But I do know he's going to be a permanent fixture in Ethan's life, and it's not fair for my son to get caught up in your War of the Machos with

Mike."

"War of the Machos?"

A reluctant grin curved her lips. "You know what I mean. I don't expect the two of you to start singing folk songs, but you *could* make an effort to be civil. For Ethan's sake." She closed the magazine and sat up, desperate to make him understand. "Mike's so good with him, Garrett. You should see them together."

He sat down on the bed beside her. "You've never stopped loving him, have you?"

"No, I never have. And I've tried. Trust me, I've tried." Until she'd thought her heart would explode from the effort. Eventually, she'd forced herself to leave Mike in the past and look toward the future. For Ethan's sake if not her own. But she'd never truly gotten over him, and that fact became clear the moment he'd stepped into her bakery and back into her life.

"I suppose it would be pretty hard to forget a man when you're looking into his son's eyes every day," Garrett conceded, empathy shining in his eyes.

She smiled, relieved not to be at each other's throats anymore. "There is that."

"Listen, I promise not to snarl and shoot flames out of my nose every time Mike and I are in the same room. Other than that, let's just take it day by day. Agreed?"

"Agreed," she said, feeling better by the minute. "Now, since you're in such a magnanimous mood, think you can give Jason a call and break up with him for me?"

Garrett laughed. "I'll tell you what. Since I do sort of owe you one, I'll buy you some time. I'll call and tell him you can't make dinner because Ethan's puking his guts up, and you're by his side wiping his brow."

"You'd really do that for me?"

"Sure. What else are big brothers for?"

Sara sat at the kitchen table flipping through a Sears catalog when the phone rang. She got up to answer it, but then hesitated. What if it was Jason calling to find out how Ethan was? She'd always been such a terrible liar. Though he wouldn't be able to see her facial expression, so maybe she could pull it off.

"Hello?"

"Hey, beautiful, whatcha doing?"

Mike. Her shoulders slumped in relief. "Nothing. Just looking through a catalog. You?"

"Just sitting here in my new house waiting for that ugly yellow truck to pull into your driveway."

"Well wait no longer. Garrett got me out of my date, though I can't put it off forever. I'll have to give Jason a call tomorrow and—" It suddenly dawned on her what he'd said. "You're in your new house? As in the one just down the block from me?"

He chuckled. "That would be the one."

"But I thought you had to wait until tomorrow." Her pulse picked up speed knowing he was so close…which scared the hell out of her. As much as she wanted to throw caution to the wind and jump in with both feet, she had to be careful, take things slow. Trust was a hard thing to rebuild, and though she had no doubts anymore about Mike's commitment to his son, she wasn't quite as confident when it came to their newly budding relationship.

"Mr. Pankovich's family moved the rest of his things out today. Didn't you see the huge moving truck that was parked in his driveway most of the day?"

"No. I didn't even notice it, to tell you the truth. I was kind of busy."

"Yeah? Doing what?"

Besides thinking about you and last night? "Brooding. Garrett and I had words earlier. We already made up, though."

"Why?"

"Because he's my brother, and I love him, despite his faults."

She heard him sigh and fought to hold back a giggle.

"Why did you and Garrett get into it?" Mike clarified.

"Let's just say he walked in and heard something I wish he hadn't." She absently flipped to the next page of the catalog.

"You're killing me here, you know that, don't you?"

She laughed. "I'll tell you later. When there isn't a pair of nosy little ears within the sound of my voice."

"Ah. Well, listen, since you no longer have dinner plans, how would you and Ethan like to join me for a burger? We can take a ride to that place next to the stadium. I rode past there the other day and was thrilled to see they're still in business."

"Ooh, I love *Perelli's*. They put a glob of butter on top and the buns are nice and crispy. Count me in."

He laughed. "I take it you're hungry?"

"Starving. I didn't eat with the guys since I was planning on going out—well, you know. I was just thinking about throwing some leftover pizza in the microwave when you called."

"Ethan's already eaten then?"

"Yeah, but that was over an hour ago. I guarantee, by the time we get there, he'll be hungry again. A little boy's metabolism is an amazing thing."

"Great. Then I'll be by to pick you up in about...thirty seconds?"

Sara laughed. "We'll be ready."

She hung up the phone and skipped down the stairs, ridiculously excited to see him. Uncle Luke sat on the couch watching Nicky and Ethan play video games. Garrett had gone out to shoot pool, as he often did on Friday nights.

At least I know he won't be getting into a fight tonight.

"Mom, guess who's winning!" Her son looked possessed as his thumbs went crazy on the game controller.

"Um, you?" she assumed, watching the television screen in amazement. *He's so good*, she thought, unsure whether to be proud of him or ashamed of herself for letting him spend so much time playing the darn thing.

"Yep. And Uncle Nicky's trying his hardest. Aren't you?"

"Sure am." Her brother cast her a sidelong grin. "You're just too good for me, big guy. Maybe I'll get a chance to practice this weekend."

"Actually, you can get some practice in right now. Ethan, your father's on his way over. He wants to take us out for *Perelli* burgers. If you're interested, that is."

Ethan dropped the controller and jumped to his feet. "Yeah! But I don't want a burger, Mom. I want a double-decker sundae with extra whipped cream."

She pursed her lips. "Well, since you've already eaten supper, I suppose. Now go put your shoes on. He'll be here any second."

"Any second? Didn't he just call?" Nicky asked.

"Yeah, but he called from old man Pankovich's house.

Or, I guess I should say, Mike's house."

Uncle Luke whistled. "That may be the fastest closing in the history of real estate."

Mike certainly did seem to be able to make things happen. And though it still stung a bit to have lost the house she'd had her heart set on for her and her son, maybe, thanks to a twist of fate, everything had worked out exactly the way it was supposed to.

"Come on, let's go," Ethan said as he finished tying his shoes. "Dad's probably already out there waiting."

"All right, all right." She shook her head and smiled. "We'll be back in about an hour."

"Have a good time," Uncle Luke said.

At that moment, the sound of Mike's voice carried down from the vicinity of the kitchen. "Hey, starving man here! You two ready or what?"

"We're coming, Dad!" Ethan grabbed her hand and pulled her along.

Mike waited for them by the back door. As soon as their eyes met, a flush crept up her neck. She knew exactly what the man was thinking, and her nipples tightened in response.

"Let me just grab my purse," she said as she dropped her gaze and moved past him toward her bedroom. When she returned, Mike had Ethan slung over his shoulder like a sack of potatoes.

"You're going to be sorry if he pukes on your back," she predicted with raised eyebrows.

Very gently, he set Ethan back on his feet, who in turn, scowled at her.

"You always ruin my fun."

"It's what I live for."

Fifteen minutes later, they pulled into the parking lot of

Perelli's. As usual, Ethan gazed longingly over at Lambeau Field. "I'm gonna play there someday."

Mike ruffled his hair. "So, you're a football fan, are you? Good, so am I. It'll be nice to have someone to watch the games with this fall."

The smile on Sara's face turned bittersweet. Football Sunday had always been Garrett and Ethan's special time.

"Can Uncle Garrett come, too? I always watch football with Uncle Garrett."

Much to his credit, Mike's expression never faltered. "Of course he can. The more, the merrier. Maybe it'll become a tradition and everybody can come down to my place for football Sunday. Even your mom." He glanced up at her, a gleam in his eye.

She shivered in response.

Crossing her arms over her chest, she said, "Hey, I like football. And I'll even make lunch for everyone. Brats, breaded cheese curds, and a big ol' pot of Chicken Booyah."

Mike laughed. "You're such a Cheesehead."

"Well, so is your son," she reminded him, hands on hips, "so you'd better say it with respect."

He shrugged. "Hell, so am I at heart. I always root for the Packers. I have to admit, though, I've become quite a Bears fan over the years."

Sara glanced around in mock horror. "Are you trying to get us lynched?"

Ethan giggled and Mike rolled his eyes.

"Well, come on, you two. I'm so hungry I could eat your Uncle Luke's Spam casserole. And that's saying something."

"That lying bitch," Jason muttered, as he watched Sara and a well-enough looking Ethan walk across the parking lot toward the restaurant. And he was fairly certain the big dude with them wasn't one of her brothers.

Carl Montgomery, who sat next to him in the truck, said, "Hey, isn't that Sara Jamison? Wow, she still looks hot as hell."

Jason glanced over at him, surprised. "You know Sara?"

Carl shrugged. "Sure. We went to school together. She and my sister were pretty chummy back in the day." He reached up and fingered his bandaged nose. "At least until that Andrews jerk-off started coming around."

"So who's the guy with her? You know him?"

Carl squinted. "Yeah, *that's* the jerk-off. I guess they finally kissed and made up."

Jason cocked a brow. "What do you mean, 'kissed and made up?' What do you know that I don't?"

"That's the prick that busted my nose and pulled a gun on me. He and Sara were a hot item back in high school."

"That's a coincidence, now isn't it?" Jason murmured, drumming his fingers against the dashboard. "He's the one who showed up the other night after I left? The one who broke your nose? You're sure of it?"

"'Course I'm sure. Why're you so interested anyway? You know Sara?"

Jason waited until the restaurant door closed behind them before starting up his truck. "I took the two-timing bitch out to the movies the other night."

"Well, if I were you, I'd steer clear of her. Besides being a grudge holder, Andrews has one hell of a temper."

"And you say he pulled a gun on you? That's kind of strange, isn't it? I mean, the average guy doesn't walk around carrying a gun." Jason pulled out of his parking spot and stopped in front of the black pickup Sara and Andrews had gotten out of. He wrote down the license plate number, surprised by the fact they were Illinois-issued. "He's from Illinois?"

Carl leaned forward and peered at Andrews' truck plates. He shrugged. "I guess so. It didn't come up in our conversation. But I do know he moved away a long time ago, and I'm pretty sure he hasn't been back in town all that long."

"Huh." Jason took his foot off the brake and pulled out of the parking lot. Just to be safe, he'd run the guy's plates. No sense taking a chance. Jason had learned that lesson a long time ago.

Eighteen

Sara gazed down at her unusually quiet son as Mike parked his truck in front of the house. After they'd eaten their fill of burgers and ice cream, Mike suggested they stop at *Toy's R Us* so he could make up for at least one of Ethan's birthdays. She'd insisted it wasn't necessary, but Ethan had begged until she'd given in. The Transformer robot he'd picked out was clutched in his fist, his eyes so heavy Sara knew he'd be out like a light before his head even hit the pillow.

Mike lifted Ethan into his arms, carried him up the porch steps and into the house. The sight of him holding their son with such tender care caused a lump to form in her throat.

She led the way to his room and lit the small lamp on his nightstand, then pulled down the comforter so his father could lay him on the bed. After tugging off his shoes, she pulled the comforter up over him and kissed him on the cheek. Mike did the same, and as their gazes met across the bed, Sara's throat grew thick at the boundless love reflected back in Mike's eyes for this wonderful little person they created.

Ethan was proof that kismet had been working in their favor, even when the forces of evil had been working so hard to tear them apart. And now here she was, daring to dream about a future together after all these years. Nothing stood in their way anymore.

Except for the fact she was scared spitless to trust him again with her heart. Though it was headed that way, and fast.

When Sara pulled Ethan's bedroom door shut behind them, Mike bent down and kissed her. A slow, lingering kiss that nearly curled her toes.

"Come with me down to the house. I'll give you a guided tour."

Sure, and guide me right into the bedroom. "Oh, I've seen the inside of that house lots of times," she teased.

"Yeah, but it looks so much bigger without furniture. You can look around, get an idea of what you'd like to do with each room."

Sara chewed on her bottom lip, knowing that if she went with him, they'd end up in bed together. It was something they both wanted, and if they were alone together, it would happen. No question about it. Mike made her ache in a way no other man ever had.

"All right, I'll come."

His eyes gleamed in the darkened hallway. "Yes, you will."

He pulled her against his chest and kissed her again, coaxing her lips with his tongue while his hands caressed her back, her hips, her backside.

She tore her mouth away, her breathing labored. "Let me just go tell someone where I'll be. I'll meet you out in your truck."

Mike chuckled. "Hell, it's like we're teenagers again, only we're hiding from our son instead of your uncle and brothers."

Sara laughed softly. "You're right, it is."

She found Nicky and Uncle Luke in the kitchen polishing off the rest of a strawberry-rhubarb pie. As always, a fresh pot of coffee was brewing on the counter.

"Thought I heard you come in," her uncle said, smiling.

Nicky took a sip of his coffee before asking, "You guys have a good time?"

"We stuffed ourselves at *Perelli's*, then headed to *Toys R Us* so Mike could buy Ethan a toy, make up for one of his birthdays. We just tucked him into bed."

Nicky peered around her. "Where's Mike?"

God, she hoped her face wasn't as red as it felt. *You are a grown woman for cripe's sake, and have nothing to feel ashamed about.* "Waiting out in the truck. He's going to give me a tour of house, get my opinion on a few things. I shouldn't be too long. Just wanted to let someone know in case Ethan woke up before I got back."

A knowing grin lit her brother's face. He shared a quick glance with Uncle Luke who hurriedly shoved a bite of pie in his mouth. Nicky said, "Well, you kids have fun. And don't worry about Ethan. I'll check in on him in a little while."

The shit was really enjoying this. She playfully narrowed her eyes. "Thanks. I shouldn't be more than an hour or so."

Nicky winked at her, and she fled the house before she accidentally made eye contact with her uncle.

Minutes later, Mike parked his truck in his new garage and closed the overhead door with the press of a button. They entered the house through the garage, which led into a breezeway.

Sara felt like a little kid again as she walked into the

house. She could almost taste the homemade chocolate fudge Mrs. Pankovich used to make right in this very kitchen, smell the fresh-brewed tea the older woman had been so fond of. Besides fudge, she'd also mixed up huge batches of popcorn balls every Halloween and invited Sara down to help her wrap them. One of Sara's best childhood memories.

She'd always thought of this place as such a grand house and imagined living in it someday. How ironic that her son's father now owned the house she'd coveted most of her life. Surprisingly, the thought didn't cause her any pangs of jealousy, like it had at first.

Okay, maybe a teensy one.

"I'd almost forgotten how big the kitchen is in this old house," she said, running her hand over the smooth Formica countertop. The harvest gold appliances were outdated, but they'd been well-taken care of. Mrs. Pankovich had taken pride in her home, and when she passed on, her husband had obviously done the same.

"I fell in love with the place as soon as I walked in. And the fact that it was so close to you and Ethan was, of course, an added bonus." He walked up behind her and placed his hands on her shoulders. "Maybe every once in a while you can take pity on me and come fix me a home-cooked meal."

She looked up at him through her lashes. "Maybe I will—*if* you're nice to me."

"Sweetheart, I plan on being real nice to you. Starting right now."

He leaned down and captured her lips. Sara turned so she could wrap her arms around his neck. Lord, how she loved the rasp of his tongue against hers, the warmth of his breath as it feathered across her cheek, the softness of his lips. He deepened the kiss, cupped her backside with both hands and pulled her up hard against him.

His breathing grew heavy and he tore his mouth away to ask, "Which room should we christen?"

She grinned up at him. "Preferably one with carpeting. The softer, the better."

"Don't worry, I bought one of those bed-in-a-bag sets today. I even remembered to wash it all."

"Oh? Pretty damn sure of yourself, aren't you?" She playfully tweaked the hair at the nape of his neck.

"I planned to sleep here tonight either way. I can't spend another night in that house."

"I know." She reached up to caress his cheek.

"Hey now, no sad face. It'll ruin the mood." He swung her up into his arms and headed for the staircase.

"Somehow, I doubt anything could ruin the mood for you."

He laughed. "True enough. But it's your fault. You're just so damn sexy."

She rolled her eyes. "Yeah, that's me. A regular sex kitten."

"You're the sexiest woman I've ever known."

"And just how many women *have* you known?" The words slipped out before she could stop them. She tried to make light of it. "Please tell me I didn't say that out loud."

"The only woman who matters—who's *ever* mattered—is the one in my arms right now."

Her throat thick over his heartfelt declaration, she reached up and cupped his cheek. More than anything she wanted to believe him. Believe *in* him.

He reached the second floor, made a right, and kicked open the first door on the left. The room was empty except for the new bedding he'd mentioned, which he'd already set up on the carpet. He dropped to his knees and gently laid her on the comforter before reaching over to flip the light on in the closet.

"You could've left the light off," she said, stretching out on the comforter. "I'm not afraid of the dark."

"But then I wouldn't be able to see that gorgeous body of yours, and that just won't do." He leaned over and kissed her again.

Sara twined her arms around his neck and pulled him down. Her hands found their way beneath his shirt, desperate to feel his warm, naked flesh. She didn't feel as awkward as she had last night at the hotel. This was Mike, the only lover she'd ever known—the only man she ever wanted inside her.

He peeled off his shirt and tossed it aside before reaching down to help with hers. Once the last button was undone, he pushed the blouse open and smiled. Her bra unclasped in the front, and after opening it with deft fingers, he bent down and drew one of her nipples into his mouth.

She sighed, arching her back, the feel of his hot mouth on her breast almost too much to bear. He released it, but only to lavish the other nipple with the same sweet attention.

Mike leaned back, pulling her up with him, and stripped her of her blouse and bra, then reached down to unbutton her pants. Sara tried to do the same, but he stopped her with a whispered, "No, you first."

Gently, he pushed her back down onto the downy-soft comforter and literally peeled her pants down her legs. Sara laughed softly. "Sorry. If I'd known we were going to end up here, I'd have worn something a little looser."

Her smile faded when he tossed her pants aside and

turned back to stare hotly at her panties.

"I swear, just looking at you I could come in my pants." He reached up and hooked both his index fingers into the waistband of her panties, then slowly started pulling them down. He looked up in surprise when her legs tensed. "Sara? What is it?"

"It's just...well, the closet light is shining right...there," she finished, feeling like an idiot for this sudden display of shyness. Sheesh, she was acting like a frigging virgin!

His lips curved. "Yeah, that was sort of the point. But if you're uncomfortable—"

"No." She swallowed and tried to steel her nerves. "No, you're the only man I've ever felt comfortable enough with to..."

When her words trailed off, he reached back up and flipped off the closet light.

"Mike, you didn't have to do that." She sighed, feeling silly for making a big deal about it. *Good lord, you're a grown woman, not an adolescent girl!*

"I want you to feel completely comfortable whenever we make love. Now, tell me what you meant by, 'I'm the only man you've ever felt comfortable with.' You've...never felt like someone was trying to force you to—"

Her eyes widened when she realized what he was so delicately trying to say. "No! Of course not. That's not what I meant."

Her panties forgotten halfway down her thighs, he pressed a gentle kiss to her lips. "Then what did you mean?"

Gazing up at him, all she could make out were those incredible blue eyes. She wanted to tell him he was the only man she'd ever been with, but was afraid. Afraid he'd think there was something wrong with her. Because for a long time, *she'd* thought there was something wrong with her. What if he were disappointed by her lack of experience? Mike had no doubt been with lots of women. What if he found her lacking? She bit her lip. She knew she was being silly. They'd made love last night and it'd been wonderful—hot, passionate, intense.

"Sweetheart, if there's something bothering you, just tell me. I told you before, you can tell me anything."

"It's, well...kind of embarrassing. I mean, I'm not ashamed or anything. It's just kind of hard to explain."

"Well, you certainly have me curious now." He shifted so that he was lying on his side, his head resting on his elbow.

She turned toward him, mainly in an effort to gain a little modesty. Mike reached over and caressed her hip. His big, warm hand felt so good on her hot flesh, she almost forgot what they were talking about.

"Maybe we should...can we just forget about this?"

"Sara, tell me."

She took a deep breath. "There's only been you."

His hand stilled. "What?"

"I've never, you know, slept with anyone but you. I don't have that much experience. Just what you and I have...are you laughing? Dammit, this is not the least bit funny!"

She tried to sit up, but he anchored her down with an arm around her waist.

"Honey, I'm not laughing at you. It's just, my God, you had me imagining all kinds of things, when all you had to tell me was the best news I've ever heard? Well, with the exception of finding out I have a son."

"You say, 'all I had to tell you' as if it wasn't a big

deal. Well, it's a big deal to me."

"That's not what I meant, and you know it. Come on, sweetheart, I don't want to fight. The fact that I'm the only man you've ever been with is surprising, yes, but in a good way." He leaned down and kissed her. "A very good way."

Okay, so she knew she was being overly sensitive. Truth was, she hadn't known what kind of reaction to expect from him, but a huge, smug smile hadn't even been on the list. She supposed it made sense, though. Men were territorial by nature...hell, so were women. The thought of Mike sleeping with other women had always haunted her, so discovering she'd been faithful, in a sense, all this time must have made him pretty damn happy. She'd been on a handful of dates over the years, but for one reason or another, had never felt an intimate connection with anyone other than Mike. Her first lover—her only love.

She palmed his cheek, her heart full as she gazed into those amazing blue eyes. "I don't want to fight either."

His relief evident, he kissed her again before gently guiding her until she was once again lying on her back. "Now, the only thing I want you to think about right now is how good I'm going to make you feel."

Sara offered no resistance as he stripped off her panties and tossed them to the side with the rest of her clothes. She'd ached for this man for eight long years, and nothing mattered right now but having him deep inside. Her core wept at the thought of how perfectly they fit together.

As if starting over, he feathered his hand slowly, almost reverently, down her throat, over one aching breast and then the other. She moaned, arching into him, her fingers clenching his hair, silently urging him on as the throbbing between her legs intensified. He hadn't even touched her below the navel, yet she could already feel how wet she'd become.

As teenagers experimenting with sex, she remembered how mortified she'd been when he'd reached inside her underwear that first time and discovered her wetness. But Mike, who'd been almost as inexperienced as she, had assured her it was normal and even seemed to become more aroused by it. And then he'd stroked and caressed her until she'd had her first orgasm.

She'd thought of that night often over the years.

Mike gazed down at the love of his life, awed by her beauty as the moonlight washed across her alabaster skin. He replaced his hands with his mouth, eager to taste those luscious nipples again. He lavished one pink tip with his absolute thoroughness, then the other while her intoxicating scent drove him mad with lust.

Continuing his exploration, he trailed a hot, wet path with his lips and tongue across her stomach, stopping to dip his tongue inside her navel. She made a sound that was a cross between a sigh and a moan. After another playful dip, he leaned back and palmed her knees, then slowly spread her legs. She stiffened for a moment, but let him do as he pleased.

His mind still reeled over the fact he was the only man she'd ever been with. The only man she'd ever allowed inside her body. And inside her heart. He knew he wasn't deserving of such loyalty and fidelity, but somehow, he'd find a way to make up for his past mistakes.

Now was definitely a good time to start.

Eager to make this experience perfect for her, Mike slid back, leaned down, and pressed his mouth against her silken flesh just above the V of flame-colored curls.

Sara half-lifted off the floor. "Mike? I-I'm not ready

for that."

He gently pressed her back down into the soft folds of the comforter. "Relax, sweetheart."

"But, Mike—"

Not wanting to overwhelm her to the point of embarrassment, he propped himself on his elbow again and placed his hand on her thigh, caressing his way gradually upward until his fingers were wet with the proof of her need. He watched that beautifully expressive face, as her eyes clenched, and that sexy pink tongue darted out to wet her lips.

Fuck. His cock grew so hard it'd be a miracle if he could bend back down.

When he felt her relax a bit, he slowly stroked his finger back and forth across her moist flesh, then slipped inside her, just an inch. Sara made a mewling sound and lifted her hips off the floor, her body as taut as a tightly strung bow.

He glanced up and searched her face in the moonlight. "My God, you're about to explode, aren't you?"

She gave a jerky nod. "I can't help it."

"It's okay, sweetheart, I don't want you to hold back. I want you to let it happen and enjoy every second of it. You can scream your heart out, baby, and no one can hear you but me. It's just you, me, and this big empty house."

He moved down the length of her until he was lying between her legs. He gripped her by the back of each knee and gently positioned her until her thighs were lying wide open, her knees practically resting against the floor.

"Oh my God, *Mike*—"

"Shhhh," he whispered. He skimmed his hands up silken legs, over quivering thighs, to the heart of her. With his thumb, Mike found her clitoris and caressed tiny circles on it before leaning forward to stroke her moist flesh with his tongue.

Sara cried out and gripped his hair in both hands. Mike wasn't sure whether she was trying to push him off or pull him in, but either way his tongue never stopped its relentless assault. He felt her convulsing, her hips moving furiously against his mouth, and it took every ounce of willpower he possessed not to come in his pants.

When her hips ceased moving and all he could hear was her ragged breathing, he rose to his knees and reached for the button of his jeans.

Sara let out a sound of distress and dragged herself to her knees in front of him. She brushed his hands away. "Your turn."

Though surprised she had the energy, Mike had no intention of arguing. He dropped his hands and watched in fascination as she unbuttoned his jeans, stroked the zipper down his straining erection, and worked both his jeans and boxer briefs down his hips. When he sprang free, she laughed softly, and Mike knew his torture had just begun.

Sara had never performed oral sex on him, but somehow he knew this would definitely be worth the wait. She held his gaze as she wrapped her hands around his shaft and gave a gentle squeeze. He swallowed and dropped his head back as she stroked him up and down a few times, growing more confident, it seemed, with each groan she wrung from him.

"Lie down so I can finish undressing you," she ordered, releasing him.

He complied, loving this dominant new side of her. She wasted no time stripping off the rest of his clothes, and when he was completely naked, she sat astride his thighs and reclaimed his cock.

Mike watched her through heavy-lidded eyes as she stroked him, caressed him, relearned every inch of him from the tip of his head to the base of his shaft. When she cupped his balls, he bucked, practically tossing her off of him.

Her soft laughter filled the room. "I guess I'm not the only one who's sensitive."

With a half groan, half laugh, he muttered, "You're a fast learner, that's for sure."

"And I haven't even gotten to the best part yet," she promised, pushing him back down.

"Sweetheart, I don't know how much more I can take." He reached for her, intending to sink himself deep inside her and end both their torment.

But Sara was not to be denied. She shook off his hands and tossed her head. "I let you. Now you let me."

Mike licked his lips, but remained still. She was right, though the thought of what she planned to do next had him clenching his jaw.

She knelt before him again, braced one hand on the floor and curled the other around his erection. Mike watched, frozen, as she leaned over and took him into her mouth. His neck arched, and it was his turn to clench the comforter in his fists. It took every bit of his self-control not to cup the back of her head and pump himself into her mouth. Instead, he let her torture him, her lips moving slowly down, taking in more than he'd ever imagined she could, then pulling back up, stroking him with her tongue.

When he couldn't take it a second longer, he grasped her head and pulled free of her mouth, then rose to his knees again. In the sliver of moonlight that slashed across her face, he could see the glazed look in her eyes. Sara had enjoyed what she'd been doing.

He crushed her against him, slanting his mouth across hers, cupping her backside in one hand while reaching down to stroke her swollen flesh with the other. She gyrated her hips in urgent rhythm against his slick fingers, and he almost lost it then and there. He dug one of the little foil packets he'd forgotten the night before from his jeans, tore it open with his teeth, and quickly sheathed himself. Then he positioned her legs around his waist and entered her with a guttural moan.

With a soft cry, Sara buried her face in the crook of his neck. He clasped her to him and thrust inside her, slow and easy. She cried out, her movements becoming frenzied as he brought her to orgasm for the second time that night.

Mike arched his neck and groaned his own release, coming so hard tears stung his eyes. What the hell...? He held Sara tight as he collapsed with her in a tangle of limbs against the pillow-soft comforter, his heart hammering in his chest.

When his breathing slowed down enough so that he could speak, he moved to the side, scooped her into his arms, and kissed the top of her head. "You have no idea how much I love you."

Sara let out one last shuddering breath and pressed her lips to his chest, but no reciprocal declaration of love came his way. Disappointment sank like a rock to the bottom of his stomach.

"Well, I guess I'd better get dressed." She paused, then added, "I told Nicky I'd be back in about an hour."

Mike released her and sat up. "I'll walk you home." He climbed to his feet and headed into the bathroom to dispose of the used condom. Maybe she wasn't ready to say the words just yet, he could understand that. But there wasn't a doubt in Mike's mind that she still loved him. Eight years and she hadn't hooked up even once? That alone told him all he needed to know. Sara was his—Mike just needed to stay patient and keep his eye on the prize.

"You don't have to," she said when he returned. "It's only a few houses down." She shimmied back into her pants.

"I want to. It'll give me a chance to steal one last kiss."

"Sounds good to me." She finished dressing and slipped her feet back into her sandals.

Not bothering with socks or shoes, he wrapped his arm around her. "We'd better go. Before I change my mind and cuff you to the doorknob."

"Hmmm." Sara pursed her lips as if thinking it over.

Mike laughed as he led her out of the room. "Come along, my little sexual deviant. My self-control isn't very good when it comes to you, and the last thing I need is the Jamison posse banging down my door."

"He's a fucking cop? I knew it!"

Jason slammed the phone down and whipped his beer can across the room. He turned to glare at Carl who wisely kept his mouth shut.

His mind worked overtime as he stared blankly at the television. Should've taken them out when he had the chance, dammit. But it was one thing, putting a bullet into a civilian. Shooting a cop? Man, if he were to get caught... Jason knew better than anyone what happened to cop killers in prison. And if there's one thing he'd never done, it was take out one of his own. It just went against the grain.

But he wanted Garrett Jamison's head on a platter. The son of a bitch had set him up good, using his hot little sister to distract him so he'd been thinking with his dick instead of his brain.

It was only by sheer luck he'd seen her with that other cop. Having Carl in the truck with him had been an added bonus, because he'd have simply figured the bitch was fickle when he saw her with Andrews.

He still couldn't figure out what the connection was, though. He knew Sara and Andrews had dated in high school, but then Andrews had moved down to Chicago where, as far as anyone knew, he still resided. Maybe they were friends who'd kept touch over the years?

Not that it really mattered. However it happened, Garrett was obviously on to him, and Andrews was no doubt here to help him make the bust. But since this certainly wasn't Andrews' jurisdiction, he must be working for DCI, which meant Jason had more than likely been under investigation since before he'd arrived in Green Bay.

And he hadn't escaped drug charges all these years just to get taken down by Deputy Dawg and Scooby-Doo—in fucking *Wisconsin* of all places.

Son-of-a-motherfucking-bitch!

He reached up to massage his temples. Not only was he a hair's breadth away from ending up in the clink, it looked as if the only chance he had to remain a free man, and maybe even a police officer, was to murder two of his own.

"Hey, you gonna kill that rat bastard or not? 'Cause if so, I wanna be there. Maybe I'll even break *his* goddamn nose."

Jason glanced over at the weasel-faced little prick

sitting next to him. *What a waste of oxygen*, he thought, unable to hide his disgust. Then an idea struck. Maybe there was a way to take out both cops without getting a single speck of dirt on his own hands. And it's not as if Montgomery here was any great sacrifice.

Shit, who'd miss him?

Jason grinned as the perfect plan formed in his mind.

Nineteen

Sara had just put on a pot of coffee when Ethan ran into the kitchen and skidded to a halt in front of her.

"Mom! Mom! There's a big truck in old man—I mean, Dad's driveway! I bet it's my bunk beds! How much you wanna bet?"

She let out a huge yawn. "Actually, I'm pretty sure you're right. I think he paid extra to have it delivered today."

"Well, come on, hurry up so we can get over there. He's probably waiting for us."

Sara glanced down at him, and a reluctant smile settled on her lips. "Ethan, I know you're excited, but it's only eight o'clock in the morning, and I'm not going anywhere until I've had my coffee. Besides, we'd just be in the way. The delivery men will be making several trips in and out of the house, so we're going to wait until your father calls and invites us down."

"But, Mom—"

"Ethan, please, no whining before I've had my coffee." She pulled out a loaf of bread from the fridge. "Toast?"

Pouting, he nodded, then hopped up on his chair.

Sara put four slices in the toaster, set the butter dish, two knives and the strawberry jam on the table. Then she poured him a glass of orange juice and fixed him a bowl of cereal.

Nicky and Uncle Luke both entered the kitchen just as she was filling the carafe with hot coffee. She set mugs on the table for both of them.

"Good morning. Would either of you like some toast?"

Her brother grunted, but Uncle Luke said, "Sure, I'll take a couple slices."

Sara popped more bread into the toaster and carried the carafe over to the table. She didn't even realize she was humming until Nicky said, "Someone must have had a good night."

Before Sara could offer up a reply, Ethan said, "We did! We had cheeseburgers, fries, and ice cream. All three of us had hot fudge sundaes. And then we went to *Toy's R Us*. Dad bought me a Transformer. It's in my room, wanna see it?"

Nicky smiled. "Sure, sport. But why don't we wait until after breakfast."

"Okay." Ethan returned his attention to his cereal.

Sara set a plate in front of her uncle, then took a seat at the table. She sipped her coffee and nibbled on her own toast, trying not to make eye contact with either one of them. Reluctantly, she glanced at Nicky who was grinning from ear-to-ear. She frowned and gestured toward Ethan. Nicky cast her a 'we'll-talk-about-this-later' look and took another sip of his coffee.

Garrett entered the kitchen a few minutes later, looking very much like death warmed over. He poured himself a cup of coffee, carried it to the table and collapsed down on the chair as if his legs could barely hold him.

"Man, you look terrible," Nicky told him. "What time did you get in?"

"Around two. And I don't want any lectures."

Sara got up and dropped a few more pieces of bread in the toaster. "I'll make you some toast. It'll help to soak of some of the alcohol that's no doubt still sitting in your stomach."

He laid his head on the table and groaned.

"Do you want Mom to make you some peanut butter and jelly pancakes?" Ethan asked him. "They always make me feel better."

Garrett gagged, and everybody, with the exception of Ethan, burst out laughing.

"No thanks, big guy," he finally managed. "Just some toast will be fine. Dry, please," he added, in Sara's direction.

"So, today's the day Mike officially moves into old man Pankovich's house," Uncle Luke said, folding his toast and dunking it in his coffee. "Life sure is funny, you know?" He shook his head, as if he still couldn't believe all that had transpired in the past week.

Nicky ruffled Ethan's hair. "Yeah, but in a good way. Right, sport?"

His nephew grinned up at him. "You guys are talking about my dad, aren't you? 'Cause I sure am happy he came back to me. He bought me the best bunk beds in the whole store!"

Garrett managed to lift his head and joke, "At least the kid's got his priorities straight."

The phone rang. Ethan jumped off his chair and announced, "It's Dad! He wants to show me my new bunk beds!"

Sara answered on the second ring. "Hello?"

"Good morning, Sara."

"Uh...who is this?"

"It's Jason. I was looking forward to seeing you last night. I hope Ethan's feeling better."

She turned and shook her head to let them know it wasn't Mike. Garrett raised an eyebrow, and Sara mouthed Jason's name. Nicky, who'd been leaning back in his chair, shot forward so fast he splashed his coffee all over the floor. He set his cup down and met Garrett's questioning look with a scowl. *What in the world...?*

Forcing her attention back to the phone call, she said, "Jason, how are you? And thanks for asking, he's feeling much better today."

"She must be talking about you," Ethan said to Garrett.

"Maybe you and I can try it again sometime. Maybe next weekend?"

Sara closed her eyes for a brief moment in frustration. She hated to keep stringing the guy along, but she had no intention of having this particular conversation in front of her son. "Let me check my calendar, and I'll give you a call back. Mmm hmm. Uh-huh. Yes, he's right here. Hold on." She walked over, shrugged, and handed Garrett the phone.

Garrett took a quick gulp of his coffee before pressing the phone to his ear. "Hey, Jason, what's up?"

"Listen man, I was wondering if you'd meet me later for a beer, maybe shoot some darts?"

He barely held back a groan at the mention of alcohol. "I think I'm gonna have to take a pass. I've got myself one hell of a hangover this morning."

"So, you can drink soda. Come on, man. I'm still new in town, and I'm damn tired of sitting alone in my apartment."

Garrett rubbed his eyes, feeling a measure of guilt for lying to the guy yesterday. He blew out a hard breath and conceded. "All right. What the hell. What time did you want to hook up?"

"Seven?"

"Yeah, I should be able to shake this pounding headache by then. Where do you want me to meet you?"

"The corner of Military and Vine. There's a little tavern there with dart boards and even a couple of pool tables."

"I know the place. All right, man, I'll see you later."

Garrett hit the disconnect button and let out a frustrated sigh.

"What's going on?" Nicky asked as he mopped up his mess.

"I'm gonna meet up with Jason later to shoot some darts." He looked at Sara. "Don't worry. The only thing I plan to drink is soda."

Sara nodded. She glanced over at her son. "Hey, sweetie, why don't you go brush your teeth and get dressed. Your dad will probably be calling soon and—"

Ethan raced out of the kitchen, chattering about his bunk beds all the way down the hall. She laughed before returning her attention to Garrett.

"Maybe you could tell Jason I have a terrible disease...?"

He grinned. "Sorry, but you have to do your own breaking up. I got you out of last night's date, and that's as much as I'm willing to do."

"Come on, Garrett. You're the one who got her into this situation; you should be the one to end it."

All heads swung toward Nicky. Garrett eyed his brother with mild concern. Something was going on with him...maybe second thoughts about that job promotion in New York?

"I was only kidding," Sara said, frowning. "I don't expect him to clean up my messes. What's gotten into you?"

He looked first at Sara, then Garrett. "I, uh, I was just kidding, too. But maybe you should explain the situation to Mike. He could have a talk with Jason. I mean, what if the guy doesn't take kindly to getting dumped?"

"Son, are you feeling all right?" Uncle Luke asked, his forehead creased with concern.

Garrett arched a brow. "I think you'd better put in for an early vacation, bro. You need it."

"I had a hell of a dream last night," Nicky said, rubbing his eyes, "and I guess I let it get to me. Please, forget what I said."

"What was it about?" Sara asked, concerned for her workaholic brother.

"Nothing. Truth is, I can barely even remember it." He yawned, stretching his arms over his head. "Well, I think I'll go jump in the shower. Clear the cobwebs from my head."

Once he was gone, Sara swung a concerned look between Garrett and Uncle Luke. "It's not like him to act so strange. Do you think he's all right?"

Garrett pushed slowly to his feet before waving off her concerns. "He's fine. Probably just some work-related stress. Sitting in front of a monitor all day will do that to a person."

"I guess," she said. "But I want you to keep an eye on him anyway, okay?"

"I will, don't worry about it." He bent down and kissed her on the top of the head. "Now if you'll both excuse me, I think I'm going to lie back down for a while."

After breakfast, Sara called the bakery to check in, make sure the new coffee machine was running smoothly, and remind Amanda to inventory the bags, cups, napkins, and plastic clamshell containers for Monday's order. Normally, she stopped in for a couple hours every weekend to take care of it herself, but decided to indulge in a few days off—something she hadn't done in ages. Once assured all was well on the business front, she headed into the bathroom for a quick shower.

Ethan, eager to get a look at his new bunk beds, pounded on the bathroom door and shouted, "Come on, Mom! Hurry up!"

It took her ten minutes to dress and pull her damp hair back into a ponytail. She'd decided that instead of waiting for Mike to call, they would just take a stroll down there.

Sara's heart started racing the moment she laid eyes on him. He was helping the delivery men carry in the king-sized mattress, and when he glanced up and caught sight of her, a slow sensual smile curved his lips.

He came back out a few minutes later, and Ethan took off running. Mike laughed and caught him around the waist, hoisting him up to sit on his shoulder. When Sara approached, he wrapped his free arm around her. "Sleep well?" he asked, his voice a low rumble.

She smiled up at him. "Like a rock. You?"

"Even better than the night before."

"Hey, are my bunk beds ready yet?" Ethan asked, dragging them both back to the present.

"Sure are. Want to go see your new room?"

"Yeah! Come on, Mom, let's go!"

As soon as his feet hit the driveway, he took off like a

shot. They both chuckled as they followed their little bundle of excitement into the house. Ethan's footsteps echoed overhead as he ran from room to room. Mike smiled and took a hold of Sara's hand.

"Since it holds such wonderful memories for me, I chose our room from last night as the master bedroom," he said, as he led her upstairs.

She peered up at him through her lashes. "And that was a king-sized bed you bought for the master bedroom?"

"Oh, yeah. California king, to be exact."

"Nice and roomy," she purred, looking forward to helping him christen it.

When they reached the second floor, he pulled her into his arms and leaned down for a kiss, but before his lips even reached hers, Ethan came running up.

"I found it! Mom, you *gotta* come see my new room! It's huge!" He grabbed her arm and started tugging her along.

Sara pouted over her shoulder as Ethan led her away, and Mike laughed as he followed after them.

Ethan's room was indeed large; roughly twenty by twenty feet—nearly twice the size of the cubicle he called a room back home. Sara tried to ignore the pangs of jealousy eating at her craw, but couldn't. She knew she was being silly. She'd probably be spending a lot of time here herself, now that she and Mike were...

Were what? What exactly *were* they doing, besides having really great sex? Oh, he'd said he loved her. Always had, always will. But what if he got tired of her? It wasn't as if he'd asked her to marry him.

What the hell am I thinking? Marriage? Good lord, girl, you're getting way ahead of yourself! Great sex was one thing, but—

Mike came up behind her and set his hands on her shoulders. "Penny for your thoughts," he whispered against her ear.

Sara melted against him. All those negative thoughts were wiped from her mind as the heat of his body started her blood flowing to all the right places.

"I was just thinking there's plenty of room here for some of Ethan's toys. His room back home is busting at the seams, as I'm sure you've noticed."

"I did. And you're welcome to send down whatever you like."

"You may be sorry you said that when the dump truck arrives with his things," she teased.

Mike bent down and wrapped his arms around her. "And will some of your things be in this dump truck?"

She frowned. Was he making a declaration? Asking a pointed question?

With a shrug, she asked, deciding to feel him out, "As close as I live, what need would there be?"

She couldn't tell whether or not he was disappointed since he didn't bother to reply. She returned her attention to Ethan, who had climbed to the top bunk and looked as if he were about to start bouncing.

"No jumping on the top bunk," Mike told him. "You'll crack your head on the ceiling."

No doubt just to prove he could, the little stinker bent at the waist and proceeded to jump. He grinned down at them. "Nuh-uh, see? I haven't hit my head one time, I—ow!"

Sara fought to hide a smile while Mike gave his head an exasperated shake. "I warned you, kid. Now, climb down from there before you knock yourself out cold."

When Ethan's feet hit the ground, he asked, "Can I put

my Spiderman posters on the wall? And my Incredible Hulk poster, too?"

"You can decorate anyway you like," his father told him, smiling. "It's your room."

"Cool! Mom, can we go to the store? I wanna buy that Spiderman alarm clock."

"You mean right now?"

"Yeah, can we, huh?"

Not wanting to rain on his excitement, and since she *had* promised he could spend his allowance any way he liked, she said, "Sure, why not. Mike, is there anything I can pick up for you while we're there?"

"As a matter of fact, I forgot to pick up bath towels and washcloths. Would you mind?" He pulled out his wallet and handed her two one-hundred dollar bills.

"Not at all. What color is your bathroom?"

His brow creased. "Hell, I have no idea. Let's go take a look."

Sara followed him into the upstairs bathroom, and her eyes widened when they landed on the bathtub in the corner. "No way! A whirlpool tub? You lucky duck!"

Mike laughed. "Hey, you're welcome over any time to try it out. Mr. Pankovich had the bathroom remodeled a few years ago, but I don't think he got much use out of it."

She ran her hand over the shiny tile surrounding the tub. "It does look brand new." The fixtures were all white, with gleaming chrome faucets in the sink and bathtub. The ceramic tiled floor was also white, as were the walls. The only thing to break the monotony was a thin strip of blue ceramic tile around the base of the tub.

"Well, I hope blue's all right with you."

"Absolutely. And I really appreciate all your help, in case I haven't already said so."

Much to her delight, he pulled her into his arms for the kiss she'd been deprived of a few minutes ago.

He brought his mouth down on hers and Sara twined her arms around his neck. She couldn't believe how soft his lips were, and the rasp of his tongue on hers was enough to turn her legs to mush.

"Oh, man, *gross*."

Ethan. With a muffled shriek, Sara broke off the kiss and shoved Mike away.

The impossible man grinned as he ruffled their son's hair. "You won't think so in about ten years, pal."

The appalled look on his little face said otherwise, and Sara coughed to cover up a laugh. "Are you ready to go?"

"Yep. I know exactly what I want." Ethan grabbed her arm and pulled her out of the bathroom. "Hey, you ain't gonna kiss Jason, too, when you go on a date with him, are you?"

Sara stopped dead in her tracks at his innocently spoken question. She bit her bottom lip and glanced back at Mike. His smiled faded.

"You have a date with Jason?"

"No," she grinned, "but Garrett does. Jason called earlier, and they made plans to go shoot darts tonight."

Mike crossed his arms over his chest and leaned against the bathroom sink. "Which reminds me, you never did tell me why you and Garrett got into it yesterday."

She gestured toward Ethan with her eyes, making it clear she didn't want to talk about it in front of him.

Ironically, it was Ethan who replied, "Uncle Garrett heard me and Mom talking about how she slept with you instead of me, and he got real mad. He yelled and stuff, but then he apologized, so I'm not mad at him anymore."

Mike's lips twisted as if trying to hold back a grin.

"Well, that's good, you shouldn't be mad at your uncle. He was only trying to protect your mom."

"From you? You'd never hurt my mom, would you?"

"Of course not. But you can never be too careful when it comes to the people you love. I'm glad you and your mom have your Uncle Garrett to look after you."

"Hey, Mr. Andrews, we have a question," one of the delivery men called out from the bottom of the stairs.

"I'm on my way!" Mike chucked their son under the chin and gave her one last, quick kiss. "See you when you get back."

Ethan grabbed her arm again and started tugging. "Come on, Mom, before they sell all the Spiderman alarm clocks!"

She grinned. "If they do, I'm sure we can find you a nice Hello Kitty clock instead."

"All right, Jamison is meeting me here at seven," Jason muttered, anxious to get this shit over with. "Are you clear on what you have to do?"

He sat in his truck with Montgomery at the corner of Military and Vine, where in less than six hours, Garrett Jamison, and hopefully that Andrews prick, would both meet with an untimely end. They were going to be the victims of a cop-hating maniac, and if things worked out the way Jason expected them to, he'd come out of this smelling like a rose. He'd considered having Carl pump a bullet into *his* arm or shoulder, just to make it look good. But some cuts and scrapes should be just as effective, he decided.

Carl fidgeted in his seat and reached up to dig in his

ear. "Man, I don't know if I can do this. I never shot anyone before. Especially no cops."

Jason reached out and twisted Carl's bandaged nose.

"Owww! Goddamn it! What the fuck did you do that for?"

"I'm reminding you of exactly why you're doing this. Are you going to let that prick get away with busting your nose? I bet he's still laughing about it. Him and Jamison both."

Jason had to resist the urge to roll his eyes. God, how he hated dealing with this whiny bastard.

"Believe me, I wanna get even with that sonofabitch. But Jamison never did anything to me. Why do I have to take him out?"

Jason gave Carl a look designed to make the hair on the back of his neck stand up. "Because if you don't, they'll be fishing your dead bloated ass out of the bay. Now I repeat, are you clear on what you have to do?"

Carl glared at him. "I'm clear. You just make sure nothing goes wrong. 'Cause if I get busted for killing a cop, I ain't going down alone."

"Don't worry, my plan is foolproof." *Not that it matters, you pathetic piece of garbage. You'll be lying on a slab in the morgue, right next to Jamison and Andrews.*

Twenty

Sara spent most of the afternoon helping Mike make his new house feel like a home, while their son eagerly decorated his new room, hanging posters and filling shelves with toys and superhero paraphernalia he'd brought from home. She'd purchased plenty of bath towels, hand towels, and washcloths to get Mike started, and because she'd gotten them on clearance, there'd been enough money left over for a bathroom rug, tank set, as well as a new shower curtain.

Uncle Luke, Nicky, and even Garrett came down to see if they could help, and Mike wasted no time in putting them all to work.

He explained that, because he'd wanted to move in as soon as possible, he'd agreed to let Pankovich's family leave behind a lot of odds and ends. Especially downstairs in the basement, which was nothing more than a huge storage room at the moment. Otherwise, they'd have needed at least another week to get everything packed up and moved out.

She smiled as she listened to Mike tell the guys how he planned to remodel the basement into a sports bar, which was pretty much all they talked about for hours.

Sara was as happy as she'd been in a long time. All the

men in her life were getting along famously—even Garrett and Mike were exchanging complete sentences. Ethan was in his glory, following the men around, being passed from one shoulder to another. She couldn't remember the last time she'd heard him laugh so much.

And while the guys were working downstairs, she decided to keep busy upstairs—washing curtains and drapes, vacuuming, dusting the ceilings and walls, wiping the baseboards down with furniture polish. The house had been kept up surprisingly well, but once Mr. Pankovich's furniture had been moved out, it became obvious there was plenty of cleaning that needed to be done. Also, a few of the rooms could use new carpeting, particularly the living room.

By two o'clock, everyone was starving, so Mike sprung for lunch, and the first meal was officially eaten in Mike's new home.

By five o'clock, the men had the entire basement cleared out, and Sara had re-hung all the freshly laundered curtains and drapes, plus dry dusted every square inch of the house. Several times she'd found herself fantasizing about living here with Mike and Ethan, as a family. And she knew, deep down, the reason she'd worked her fingers to bone today was because in her heart of hearts, she'd already started to think of this place as *their home*. Hers, Mike's, and Ethan's.

Mike thanked and shook hands with the guys as they headed out, and Sara's chest swelled with…hope—hope for the future.

Once the door closed behind them, he pulled her into his arms and proceeded to kiss her breathless.

As if on cue, Ethan came sprinting around the corner. A look of complete disgust twisted his little face. "Oh, man, not again."

Sara managed to hold back a grin, but Mike said, "You'd better get used to it, little man. Because I plan on kissing your mother every chance I get." To drive his point home, he bent her over his arm and planted another one on her.

Their son rolled his eyes, but a reluctant smile broke out on his face. "Whatever," he said, before racing back up the stairs.

Sara gazed up at Mike in thoughtful contemplation as a sudden peacefulness settled over her.

"What?" He slipped his hands into the back pockets of her jeans and cupped her ass.

She cleared her throat, fighting to regain her train of thought as he gently massaged her backside. "I was just thinking."

"About...?" he prompted, brows raised expectantly.

"About what a great guy you are. And what a fantastic father you've turned out to be."

Mike blinked, as if he wasn't quite sure he'd heard her correctly. "I'm sorry, but did you just compliment me?"

"Yep. How's that for a total shocker?" For her as well.

It was Mike's turn to look thoughtful. "And what exactly brought you to this grand conclusion?"

She shrugged. "Just...everything. I mean, you're terrific with Ethan, and he obviously adores you."

"When I'm not kissing his mother."

She smiled. "Yeah, but don't worry, because that's when *I* adore you, so it kind of evens out."

He bent down and kissed her again, gently this time, then lifted his head to say, "Well, if I'm so wonderful, how come you won't move in with me?"

Her pulse sped up at his casually tossed out question.

As if he'd read her mind or something. "Umm, for starters, I haven't been asked."

"I kind of thought it was implied by, 'then how come you won't move in with me?'"

"That's not asking, it's assuming. And since we've barely been back in each other's lives a week, it's an awfully big assumption."

Disappointment tightened Sara's chest. He wanted her to move in with him; shack up for the sake of convenience. Not a word about marriage. Apparently, bearing his child wasn't a good enough reason to put a ring on it. And just what kind of message would that send to their son?

Mike stared down at her, very much tempted to argue the point. He surprised himself by saying, "You're right. It *was* a big assumption. It just kills me when I think about how different our lives would be if...well, if I wasn't a complete idiot. But haven't we missed out on enough? Dammit, Sara, I don't want to waste any more time."

She gazed up at him and admitted, "Neither do I. But on the other hand, the thought that you could just up and leave again one day, and I'd be left to explain to our son why, scares the hell out of me."

Mike pulled his hands from her back pockets and took a step back. Hands on hips, head hung low, he took a couple of deep breaths to rein in his temper. "I would never, *never* leave my son. Period. No matter what ends up happening between the two of us, I will forever be a part of Ethan's life. So I want this to be the last time you ever suggest I'd walk out on my kid. Understand?"

Sara stared at him without responding for what seemed like an eternity. Then silent tears began to fall. She angrily swiped them away as a barely audible sob escaped her.

The anguish shimmering in her eyes broke his heart.

With a muttered curse, Mike took her into his arms, infuriated with himself for losing his temper and causing her even a moment's more pain than he already had. He reminded himself that her wounds were still open and fresh, and her insecurities, as far as his intentions were concerned, were valid and quite justified.

"Sara, please don't cry," he said, running his hands over her back. "I'm sorry. I didn't mean to take my frustrations out on you. It's just...the guilt I feel sometimes is more than I can handle, and I don't know what the hell to do with it."

She took a shuddering breath against his chest. "I didn't mean to make you feel guilty. I just don't know what to think. My heart tells me you mean everything you say. But I've spent the last eight years believing I can't trust my heart where you're concerned."

He cuddled her against him, his chin resting on top of her head. "Sweetheart, as long as you believe I love you, and that I love our son, I'm content to wait until you're ready to trust in me again. Patience has never been my strong suit, but for you, I'll wait forever if I have to."

"Mom? Are you all right? Dad, why is she crying?"

Mike hadn't heard Ethan come in, and he suddenly felt like an even bigger jackass than he had a second ago.

Before he could answer, Sara sniffled, wiped her eyes against his T-shirt, and turned a watery smile on her son. "I'm fine, sweetie. You know how silly I get sometimes. Remember when that mayonnaise commercial made me cry?"

Ethan rolled his eyes. "Yeah, I remember." He looked up at his father and said in a conspiratorial manner, "Girls cry about stupid stuff sometimes. You'll get used to it."

Mike couldn't help but grin. "I'm sure I will."

"Hey, do you wanna come down to our house and play my new video game? I can already beat Uncle Nicky at it, and he gets really grumpy."

"I'd love to see that, believe me. But I'll have to take a rain check. There're a few things I need to take care of tonight."

Sara gazed up at him, her eyes brimming with curiosity. "Oh, well, we'd better get going then. Will we, uh, see you tomorrow?"

"Absolutely." Mike knew that look. She wanted to know exactly what it was he had to do tonight. Unfortunately, he had to keep her in the dark a while longer. "We can head over to that furniture store in Pulaski, try to find something for the living and dining rooms. Oh, and I also need to pick up a few TVs, so maybe we could hit a couple of other stores, too."

"Yeah, you gotta buy a big one for my room," Ethan said, casting a surreptitious glance at his mother.

"It's up to your father whether or not he wants you to have a television in your room."

Mike wasn't sure how to respond to that. Was this some sort of test? He eyed Sara suspiciously before replying, "I don't see why you shouldn't have one in your room. But nothing too big. Maybe a twenty-inch."

"Are you gonna buy a big-screen for your room?" Ethan asked, his eyes lighting up.

"Nah, not for my bedroom. But I might put one down in the rec room," he admitted, grinning.

"Cool! We can hook my Wii up to it. Just wait 'til you see how awesome it looks on a big screen."

"All right, kid, we'd better get going so your father can get to...whatever it is he needs to get to."

Mike picked his son up in his arms and squeezed the stuffing out of him. Ethan leaned back and asked, "When can I sleep in my new bunk beds?"

"Well, if it's all right with your mother, how about tomorrow night?" They both looked to Sara for an answer.

She reached up and tweaked Ethan's nose. "Tomorrow night will be fine."

"Mom, you could spend the night, too. You and dad slept together at the hotel, so he already knows you kick in your sleep."

Mike snickered and Sara coughed to cover up a laugh. "I think I'll let you two guys have the night to yourself. Maybe I'll send down some treats, though, just so you don't starve."

"How about fried chicken? That's my favorite. And chocolate chip cookies for dessert!"

"Sounds good to me." Mike gave Ethan one last squeeze before setting him on his feet. "Now, you'd better close your eyes, because I have every intention of giving your mother a kiss."

And as Ethan groaned, Mike took Sara into his arms and laid one on her.

With a heavy heart and an ache in his gut, he watched Sara and Ethan head home. Damn, it was hard watching them go. They were *his* family and should be living under *his* roof.

With a sigh, he shut the door and headed for the bathroom. Covered in dust and grime, he desperately needed a shower.

Twenty minutes later, he hopped in his truck and headed to his parents' house to see if the painters had finished the job. They'd assured him the entire house would be painted by today, and Mike prayed they were true to their word. The sooner he sold the place, the sooner he could move forward with his life. He had a son to take care of now, and hopefully soon, a wife.

The painters' van was parked in the driveway, but when he walked through the door, he realized they were packing up. He'd send the realtor an email tonight, and hopefully there'd be a 'For Sale' sign staked in the front yard by tomorrow afternoon.

He walked through the house to inspect their work, and was satisfied enough to write them a check right then. He walked through the house again once they left, but this time felt a chill run through him as a vision of his mother's beautiful face swam before him. God, how he missed her. He regretted so much the horrors she'd had to live through. But almost more, that she hadn't lived long enough to meet her first grandchild. She would have adored Ethan.

Which reminded him, the boxes full of his mother's things were still down in the basement. After loading them into the back of his truck, he glanced at the clock; six-thirty. Mike hopped in his truck and headed for Jason's apartment.

He knew the guy had plans to meet up with Garrett sometime tonight, but some nagging instinct told him to tail him, make sure Jamison had back-up. Just in case Thomas tried to lure him in to his nefarious dealings. Not that Mike thought for a second Garrett would ever get mixed up in drugs. But Sara's brother had a devil of a temper, and if he lost his cool, he could land himself in some serious trouble. Who knew what Jason could be capable of if backed into a corner?

Mike spotted Jason's truck as he drove past his building, and breathed a sigh of relief. Flipping a U-turn at the end of the block, he parked in the lot across the street and killed the engine. Hopefully, he wouldn't have long to wait.

Jason watched from an angle out his bedroom window as Andrews drove past, turned around at the corner, and pulled into the parking lot across the street to wait him out. Just as he'd suspected, Garrett had filled the guy in on their plans.

Jason smiled with smug satisfaction. In just a few minutes, he'd lead the poor bastard to the corner of Military and Vine, where Montgomery was already lying in wait. Once that idiot took care of Jamison and Andrews, Jason would put a bullet between *his* eyes, and there wouldn't be a single shred of evidence to tie him to the murders.

His story was perfect. He and Jamison had met up for a beer and a game of darts when some maniac opened fire on them in the parking lot. Before Jason could even pull his gun, Jamison and a third guy he'd never seen before were dead, and Jason had shot and killed the perp.

There'd probably be some suspicion, especially from Jamison's family, but they were the least of his worries at the moment. He'd simply play the model officer until he was sure DCI didn't have anything on him, then get the ball rolling again. Or he could put in for another transfer. Claim nightmares were plaguing him, or some shit like that.

Jason stuck his pistol into its holster inside his flannel shirt, grabbed his keys off the table, and headed down to the parking lot with single-minded focus.

Garrett stood bare-chested in front of the bathroom mirror, combing his damp hair, when someone knocked on the door. "Come in, it's open."

His nephew shuffled in and propped his elbows on the sink, his face in his hands. He watched him comb his hair and put on deodorant before asking, "Will you cancel your date with Jason and go out with me instead? We could go to that arcade again."

Garrett grinned down at him. "First of all, I don't have a 'date' with Jason, silly. I'm just going to meet him for a drink and to shoot some darts."

"Well, that's what Mom said. She told my dad that you and Jason are going on a date."

He laughed. "I'll have a talk with your mother later. A date is something you do with a girl, sport."

"Oh." Ethan shrugged. "Well, whatever you wanna call it, could you cancel and spend the night with me instead?"

Peering down, Garrett lifted a questioning brow. "Ethan, what's going on here?"

"Nothing. I just wanna hang out with you, that's all. And my dad had some stuff to take care of, so I got nothing else to do."

Ah. He tried not to take it to heart that boredom was the main reason his nephew had sought him out. "Bored out of your skull, huh?"

"Yeah, I guess. But also, you're the best at Combat Commando, and I really feel like playing it at the arcade. We can get some pizza there, too."

Garrett gazed down at him, hands on hips. "You know I'd much rather spend my time with you, sport. But it wouldn't be nice to cancel out on Jason. He's still pretty new in town and doesn't have that many friends.

"Well, he could come with us. They have dartboards at the arcade. And we could show him how to play Combat Commando. Skeeball, too."

He considered it. Hell, Jason seemed to like Ethan, and Garrett already told him he had no intention of drinking tonight. And let's face it, it didn't matter how old a man was, the minute he walked through the doors of an arcade, he was instantly ten-years-old again.

"You know, I think that's a great idea. We'll head over to where Jason and I are meeting, and I'll have him follow us to the arcade. I'm sure he'll get a kick out of it."

Mike followed Jason from a safe distance behind, half expecting to end up at that dump *T&R's Place*. Instead, he headed several miles south on Velp Avenue and turned into the parking lot of a little dive set a good quarter mile back from the road. Mike rode past, then doubled back around, giving the guy plenty of time to exit his truck and enter the bar. Mike pulled into a spot out of eyeshot of the door and killed the engine.

The lot was less than half full, and Mike did a quick sweep to make sure every vehicle was empty. Then he hunkered down and waited for Garrett to show up.

He didn't have long to wait. Less than five minutes later, Jamison pulled into the lot and parked right alongside Jason's truck.

Out of his peripheral vision, Mike saw the glint of something shiny as it reflected off the last of the fading sunlight. He swung his head just in time to see an arm unfold and a figure step out from behind the stand of trees that ran the length of the back lot. The figure held a gun, and it was pointed directly at Garrett's truck.

As if in slow motion, Mike watched Garrett step out of the truck only to reveal he hadn't come alone. There, sitting in the passenger seat, was Ethan.

Dear God! Mike swung his door open and jumped out of the truck. He aimed his pistol, fired, and heard the figure cry out right as a second shot rent the air. He swung back around and saw Garrett clutch his right side before diving back inside his truck. Mike raced across the parking lot as he dialed 9-1-1 on his cell phone.

He swung the driver's side door open and crouched down. Garrett lay sprawled across the seat, shielding Ethan, who was curled up on the floor.

"Ethan, stay down on the floor. Everything's going to be fine, I promise."

"D-Dad?" Ethan sounded on the verge of hysteria, and tears streamed down his face. Mike wished he could take him in his arms and comfort him, but it would have to wait.

"Yeah, it's me. You're being a very brave boy. I'm proud of you. Garrett, how bad is it?"

Jamison attempted to pull up his shirt. Mike assisted and breathed a huge sigh of relief. He'd only been grazed, although quite a chunk of flesh was missing. Mike knew it had to hurt like hell.

"Hey, it's only a scratch, you big baby," he said, trying to take Garrett's mind off the pain and reassure Ethan at the same time. "I've nicked myself worse than that shaving."

Garrett managed a strangled laugh. "Christ, it feels like someone set fire to me. Ethan? Sport, are you okay? Don't cry, please don't cry. I'm fine, I swear I am."

"But you're bleeding a lot. It's all over m-my shirt."

"Sorry about that, sport," Garrett said, his voice strained as he sucked in a ragged breath. "You're wearing your favorite Spiderman shirt, too. Don't worry, I'll buy you a new one."

"I don't care about my dumb old shirt."

Mike heard the sirens and muttered, "About damn time." Under normal circumstances, he would have raced after the shooter immediately after calling 9-1-1. But there wasn't a chance in hell he'd leave his son's side until backup arrived.

Ethan attempted to sit up, but Mike put a hand on his head and insisted, "Stay down, son. Just to be safe. I promise you, your uncle's going to be fine. He'll probably be crabby for a few days, but then you're already used to that, aren't you?"

He nodded, the solemn look on his face breaking Mike's heart.

The wail of sirens grew so loud that Ethan clapped his hands over his ears. An ambulance pulled into the parking lot, as well as two squad cars, all of them surrounding Garrett's truck.

Mike climbed out, and as the paramedics took care of Garrett, he turned to the nearest officer and flashed his badge. "Detective Mike Andrews with the Oak Lawn Police Department, south of Chicago. I'm going after the shooter. I'm sure I hit him, and if I did more than clip him, he may be lying right behind those trees."

"I'm coming with you," the officer said, drawing his gun.

They approached the area from different sides and Mike cursed when he realized the bastard had managed to escape. But as they searched a little further into the woods, he spotted him, lying face down over a huge rock. His gun had slipped from his hand and was dangling from his trigger finger. Mike knelt down and carefully extracted the gun, then flipped him over.

Carl Montgomery.

Which meant Jason had set Garrett up for an ambush.

And Ethan had come within a hair's breadth of taking a bullet himself.

The thought brought on a wave of nausea so strong he nearly doubled over. He took a couple of slow, deep breaths until the urge passed.

Mike's shot had hit Carl in the chest, on the left side just below his collarbone. He felt for a pulse and blew out a relieved breath when he found one. They needed him alive so he could testify against Thomas in court. Mike had heard enough of their conversation last Saturday night to know Carl was key in nailing Thomas to the wall. But the question remained, why the hell had they gone after Sara's brother?

The officer with him called for one of the paramedics to come take care of Montgomery. Mike rose to his feet and made his way back to Garrett's truck. Ethan had calmed down considerably, and was now curled up against his uncle's good side.

"Are you all right?" Mike asked his son as he approached.

Ethan looked up in surprise, as if in all the excitement he'd forgotten Mike was there. He rubbed his eyes and said, "Yeah, I'm okay. But Uncle Garrett's gotta go to the hospital. Mom's gonna be really mad when she finds out he got shot."

Mike took his son in his arms and held him tight, squeezing his eyes shut for a brief moment to collect himself. He'd give Sara a call as soon as Garrett was safely inside the ambulance and on his way to the hospital.

He looked up, and his jaw clenched as he caught sight of Thomas. The bastard had finally shown his face and was busy chatting with one of the officers. He looked up and made eye contact with Mike, then strode over and approached on Garrett's other side, laying a hand on his shoulder. "Man, you are one lucky guy. What in the world happened?"

You happened, you sonofabitch. It took every bit of self-control Mike possessed not to throw the prick up against the truck and beat the living shit out of him. "Someone took a shot at him from over in those trees. Luckily, I was able to wing the guy before he pulled the trigger, so his shot was off. But we've got him, and it looks like he's going to live."

"Christ, what a relief." Thomas held his gaze for a brief moment, the alarm in his eyes unmistakable.

Yeah, you'd better sweat, you motherfucker.

The bastard cleared his throat, scratched under his chin, and switched his attention back to Garrett. "I take it you're going to live as well?"

Jamison smiled through clenched teeth as the paramedic bandaged the wound. "Yeah, I'll live. Ain't nothing a bottle of brandy and some Vicodin won't cure."

"Vicodin, yes," the paramedic said. "But not mixed with alcohol. Got it?"

Garrett winked at Ethan. "Sure. I'll be a regular choirboy."

Mike dragged his gaze from Thomas and forced a smile for his son's sake. "If your sister has anything to say about it, you will be."

"Damn, I almost forgot about Sara. This is her biggest

fear come true."

"She'll be so happy you're alive, nothing else will matter," Jason assured him. Then he turned back to Mike and held out his hand. "By the way, I'm Officer Jason Thomas with the Green Bay Police Department."

Mike ignored Jason's outstretched hand. "Detective Mike Andrews. I'm an old friend of the family. I'm also Ethan's father."

Jason dropped his arm, seeming genuinely surprised by that. "Interesting." He glanced over at Garrett. "I could have sworn you told me Ethan's father was dead."

Garrett grimaced and shot Mike a 'thanks a lot, jackass' look. With a nod in Ethan's direction, he said, "Could we have this conversation later? Maybe after I've had a dozen or so pain killers?"

A second ambulance arrived for Carl. Without taking his gaze off Thomas, Mike pulled out his cell phone and punched in the Jamison's phone number.

Jason's pulse raced as he watched Carl get lifted into the ambulance. No doubt as soon as the fucking weasel was able to, he'd spill his guts, and Jason would find himself sitting in a jail cell awaiting trial.

He glanced over at Andrews, but quickly looked away when he realized the guy was staring at him. He hadn't gotten a good enough look at him last night to make the connection, but up close, there was no mistaking the resemblance between him and the kid.

And there was the link he'd been looking for.

Andrews was on the phone, most likely with Sara or one of their brothers. Jason returned his attention to

Garrett and said, "Since you seem to be in good hands, I think I'll head over to the station. There's no doubt going to be a lot of questions, and maybe I can get a heads up on who wanted you dead, and why."

"Thanks, Jason, I'd appreciate it."

Mike slid his cell phone shut as he strode back over to Ethan's side. He stuffed the phone in his front jeans pocket then picked Ethan up in his arms. "I'm going to have you ride with me to the hospital."

"But I wanna ride with Uncle Garrett."

He gave him a hug, and Ethan laid his head on his shoulder. "I know you do, son, but you can't. They won't allow it. We'll follow the ambulance to the hospital, and as soon as the doctor's done fixing up your uncle, you can go in to see him."

"Your father's right, sport," Garrett said, as he was made to lie down on the stretcher. He scowled at the paramedic before returning his attention to Ethan. "And I may need you to calm your mother down when she gets to the hospital. You know how upset she's going to be."

Ethan gave a solemn nod and leaned over to kiss his uncle's cheek.

"We'll be right behind you," Mike said. "Sara was in the shower when I called, so I spoke to Luke. They're all going to meet us at the hospital."

Garrett nodded, but said nothing. Mike knew the pain had to be damn near excruciating, but was pretty sure the thought of what could've happened to Ethan was the cause of the strained look in his eyes.

And then Garrett surprised him by saying in a voice

low enough so Ethan couldn't overhear, "Later, you're going to tell me exactly what the hell is going on, and why Jason just tried to have me killed."

Twenty-One

Mike and Ethan had been waiting about ten minutes by the time Sara, Nicky and Uncle Luke came through the automatic doors of the Emergency Room entrance. As soon as he saw his mother, Ethan wiggled to be free and took off running. Sara scooped him up into her arms and both of them burst into tears.

Mike walked up hesitantly, unsure of their reaction to his involvement in the situation. At the very least, Nicky would ream his ass for not letting him tell Garrett the truth about Jason. And he still hadn't told anyone that Carl was the shooter.

Much to his surprise, the first words out of Nicky's mouth were, "Thank God you were there. Uncle Luke said you winged the guy just before he got his shot off. Garrett might be dead right now if not for you." He threw his arms around him and thumped him on the back.

Mike let out a shaky breath. "I was afraid you might blame me for this after the talk we had the other night. If Garrett had known what Jason was about, he certainly wouldn't have brought Ethan along with him."

Nicky lowered his voice. "Jesus, are you saying Jason shot Garrett?"

"I promise I'll explain everything later," Mike

whispered. "Here comes your sister."

With Ethan still held tightly in her arms, Sara walked up and met Mike's gaze. Her eyes were red, wet with tears, and he wanted nothing more than to take her into his arms and never let her go.

"Are you all right?" he asked, searching her face for the truth.

"I should be asking you that question. Do you have any idea how grateful I am that you were there? You saved Garrett's life, and possibly even..."

Mike stepped forward, took Ethan from her, and wrapped his arms around both of them.

Luke came up from behind Sara and said, "I don't know what you were doing there, son, and frankly I don't care. I'm just damn grateful you were." He walked off toward the coffee machine with Nicky following behind him.

Sara looked up at Mike, frowning. "What exactly *were* you doing there? Were you following Garrett and Ethan?"

"Sweetheart, I promise I'll explain everything later." He gestured with his eyes toward Ethan, and Sara nodded her understanding.

After a moment, she whispered, "I'm just so grateful you're all right. I don't know what I would have done if something had happened..." Once again, she couldn't finish her sentence, and Mike tightened his arms around them.

Nicky and Luke returned a minute later with steaming paper cups. "Hey, we can go see him now," his friend announced, grinning. "I could hear him cursing from out in the hallway."

They all filed into the vinyl-curtained cubicle and surrounded the small hospital bed, which seemed even tinier with Garrett's massive frame draped over it. The first thing he did was open his arms to Sara.

"You are quitting the force as soon as we get home," she said against his shoulder. Then she looked over at Mike and added, "You, too."

"But I wasn't even shot in the line of duty," Garrett pointed out.

"And I wasn't shot at all," Mike chimed in.

"I don't care. I don't think my heart can take this again."

"You doing all right, sport?" Garrett asked, examining his nephew's tear-stained face.

Ethan nodded, and showing the first sign of life since the shooting, said, "But ice cream would make me feel even better."

Mike laughed, and everyone followed suit as the gut-wrenching terror of what happened—and what could have happened—slowly drained away.

Sara kissed Ethan on top of his head and smiled as she wiped away tears. "I have a half-gallon of both vanilla and chocolate in the freezer at home."

The ER doctor finally came in and released Garrett, giving him prescriptions for both antibiotics and pain killers, and Sara explicit instructions for cleaning and bandaging the wound. Then he ordered Garrett to take it easy for at least a week, get plenty of rest, and absolutely no alcohol while taking the pain killers. Garrett rolled his eyes, Sara scolded, and Garrett promised to be a good boy.

Out in the parking lot, Mike watched Danny's truck pull into the spot next to Nicky's Jeep.

"Sorry I'm late. I blew a damn tire, if you can believe it." He came up on Garrett's right side. "Good thing you've got thick skin, huh?"

Garrett arched a brow. "Your concern is touching. I may weep."

Danny laughed. "Don't be a grouch. You know I was worried as hell."

"I know."

Mike buckled an exhausted Ethan into his truck, while Sara watched Garrett step gingerly into Nicky's Jeep, her beautiful face creased with worry.

"He's going to be fine, honey," he assured her. "Come on, let's get you guys home."

She nodded and attempted a smile, though Mike wasn't fooled. As she climbed in next to her son and kissed him gently on the brow, a surge of anger took Mike by surprise, nearly overpowering him. He tamped it down for Sara's sake. She was already anxious enough over Garrett's injury. The last thing he wanted to do was add to her stress.

But one way or another, Thomas was going to pay for this. Mike would make sure of it.

They'd ordered a late supper as soon as they got home, so while they waited for the food to arrive, and while everyone else was occupied elsewhere, Mike decided to fill Garrett in on what he knew about Jason.

"Thomas is a suspected drug trafficker, and I've been tailing him since last Saturday night, trying to get something DCI can use against him in court. I've overheard enough to know he was days away from a huge buy, but after tonight, it's a pretty safe bet that deal's been postponed for a while."

Garrett tiredly rubbed his eyes with the heels of his

hands while muttered curses poured from his mouth. "This is fucking crazy...And I let that dirty SOB take my sister out on a date!"

"Yeah, I wasn't too happy about that either."

"Why the hell didn't you tell me? Shit, Mike, it could've just as easily been Ethan who got shot tonight."

Mike clenched his jaw. "I don't need you to remind me of that fact. That hair trigger temper of yours is exactly the reason I didn't tell you. And it's not like I had advance warning. The first time I tailed him, he led me straight to your front door. If it's any consolation, they weren't out of my sight for more than a few minutes that night."

"So, why put a hit on me? I'm not mixed up in that shit."

Mike glanced down at Ethan who was cradled in his lap sound asleep. "That happens to be the million-dollar question. And I don't have an answer for you, at least not yet. But there is something else you need to know."

"Jesus, what now?"

"Carl Montgomery's the one who shot you. And the reason I was at that dive last weekend where I got Carl's taped confession, is because I'd followed Thomas there. He was meeting up with Montgomery. The two of them obviously had business dealings together. They also met there Monday night." Mike stroked a gentle hand over his sleeping son's brow. "The most we can do now is pray Montgomery makes it through surgery, and offer him a deal to testify against Thomas in court."

Garrett blew out a hard breath. He pushed himself to his feet and slowly made his way to the refrigerator. After a quick glance to see if the coast was clear, he pulled down a bottle that looked suspiciously like Christian Brothers brandy, twisted off the cap, and tipped it to his lips.

"Garrett Allen Jamison! I don't believe you!"

At the sound of his sister's voice, Garrett sputtered and must have choked the fiery liquid down the wrong pipe as he started coughing his lungs up. He grimaced and clutched his side as he grabbed onto the counter for balance.

"Jesus H…Christ, Sara! You…scared the…hell out of me!"

Laughing, Mike hid his face against Ethan's head.

Hands on hips, Sara scolded, "You have no one to blame but yourself. The doctor specifically told you not to mix alcohol with those pain killers, and we're not home twenty minutes before you're disregarding his instructions."

Danny, Nicky and Uncle Luke all piled into the kitchen, and Mike continued to chuckle as Sara filled them in, much to Garrett's chagrin. Nicky shook his head as he helped his brother back to his seat.

The doorbell chimed. Mike had already pressed money into Luke's hand for the pizza, so while he and Danny answered the door, Mike kept a watchful eye on Sara as she pulled plates down from the cabinet and set them on the counter. She leaned against the kitchen sink, and though her back was to him, he knew she was attempting to pull herself together.

Mike wanted nothing more than to take her in his arms and hold her until her worries subsided. But until that bastard Thomas was safely behind bars, none of them could rest easy.

Sara walked up behind Mike, placed a hand on his shoulder, and leaned in to smooth her other hand across her son's brow. The poor little thing was out like a light, having not so much as flinched while the adults were busy shouting over his head.

Mike patted her hand, then pushed his chair back and rose to his feet with Ethan cradled in his arms. "I guess I'd better put him to bed before he wakes up," he said in a low tone.

She nodded, thanking God yet again that both of them were safe and sound. Her head ached from running all the 'what if' scenarios through her mind. She kept reminding herself to be grateful, that Mike and Ethan were both unharmed, and though Garrett had been shot, it was only a flesh wound—thanks to Mike. She had so much to be thankful for. It was just hard not to wallow in the 'what ifs.'

"I'll come with you."

Sara led the way to Ethan's room and opened the door. She watched as Mike laid their son on the bed, tugged off his shoes, and covered him with the Spiderman comforter she'd had to search four stores for. They both pressed a kiss to his cheek, then Mike took her in his arms and held her tight.

After a moment, she leaned back to gaze up at him, and Mike bent his head to kiss her, softly at first, and then more demanding as her lips parted. She twined her arms around his neck, and he practically crushed her against his chest. Sara moaned softly, and he broke off the kiss.

"We'd better stop while we still can." He kissed her forehead and added, "Besides, I'm starving."

"So am I," she whispered, moving against his semi-erection. "Just not for food."

"Damn, you really know how to torture a man."

She gazed up at him, needing him desperately, but knowing now wasn't the time. "Sorry, but I can't seem to get enough of you."

"You're insatiable," he said, dipping his head to capture her lips again.

"Hey, guys, it's going fast!" Danny hollered.

"Shhhh! They're putting Ethan to bed, you moron," was Garrett's just as loud response.

Sara laughed softly, never more grateful to hear her brothers' booming voices.

"Come on, we don't want to get caught in a compromising position in our son's bedroom." Mike took her hand and pulled her along behind him.

When they entered the kitchen, hand in hand, Sara's face grew warm as all eyes were on them. And everyone was smiling. Even Garrett, who said, "Come on, lovebirds, time to eat."

A short time later, Sara grew concerned as Garrett's eyes grew heavy and he swayed lethargically in his chair. She asked Nicky and Danny to help him to his room.

"You guys are making too much of this," Garrett said as he draped an arm over each brother's shoulders, his voice groggy from the medication. "It's just a flesh wound."

"You've always been the one to take care of us," Sara reminded him as they slowly made their way down to his room. "Now it's your turn. Besides, that bullet made a pretty big crease in your side, and you're probably going to feel a lot worse tomorrow than you do tonight."

They eased him down onto his bed, and trying to ease the tension, she teased, "Would you like me to read you a bedtime story after we tuck you in?"

Garrett made a sound she assumed was a laugh. "Yeah, as a matter of fact, there's a Penthouse in my bottom drawer—"

Sara pinched his forearm causing him to yelp. "Goodnight, Garrett. There's water on your nightstand, and if you need anything else, just holler, all right?"

"I'll be fine. Go take care of Mike. He's more shook up about what happened tonight than he's letting on."

"I was thinking the same thing," Nicky said. "It seemed like he didn't want to let Ethan go."

Sara kissed Garrett on the cheek and then adjusted the blanket for him. "I really hate what happened tonight. But if there's one positive thing that came out of it, you and Mike seem to have developed some sort of appreciation for each other."

"He more than likely saved my life, and possibly even Ethan's. I can't think of anything I appreciate more. Now please, get the hell out of here so I can get some sleep." He smiled, although it was pained, and gave her a gentle shove toward the door.

While Nicky and Danny joined Uncle Luke in the kitchen, Sara glanced into the darkened living room where Mike stood alone, gazing at a picture of Ethan hanging on the wall.

She came up behind him and snuggled against his side. "He's fine, Mike. Thanks to you, he's safe and sound, snoring away in his bed."

Mike's smile didn't quite reach his eyes. "But what if I hadn't been there? I could have lost him after only a week...I want to lock him up in his room and never let him out."

"But you *were* there. You saved my brother's life, and you saved our son."

He sighed. "Listen, I need to get going. I have a couple of things to take care of before I can head home. But I'll call you first thing in the morning to check on Ethan and Garrett." He turned and pulled her into his arms.

Frustration gnawed at her. "Mike, you promised to tell me why you were following Garrett and Ethan tonight," she reminded him.

"Tomorrow, sweetheart. I'll explain everything tomorrow."

God, how she hated being treated like fine china, as if he didn't think she could handle whatever it was he was so reluctant to tell her. "I'm not some delicate flower, Mike. I've been through a lot, and I promise nothing you can say would make me crumble like some…weak little girl."

His gaze softened as he cupped her face. "Sweetheart, you are without a doubt the strongest woman I know. That's not what this is about. It's a time issue. I have to go. But I swear, I'll explain everything to you tomorrow. You have my word."

She relented, somewhat mollified. "Fine. But Mike, I won't be put off any longer than that," she warned.

He gave her one last kiss. "Tomorrow, I promise."

Mike drove down Thomas' block for the second time that night, but came in from the opposite side and parked three buildings down. The Big Bird mobile sat in its usual spot, and his apartment was lit up, so Mike dug his binoculars out of his glove compartment and trained them up at the window.

From this angle, he couldn't see much at first. Until Thomas stalked past with a phone glued to his ear, shouting at whatever poor soul was on the other end of the line.

Mike set the binoculars down and climbed out of his truck. He'd take a quick walk past Thomas' truck and peek inside. It was a long shot, but he desperately needed to find something, anything, that could shed light on the reason he had targeted Garrett.

He approached the truck, clicked on his penlight and peered inside. He ran the thin beam of light around the interior of the truck, disappointed to find nothing more than the usual—papers and receipts strewn across the floor, a couple of candy bar wrappers, a pile of loose change in the unused ashtray, some fast food wrappers and paper cups...He stopped the light on a cup sitting in the cup holder on the passenger's side of the truck. Now, why the hell did that cup make his hackles rise? He ran the beam of light across the name stamped across the front. *Perelli's.*

Bingo.

Thomas must have seen him there with Sara and Ethan. Mike considered that for a moment. So what if he'd seen them together? That was reason enough to be pissed off, sure. But cold-blooded murder? No way. There had to be something else.

Could Carl have been with Thomas at *Perelli's* and identified Mike as the guy who'd busted his nose? A bandaged nose is surely something a person would ask about. And as a cop, if Thomas had any instincts at all, he would've questioned Carl about the connection between himself, Sara and Mike. Then he would've run Mike's plates and discovered he's a cop. Mike himself would have done no less.

He clicked off the penlight and headed back to his

truck. Thomas must have suspected Garrett was the one on to him. From there, it wouldn't have been much of a stretch to assume Mike had been aiding him in the investigation. Hell, he may even suspect Sara had been in on it. Christ, the thought of that bastard going after her was enough to freeze the blood in Mike's veins. Thomas had no way of knowing Garrett would never use his beloved sister in such a way.

So, if Thomas knew Mike was a cop, he also must have realized he'd been tailing him all week. The fact that he'd confronted Carl only minutes after his meeting with Thomas would've been a pretty obvious clue.

Christ, Mike thought as a chill ran through him, *what if Thomas had counted on me following him to that dive tonight?* Maybe Garrett hadn't been the only target after all. And Ethan could've very well been caught in the crossfire.

Mike blew out a frustrated breath as he climbed back into his truck. He glanced up just in time to watch the light go out in Thomas' apartment, and he seriously doubted the man was heading off to bed. The scumbag's only possible chance of weaseling out of an attempted murder charge would be to silence Carl. Tonight.

Mike put the truck in gear and headed for the hospital.

Sara padded into the kitchen and put a cup of water into the microwave for tea. After tossing and turning for more than an hour, she knew sleep would be impossible. She glanced up at the clock—nearly one a.m.

Sitting at the kitchen table with the steaming mug cupped between her hands, she couldn't keep her thoughts from going back to the exact moment Uncle Luke told her Garrett had been shot. And since she'd been in complete shock, it hadn't at first registered that Garrett had taken Ethan along with him. When it did, the sheer horror that had numbed her body was something she hoped to God she'd never have to feel again. But her uncle had quickly explained that Ethan was fine, and her brother's injury wasn't life-threatening.

As she sipped her tea, Sara wondered where Mike was at that moment. Out following a lead? At the hospital questioning the man who'd shot Garrett? Or was he at home, alone in that great big bed?

She ached for the comfort of his arms around her. She was also anxious to talk to him, make sure he was all right. The look on his face earlier tonight as he'd gazed at Ethan's picture had been a cross between helplessness and fury, although he'd done his best to mask the anger, probably for her benefit.

She heard the clip of footsteps on the front porch seconds before a soft rap sounded on the door. For a split second, she feared it might be the shooter come to finish Garrett off. Then her common sense returned—the shooter was lying in a hospital bed with a bullet hole in his chest. She got up to answer the door.

After a peek through the window, she breathed a deep sigh of relief. *Mike.* She unlocked the door and let him inside.

"Sorry if I startled you. I knew I wouldn't be able to sleep until I'd checked on you and Ethan again."

He opened his arms and Sara flew into them, snuggling against his chest.

"I'm glad you came back," she admitted.

"I couldn't stay away. We've been apart for so long, I

hate to spend even another minute without you." He kissed the top of her head.

She looked up and met his gaze. "Then stay with me tonight. Danny's sleeping over at his girlfriend's, a nuclear bomb wouldn't wake Garrett up, and Uncle Luke, Nicky and Ethan all sleep like the dead."

Mike bent his head and slanted his lips across hers. When she groaned, he lifted his head and said, "You have no idea how tempting that is. But out of respect to your brothers and uncle, I have to say no."

She failed to hide a slight pout.

Mike chuckled and reached up to run the pad of his thumb over her bottom lip. "If you'd just agree to marry me, we wouldn't even be having this conversation. We'd be in our own bed and—"

Her heart stopped. "What did you say?"

"I said, we'd already be in our own bed—"

"No, before that."

Mike had to think for a moment, and Sara grew slightly irritated. "How can you forget something you *just* said?"

"Sweetheart, I said the same thing I said to you yesterday. If you would just agree to marry me—"

"No, you asked me to move in with you," she clarified, "not *marry* you. I think I would've remembered something that important."

He stared down at her as if she'd just spoken gibberish. "But you knew what I meant. Of course I want to marry you. I love you."

Giddy with happiness, Sara thought her heart would burst from the joy his words caused. A tear slipped from the corner of her eye.

"Sara...? Honey, I'm sorry, I didn't mean to make you cry."

She shook her head and reached up to swipe at her eyes. "I'm crying because I'm happy. Don't you remember? Ethan explained it to you."

A small grin lifted the corners of his mouth. "Actually, he said girls cry over stupid things, but I don't think being happy falls into that category."

"Are you sure?"

Mike curled his hand around the back of her neck and caressed the flesh beneath her ear. "Am I sure I want to marry you? Sweetheart, I've never been more sure about anything."

He leaned down for another kiss, and Sara wrapped her arms around his neck, kissing him back with such fervor Mike started inching up her nightgown right there in the middle of the living room. He backed her up until her calves hit the couch, and the two of them tumbled backwards, laughing.

"Ahem."

Sara swung around and nearly died of mortification as Uncle Luke stepped into the room.

"I'm really sorry to, uh, interrupt, but I thought I heard Ethan cry out in his sleep. I saw the light on in the kitchen and...well, I had no idea Mike was here."

Face burning, she climbed off the couch with as much dignity as possible. "Thanks, Uncle Luke. I can't believe I didn't hear him." She hurried off to check on her son, feeling like the worst mother in the world.

Sara opened Ethan's bedroom door and stepped inside. "Sweetie, are you awake?"

As her eyes adjusted to the darkness, she realized with a start that his bed was empty. She flipped on the lamp.

"Ethan, this isn't funny. Not after the night we've had." Still no answer. She got down on her knees and checked under the bed. It'd been quite a while since he'd hid from her like that, but she had to look.

Empty.

Her pulse picked up speed.

Then she heard the toilet flush and her breath whooshed out in great relief.

Good lord, she'd almost worried herself into a full-blown panic. The door creaked and she looked up to see Nicky enter the room.

"I saw the light on," he said. "Figured I'd come check on him."

She smiled her appreciation. "Uncle Luke heard him cry out. I think he may have been having a nightmare, so as soon as he returns from the bathroom, I'll lay with him 'til he falls back asleep."

Nicky reached up and scratched the back of his head. "Ethan's not in the bathroom. I just came from there."

Twenty-Two

"Christ, I feel like a teenager right now," Mike admitted, hands on hips. "Please tell me my face isn't as red as it feels."

"Maybe just a little," Luke said, grinning. "But don't worry, boy. I won't be chasing you out of the house with a shotgun, if that's what you're worried about."

"Well, that's a relief, I—"

"Mike! *Mike!*"

At the sound of Sara's hysterical shrieking, a chill raced up his spine.

"Oh my God, this can't be happening! Mike! Oh, God, please!"

He took off like a shot, passing Nicky on the way, who blew past him without a word. Mike rushed into Ethan's room, his gaze ping-ponging around as he looked for Sara. "What the hell—?"

"He's gone! Mike, I looked everywhere, but he's not here! *He's not here!*" She was frantically combing the room on her hands and knees.

He grabbed her by the upper arms and hauled her to her feet. "Honey, calm down. Take a deep breath."

Garrett burst into the room clutching his side, his face pinched and drawn with pain. "What the hell's going on in here?" he demanded, looking wildly around. "Where's Ethan? Sara, where the hell is Ethan?"

"He's not in the kitchen," Nicky announced as he came up behind Garrett.

Sara sobbed uncontrollably in Mike's arms. He sat her on the end of the bed, then turned to the others. "Garrett, stay here with Sara. Nicky, Luke, you're going to search this house from top to bottom. Probably Ethan just went downstairs to play video games and fell asleep on the couch. I'm going to run down to my place, just to be thorough, make sure he didn't wander down there in hopes of sleeping in his bunk beds."

Garrett gave a curt nod. He sat with a grimace and wrapped his good arm around Sara as Mike, Nicky, and Luke all raced from the room.

By the time Mike returned, Nicky and Uncle Luke were waiting for him in the hallway, the misery in their eyes saying it all. He gave his head a grim shake to let them know he'd come up empty, too, before leading the way back into Ethan's room. Sara jumped up from the bed and ran to him, her eyes imploring him to tell her Ethan was safe and sound downstairs, just as he'd said. Only he couldn't, and the realization of that nearly destroyed him.

He grasped her shoulders to steady her, then a thought struck and he said to Nicky, "Quick, check the window. There's no wind, and the drapes are closed, so I didn't think of it 'til just now."

Garrett cursed as Nicky rushed over and pulled the drapes back, and just as Mike feared, the window stood wide open, the screen missing. He looked at Garrett and said the scariest words any parent ever wants to hear. "We need to issue an AMBER Alert."

Sara's knees gave out, and she would have fallen to the

floor if he hadn't been holding her up. "No, please, not my baby! Oh my God, this can't be happening!" She starting sobbing again, and Mike bent down and swung her up into his arms. His own eyes were burning, but he had to stay calm. For Ethan's sake as well as Sara's.

He carried her into her own room and sat on the edge of the bed with her cradled in his arms. "Sweetheart, I have to go. The sooner we get out there, the sooner we'll find him. But I can't be worrying about you, too, so I want you to promise me you'll stay put until you hear from me. Do you promise?"

Sara took a deep, shuddering breath, then reached up to swipe the tears from her eyes. "No. I'm going with you. And you obviously know who took him, so tell me right now, who has my son?"

"Sara—"

"Dammit, Mike, I deserve to know!"

He blew out a heavy breath. "Jason Thomas. And he's dangerous, Sara. I want you to stay here where I know you'll be—"

"Jason?" Her face screwed up in surprise. "But why?"

"I don't have time to explain right now. Please, just stay here and I'll call—"

"I'm not going to just curl up into a ball and do nothing! My son needs me. I'm going with you." She jumped up from the bed, yanked on a pair of jeans, a T-shirt, and slipped into a pair of tennis shoes in record time. "Let's go," she said as she swept past him.

While he understood her need to come along, to help find and rescue their son, all Mike could think about was protecting her from what Thomas might do—or may have already done—to their little boy. The scenarios running through his head were enough to make him want to vomit.

He'd only just gotten to know the little guy... God couldn't be so cruel, could he? But then, he'd taken his mother from him, leaving Mike alone with that monster to fend for himself...

Forcing himself to focus, Mike shook all negative thoughts from his head and raced after Sara.

Nicky, Luke, and Garrett all waited for them by the front door, dressed and ready to go.

With his hand resting on the pistol he'd stuck in the waistband of his jeans, his face a mask of pure fury, Garrett looked ready to commit murder. "That bastard better pray to God I don't find him first."

Sara gasped, and Mike wrapped his arm around her. "I don't give a damn what you do with him, *after* Ethan's safe and sound, got me?"

"Don't worry. I'd never do anything to endanger Ethan's life. Now let's go."

"Son, I'm driving and I don't want any arguments," Luke said as he grabbed Garrett's keys out of his hand.

"Shouldn't someone stay here?" Nicky asked. "Just in case he calls?"

"I'll give Danny a call as soon as we're on our way," Garrett said. "Explain what's going on and tell him we need him at the house. I'll also buzz the station; see who's on call tonight."

Mike nodded. "Sounds good. Okay, Sara and I'll head to Thomas's apartment first. I doubt he's that stupid, but it has to be checked out. Nicky, run past *T&R's Place*, but be careful since you're not armed, and we already know the son of a bitch isn't above murder. If you spot his truck, call us on our cells."

They quickly swapped cell phone numbers, jumped into their respective vehicles, and sped off in different directions.

Mike raced over to Jason's apartment, but just as he'd figured, the guy's truck was nowhere to be found.

He handed Sara his cell phone. "I'll be right back. Holler out the window if one of them calls."

He ran up the walkway and pressed every doorbell until someone buzzed him in. He yanked the door open and raced up the stairs. The apartment door was locked, so he kicked it open, rushed inside and did a quick sweep of the place. Nothing seemed disturbed. No drawers flung open in haste, plenty of clothes hanging in the closet, toothbrush lying beside the bathroom sink. So, if he wasn't planning to skip town, why take Ethan? What was the point...what did he hope to accomplish? A ransom demand didn't make sense; the Jamisons weren't wealthy people. And Ethan was an innocent little boy, what reason could Thomas have to kidnap him?

What the hell am I missing?

Was it possible he hadn't been there to kidnap Ethan, but to finish the job Montgomery started? Maybe he entered the wrong room by mistake, and Ethan woke up, started to scream—Luke mentioned he'd heard him cry out—so Thomas panicked and took him?

Mike's heart hammered in his chest as fear of the unknown gripped him. It seemed a likely scenario, but where did that leave his son?

Fighting to keep his fear in check, Mike flew down the stairs and raced back to his truck. "Nothing's missing as far as I can tell," he said in response to Sara's questioning gaze. He hated the confused, desolate look in her eyes and silently swore that bastard would pay dearly for causing her such torment.

As he pulled out onto the street, he switched on the

radio and scanned through the stations in search of the AMBER Alert message. His phone rang and he thought, *please God, let it be good news,* as Sara answered the call.

"He's been spotted!" she cried, the first sign of life shining in her eyes since they'd left the house. "Garrett says Jason's truck is headed south on highway forty-one, approximately one mile north of the one-seventy-two exit. He was seen taking the on-ramp off twenty-nine, and there's two squads on his tail. Garrett and Uncle Luke are maybe two miles behind them."

Mike let out a deep, shuddering breath. "Thank God." He took the phone and told Garrett, "We just left his place and nothing seems to be missing." He quickly explained his theory, which had Sara staring at him in stunned silence, and Garret cursing a blue streak. "Listen, we're heading north on Velp, so I'll hop on forty-one from here. Nicky, where are you?" he asked, never more grateful for three-way calling than now.

"I'm a couple cars behind him. I'd just hopped on forty-one when Garrett called. And I can see Ethan. The bastard didn't even buckle him in. His head keeps popping up to look out the back window...as if he's watching for us."

Mike had to swallow hard. He cast a quick glance at Sara, grateful she hadn't heard what Nicky said.

"And we will. Let's keep the phone connection going for now. I'm putting mine on speaker." He clicked the button and slid his phone into its mount on his dash. "Garrett, I'm assuming you have a radio in your truck?"

"Of course. I just got done talking to dispatch before I called. The two unmarked squads tailing Jason are good guys, and they know Ethan. They won't let him out of their sight or turn their cherries on until they have to.

Jason's driving the speed limit and staying in the left lane, so he probably plans on staying on the highway for a while."

Mike flew up the ramp onto forty-one and attempted to make up some ground. He and Sara were the farthest away, and he wished like hell he could put the pedal to the metal. But he couldn't afford to do anything that might alert Thomas to the fact he'd been spotted. Especially since the bastard hadn't even bothered to buckle Ethan in.

The thought of Ethan's small frame being bounced around the cab of Thomas's truck caused Mike to break out in a cold sweat. Ethan was big for his age, but still just a boy, and could easily end up with a few broken ribs just from being slammed against the dashboard.

He shot Sara a brief glance. "We're closing in on him. It's only a matter of time before he's safe in your arms, sweetheart, I promise."

"All I can think about is how scared he must be. Mike, if something happens to him..." She broke off on a sob and Mike cursed, frustrated he couldn't offer her the comfort she so desperately needed.

"I let you both down once, sweetheart. And as long as there's breath in my body, it'll never happen again. I swear it."

"Shit!" Nicky's voice blurted out through the phone. "Jason just tore across three lanes of traffic to take the Oneida Street exit. I don't know if he recognized me or the squads, but he knows something's up."

Mike heard Garrett talking to dispatch before he explained, "They're gonna wait to flip on their cherries. Nicky, how far behind him are you?"

"Not far, just a couple car lengths. But he's weaving through traffic like a madman, and you know how tricky this intersection is. He's heading east, toward the mall."

Garrett cursed. "Just stay calm and keep him in your sights. We're exiting onto Oneida right now, so we're not that far behind."

At that moment, Mike decided to change course, and prayed like hell his rash decision paid off. He moved into the right lane and took the one-seventy-two exit heading east.

Sara whipped her head around to face him and demanded, "Where are you going? Mike, we're going to lose him!"

Without taking his eyes off the road, he explained, "I know a short cut that'll bring us right out onto Oneida Street, down by the mall. With any luck, we'll either pull out in front of him, or not that far behind him." The only possible problem was, he hadn't been this way in years, and Lord only knew if the street still went through the same with the way some of these neighborhoods had been built up.

But he breathed a sigh of relief as the road did indeed curve around, and he ended up coming out onto Oneida right across the street from Bay Park Square Mall. He sat at the stop sign, unsure whether to turn right or left.

"There he is!" Sara shouted, pointing west, which meant, miraculously, they'd ended up in front of him. "Oh, my God, he doesn't even have him belted in!" she cried in outrage.

Mike was grateful to hear the fire back in her voice. "Calm down, honey, we're closing in on him. Ethan's a tough kid. He's hanging in there, don't you worry."

He made a left out onto Oneida, and maneuvered until he was directly in front of him.

"Okay, I'm right in front of him," Mike told the others.

"Nicky? How far back are you?"

"There's only three cars between us. And I recognize the squads, they're flanking the car behind him. Garrett, where are you and Uncle Luke?"

"We're two vehicles behind you, to the right. We have to be extremely careful now. Lord only knows what he might do to Ethan if he's scared enough."

"Let's just concentrate on boxing him in and forcing him to surrender," Nicky said. "He wouldn't dare hurt Ethan now. It would serve no purpose other than to guarantee he dies a slow, agonizing death by our hands."

Without warning, Thomas stepped on the brakes and made a hard right onto a side road. Mike had to make a quick turn into a gas station and cut through the parking lot to stay on his tail. Sara bounced off the seat and grunted.

"Christ, honey, I'm sorry."

"I'm fine. Just don't lose him, Mike. Please...don't lose him."

Her voice cracked, and he shot her a quick, sidelong glance. His gut clenched at the anguish in those huge, red-rimmed eyes, her lips moving in silent prayer. *When this is over*, he silently swore with grim determination, *I'm going to kill that cocksucker with my bare hands.*

He glanced in his rearview mirror and breathed a sigh of relief. The two squad cars were coming up fast behind him. Hopefully, Nicky, and Garrett and Luke weren't too far behind.

Thomas obviously had no intention of surrendering. He accelerated and made several quick turns—left, right, then left again. The truck skidded around every corner, and at one point, as Thomas drove under a street lamp, Mike saw Ethan slam against the dashboard. Sara cried out, and he had to fight with everything he had to keep his hands on the steering wheel and his focus on their son.

Jason couldn't believe he was in the middle of a high-speed pursuit, and *he* was the one being pursued! Snatching the kid had been a spur of the moment decision. He'd meant to climb through Garrett's window and finish the job Montgomery fucked up. Then he would've headed over to the hospital and taken care of that idiot as well. But he'd ended up in the nephew's room by mistake, and as he'd attempted to slip back out, the kid had opened his eyes and started to scream. By then, Jason had no choice but to jump on top of the little bastard to shut him up.

He'd had to change plans; there was no help for it. He figured he'd use the kid as bait to draw both Jamison and Andrews out, and then eliminate all three. Then he'd head down to Mexico, fake his death thanks to some friends he'd made down there, and return to the U.S. with a new identity. Sure, it wouldn't be easy taking out a kid, but there was no help for it. The little shit could identify him.

But then he'd noticed a couple of unmarked squads following him onto highway forty-one. He hadn't sweated it at first. Hell, he'd only snatched the kid maybe twenty minutes before then. They shouldn't have even noticed him missing yet, for chrissake.

He cast a quick glance in his rearview mirror. It would take a miracle to get him out of this one now, and frankly, he doubted God was willing to grant him one of those. Not after everything he'd done—and planned to do.

Fucking Jamison and that idiot ex of Sara's. If not for those two pricks, he'd be busy cutting up his shipment right now and letting his contacts know when and where to meet him. That deal alone would have netted him fifty large.

And thanks to Montgomery pulling through surgery, he'd be facing attempted murder charges—on top of kidnapping. The loss of his badge was a given, as was a long prison sentence. Yep, his luck had definitely run out. Thanks to the father and uncle of the little bastard sitting scared shitless beside him. His only shot at freedom would be if he could make it down to Mexico. He had an in with one of the players in Puerto Vallarta who'd offered him a place in his organization more than once.

But first, he needed to get rid of the kid and the cops tailing his ass.

He realized he was coming back up on Oneida Street. He had a string of vehicles chasing him, and possibly even a road block set up ahead somewhere. Fueled by rage and hopelessness, he smacked the steering wheel over and over as he wracked his brain for an answer. Casting the sniveling brat one last glance, he made a bold decision. One he hoped would buy him the time he needed to make his escape.

Reaching over, he grasped the passenger-side door handle and yanked it open. Then he leaned back and kicked the little bastard out of the truck.

Twenty-Three

Sara lunged forward with a roar as she watched her son fly out of the truck. "Ethan!" Cruelly yanked back by the restriction of her seatbelt, she grappled frantically with the release button, screaming her son's name so hard her throat constricted. Nothing in this life could have prepared her for the sight of her precious baby getting shoved out of a moving vehicle. What kind of evil monster could do such a thing?

Mike fish-tailed hard to the right and screeched to a halt less than twenty feet from where Ethan's body lay crumpled and unmoving. She jumped from the truck and took off running, but she slipped on gravel and fell to her knees in her haste to get to her son's side. Mike raced ahead and dropped to his knees beside him. She half ran, half crawled until she reached them, instinct compelling her to scoop Ethan up into her arms.

Mike grabbed her wrists and hauled her back against his side. "Sara, you can't touch him until I've had a chance to check for—"

A loud crash followed by the distinct crunch of shattering glass and blowing horns was so deafening Sara flew back on her haunches. Mike threw himself in front of her and Ethan, shielding them from any potentially flying debris.

After a few seconds, he pulled out his cell phone and called for an ambulance while she lay down on her side in the grass beside their son.

She gently stroked his face as tears spilled from her eyes. "Sweetie? Please talk to mommy. You're scaring me. Please say something."

Mike knelt down on Ethan's other side and felt for a pulse. "He's alive."

"Thank God," she cried as Mike ran gentle hands up their son's arms, legs, and his little chest.

"He doesn't seem to have broken anything."

Screeching tires behind them had her sitting up in a rush. She watched Nicky and Uncle Luke race across the street toward them, Garrett hobbling behind at a much slower pace. She turned back to her son and prayed the ambulance would hurry the hell up.

"Is he all right?" Nicky demanded as he dropped to his knees at his nephew's feet. "Mike, please, tell us he's all right."

Uncle Luke reached down and attempted to help her to her feet, but she shook off his hand.

"No. I'm not leaving his side."

Without a word, he sat down beside her and wrapped an arm around her shoulder.

"There doesn't appear to be any broken bones," Mike told them. "Though I can't be sure, so we'll have to be careful not to move him." He tore his flannel shirt off and gently tucked it around his head.

Ethan's eyes fluttered open, and Sara cried out her joy. Uncle Luke gave her a reassuring squeeze.

"Son, it's Dad," Mike said. "Can you hear me? I know you're scared, but if you can hear me, it's very important that you let me know."

"I-I want my mom...Mom?" Ethan croaked out, craning his neck to look for her.

Sara crouched beside him, laughing and crying at the same time. "I'm right here, sweetheart. Mommy's right here, and I'm not going anywhere."

"Ethan, we need you to hold still," Mike instructed. "Okay?"

Leaning in closer, Sara smoothed her hand over his brow, his cheek, his precious face. She could hear the whining of an ambulance in the distance, and breathed the deepest sigh of relief of her life. "You're going to be just fine, my brave little man, don't you worry." She looked up at Mike. "Can I hold him? He needs me, Mike. He needs to feel my arms around him."

Mike had never felt more helpless in his entire life—or more enraged. He was dangerously close to losing the tenuous hold he had on his temper, and it scared the living hell out of him. "Honey, I know, but we have to be cautious. The paramedics will be here any minute. If we move him now and cause an injury, we'll never forgive ourselves."

Garrett finally reached them. He braced himself against the nearest telephone pole and carefully knelt down beside her. He reached out to stroke Ethan's face. "Hey, sport. I want you to try and relax. Take slow, deep breaths. That's it, slowly. Good boy. How do you feel? Man, you're some kind of hero."

Ethan's lip started quivering, but his little face twisted with outrage when he announced, "Uncle Garrett, I-I want you to arrest Jason! He-he stealed me outta the house and wouldn't let me go! And he called me bad names, and...and...and he kicked me outta the truck!"

Sara's eyes filled with fresh tears.

Garrett's jaw hardened as he exchanged a quick glance with Mike. "Don't you worry, sport," his uncle said. "Jason won't see the outside of a jail cell for a *very* long time."

For the second time in his life, Mike literally saw red. The urge to murder Thomas with his bare hands drove him to his feet. "The only thing that bastard's gonna need when I get through with him is a toe tag."

"Mike, please!" Sara begged as he strode off toward the crash site.

"D-dad?"

Mike stopped cold as the fear in his son's voice tore him to the quick. He turned around and the anger whooshed from his chest as Ethan held out his arms. His out-of-control temper had cost him the first seven years of his son's life. No way in hell would he let it, or Jason Thomas, cost him another minute more.

With a deep, shuddering breath, Mike took one last look over his shoulder at the mangled, canary yellow truck surrounded by squad cars. Then he walked back, knelt down beside his son, and gently took him in his arms.

Mere seconds after shoving her son out of his truck, Jason had been cut off by a carload of teenagers, he'd swerved to the left and crashed head-on into a parked truck. Luckily, all four kids were fine, and the parked truck had been empty.

And as it turned out, getting shoved out of the truck had very likely saved Ethan's life.

Sara watched with hands clenched in silent prayer as

the paramedics checked her son over from head to toe. Fresh tears, this time joyful tears, slid down her cheeks as they proclaimed him to be the luckiest little boy alive having suffered nothing worse than a few scrapes on his face, hands and bare feet, and some bruising. But they insisted on taking him to the hospital so he could be fully examined by a doctor. Ethan begged and pleaded to go straight home, but for once she wasn't giving in to his puppy dog eyes and lip quiver.

"I'm sorry, sweetie, but the only place we're heading is St. Mary's Hospital."

By the time they made their way home, it was nearly four o'clock in the morning. Ethan, who'd been riding a sugar rush for the past twenty minutes thanks to the chocolate bar his father snuck him in the emergency room, looked ready to pass out from exhaustion. Sara, hesitant to put him in his own bed, had Mike lay him on hers.

"I'd like to stay here tonight, if it's okay with everyone else," he said as he pulled the comforter up to Ethan's chin. "I can sleep in Ethan's room."

"But Mike—"

"I'll be fine, sweetheart. Thomas has a broken leg and pelvic bone. Believe me, he won't be able to take a piss on his own for a very long time, let alone get out of bed and cause any more harm."

Never one to wish ill will on anyone, Sara couldn't help but hope Jason suffered horribly for everything he'd done to her family.

Mike led her out of the bedroom, and they joined the others in the kitchen. Nicky had called Danny from the hospital to fill him in and let him know Ethan would be fine. Since there was no point in him staying, he'd headed back to his girlfriend's apartment, but said he'd be back in the morning.

"I think we should all try to get some sleep," Uncle Luke said on a huge yawn. "The sun'll be up in less than an hour."

"Thank God this is over," Sara said. "But before we turn in, will one of you please tell me why the hell Jason went psycho on our family?"

Mike, Nicky, and Garrett took turns explaining the entire story to her and Uncle Luke, who was just as much in the dark as she.

"My God...How could I not have realized what a slimeball the guy is?"

"Hell, I'm the one who brought him into our lives," Garrett countered, looking as weary as Sara had ever seen him. "I hope you can all forgive me. If I wasn't so damned set on keeping the two of you apart, this never would've happened."

"Don't beat yourself up," Mike said. "You couldn't have known what kind of a lowlife the guy was. If anyone has reason to feel guilty, it's me. I should've filled you in from the beginning, right after I found out he and Sara were dating."

"We went on *one* date," Sara pointed out, exasperated. "I didn't even let him kiss me goodnight."

Mike brought her hand up to his lips. "I know."

A reluctant smile tugged at her own lips. "I can't believe you were following us the entire time."

He grinned. "I'll let you in on a little secret. Remember when something hit Jason in the face in the theater?"

Her mouth dropped open. "That was you?"

"Yep."

Sara chuckled, oddly relieved to know he'd been watching them the entire time. She reached up and kissed him on the chin.

Uncle Luke rose to his feet. "Well, I suppose I'd better hit the hay," he said, yawning again. "As tired as I am, I'll be lucky to wake up in time for supper."

"I hear you." Nicky yawned, too, and stretched his arms over his head. "Thank God tomorrow's Sunday."

"You mean, *today's* Sunday," Garrett said, rubbing his eyes. Sara gazed at him with concern. Now that the adrenaline rush had worn off, it'd be a miracle if he could make it to his room on his own two feet.

As if reading her thoughts, Nicky and Uncle Luke each grasped one of Garrett's elbows and helped him to his room—and miracle of all miracles, he didn't voice a single word of complaint.

Tired, yet still wound up, Sara got up to wash the few cups in the sink. She heard Mike come up behind her before his hands settled on her shoulders.

"Come on, sweetheart, this can wait 'til later. Right now, I think we should both get some sleep." He turned her until she was facing him, then bent his head and kissed her gently on the forehead.

Sara smiled, more content than she'd ever been in her life. How amazing to think that in just a little over a week, their lives had done a complete one-eighty. Ethan had his father in his life, and the only man she had ever loved was holding her in his arms.

She'd spent the better part of the last eight years believing Mike had betrayed her in the worst way possible. Or, at least, what seems like the worst way possible when you're only eighteen years old. She'd learned not to trust her own instincts, when in reality, they'd been dead on. The love that had shone from his eyes as a young man had been genuine and true, and although two hateful, jealous people had torn them apart, and a drug-dealing, dirty cop had even tried, fate had eventually intervened and made them whole again.

"I've always loved you, you know that, don't you?" Mike said against the top of her head.

Sara's arms tightened around him. It was time. Time to say the words that stood between them and a wonderful life together. "And I've always loved you. Oh, Mike, I'm afraid to blink for fear I'll find out this has all been an incredible dream and nothing more."

He pulled back and gazed down at her. "If this is a dream, let me sleep for the next fifty years or so." He leaned over and kissed her on the lips. "Sorry, sweetheart, but from this day forward, you're stuck with me."

Epilogue

Four days later, Mike called Nicky's cell phone, in need of a little assistance.

"Hello?"

"Hey, Nicky, it's Mike. I need to talk to you, but don't let Sara know it's me on the phone."

"She's in the shower. Where are you? You told her you'd be here for that big honkin' pancake breakfast she made for all of us, and I don't need to tell you how disappointed she was. She took the day off work and everything."

"I know, and I'm sorry. I just didn't want her to know where I'd gone, and...well, I made sort of a last minute decision."

"Which was?"

"Sorry, buddy. You'll have to wait with everyone else."

Nicky laughed. "Not even a little hint?"

"Well, I *will* need some help pulling it off, so could you and the guys keep her busy while I get everything ready?"

"Depends on how long you'll need. Because you know Sara. We may have to strap her down if she becomes suspicious."

Mike grinned. One of the many reasons he loved the spunky woman. "Then borrow Garrett's handcuffs, 'cause I need a few hours, at least."

"A few *hours?* Oh, man, you're going to owe us for this."

"Thanks, Nicky, you're the best."

"Pierogies? I thought you hated those things." Sara scowled as she eyed her brother with frustration. Lord, how she hated making those damn things—they took for-frickin'-ever.

Garrett relaxed back in the recliner and flipped through the channels. "I just suddenly got a taste for 'em. Besides, it's the sauerkraut ones I don't care for." He moaned softly, and Sara frowned, concerned.

"Are you all right? You know, your next pain pill isn't due for another hour."

"I'm okay. Just a little sore. But a batch of those cheese and potato pierogies you make sure would hit the spot."

She just barely held back an eye roll. Men could be such babies. "Well, I'll have to dig the recipe out of my cookbook—"

"You're the best, Sis."

A couple hours later, Sara scooted the savory little pockets and onions around in the pan with more force than necessary. After everything that'd happened over the past week, how could he blow off the special family breakfast she'd planned? The breakfast she'd stayed home from work to prepare. He sends her a text to say something came up and...that's it? No explanation, no apology. *Inconsiderate, insensitive, thoughtless, arrogant—*

"Man, those things sure smell good," Garrett commented from the living room. "Are they almost ready?"

Sara shook the pierogies and onions onto a plate, then spooned a large dollop of sour cream into a small bowl. She put both on a tray, stalked into the living room and handed it to him.

"Uh, is something wrong? You look...upset."

"No," she snapped. "I'm fine. Just fine." She drummed her fingers against the back of his chair, growing angrier by the second.

After casting her a quick glance—a suspiciously guilty glance if she knew her oldest brother—Garrett returned his attention to the television and dunked one of the piping hot, potato and cheese-filled pockets into the sour cream.

The phone rang. *About damn time*, she thought, heading into the kitchen to answer it. But before she even took two steps, Uncle Luke called out, "I got it!"

"That was Nicky," he informed them a minute later. "He says we all need to get down to Mike's place right away."

Sara's heart lurched in her chest. "Oh my God, what happened? Is Mike all right? I knew there had to be a good explanation—"

"Honey, all he said was that we'd better get down there right away."

"Well, would you mind staying with Ethan then? The last time I saw him he was downstairs—"

"Ethan's already down there. With Nicky," Uncle Luke said, tugging at his ear.

Sara crossed her arms over her chest. "You just insisted all Nicky said was we need to get down there right away."

He shrugged. "I, uh, forgot that he also mentioned Ethan was with him."

"Hmmm." She was almost sure he was lying...but why? And Nicky wouldn't take Ethan out of the house without letting her know. Something was definitely going on here.

Garrett pushed himself to his feet and set his plate on the end table. "Why don't we just head on down there and see what the heck's going on?"

"You're certainly all acting mighty strange," she declared. Then she strode past them and hurried out the front door.

She was practically running by the time she reached the walkway that led up to his front door. Could something have happened to Ethan? No, Nicky would have said something to Uncle Luke if that were the case.

Just as she raised her hand to knock, the door swung open and there stood her brother and Ethan, both grinning broadly. They each grasped one of her hands and guided her toward the back of the house to where the French doors stood open onto the patio. The entire patio was covered in a sea of red, white and pink roses. Sara's breath caught and her eyes misted over.

She gazed around as she walked through the French doors. Dozens of lit candles lined every inch of the porch railings and the bistro table in the middle of the patio. And then she saw Mike, looking so handsome in a white collared, button-down shirt and black slacks it nearly took her breath away.

"Hi, sweetheart."

Sara's eyes roamed once more around the patio, taking in all the gorgeous roses that were in every state from tight buds to full bloom—and the sweet smell was simply indescribable. She loved roses, always had, and loved him for remembering.

Tears stung her eyes. She could only think of one reason a man would create this kind of atmosphere, and only one reason he'd have her family here to witness it. But she didn't dare think the words…

"Mike, what's going on? A text message? Really? You could've called. I've been so worried."

"Worried?" Garrett snorted. "You were mad as hell, don't deny it."

Hands on hips, Sara scowled at her oldest brother. "And I had good reason. Really, Garrett, pierogies? You know how much I hate making those things."

"Actually, that was my idea," Nicky admitted. "I needed something that would keep you busy for a while."

Sara turned back around to face Mike. "Why?"

He covered the short distance between them and took her hands in his. "Because I asked him to."

"Why?" she repeated, her chest swelling with hope.

Mike scanned the faces behind her. "Do I have all of your blessings?"

"Absolutely," Nicky replied.

"You know you do, son." Uncle Luke smiled at him.

"You have mine," Garrett said. "And I'm not too pig-headed to admit I was wrong. You're a good man, Mike."

Ethan walked over and stood next to his father. "Dad, only priests can give blessings. But you do have my permission to marry my mom." He held out a small, maroon-colored velvet box.

Sara's hands flew to her mouth and her throat went dry. He was going to do it! He was really going to do it and…and…what the hell's that smell? She sniffed her arm and her eyes widened in horror. Good God, she smelled like onions! Sara spun around to glare at her brothers, then promptly burst into tears.

"Sweetheart, please tell me those are happy tears," Mike said as he plucked the jewelry box from Ethan's hand.

"I-I...I smell like an onion. And it's all your fault." Sara pointed an accusing finger at Nicky.

"Funny, but I was thinking you smell good enough to eat," Mike whispered into her ear.

Her tears subsided into embarrassed laughter, and she wrapped her arms around his neck, happier than she'd ever thought possible.

"Ask her already," Garrett said, followed by a chorus of agreement.

Mike untangled her arms from around his neck and took a step back. Then he got down on bended knee. Sara squealed in delight and did a little happy dance.

"Sara, I've loved you since the first moment I laid eyes on you, and that's no exaggeration. And because of my own insecurities, we've lost so much time together. But I've come to believe fate brought us back together because we were meant to be, and sweetheart, I don't want to waste another single second. Sara Lynn Jamison, will you marry me?" He flipped open the box and Sara gasped.

"Oh my God, it's beautiful," she breathed, reaching out to run a reverent finger over the most incredible engagement ring she'd ever seen. The round diamond in the center was surrounded by four smaller trapezoid pink diamonds. "But it's way too extravagant. We'll return it and I can pick out something more sensible—"

"Sara, I picked this ring out all by myself, and I promise you, I can afford it. Now, you don't want to hurt my feelings, do you?"

"Well, of course not, but—"

"Sara, *will* you marry me? With this ring, the one I picked out for you?"

"Come on, Mom, say yes already!"

Smiling through her tears, Sara nodded and held out her hand for Mike to slip on the ring.

"What was that?" Nicky teased. "We couldn't hear you all the way back here."

Mike slid the ring onto her finger, and Sara held up her hand for everyone to see. "I said yes!" she shouted, laughing joyously.

Mike picked her up in his arms and spun her around before sealing their fate with a kiss.

"All right, everyone, as much as I appreciate all of your help, the rest of the evening is just for the two of us," Mike announced as Sara nibbled on his earlobe. "So thanks for everything, but now it's time to get the hell out."

"Even me?" Ethan demanded, his brow knitting in outrage.

"Even you," Mike confirmed with a nod.

Sara pulled back and smiled at her son as understanding dawned in his eyes.

"You're gonna kiss her again," he accused. "Aren't you?"

His father nodded. "I'm afraid so, kiddo."

Ethan shook his head, his disgust evident. "Oh, man, I don't know what I'm gonna do with you two." He grabbed Garrett's hand. "Come on, you don't want to see this either. It's pretty gross."

Garrett, Nicky and Uncle Luke all chuckled as they followed Ethan out of the house.

Once they were alone, Mike set her on her feet,

grabbed the bottle of champagne he'd had chilling in ice and handed it to her. "Give me two minutes to put out all these candles," he said, licking his thumb and forefinger. Sara giggled as he raced around the patio, snuffing and blowing out every single one in record time.

With a wink, he took the bottle back from her, tore off the foil and popped the cork. He filled two champagne flutes and handed her one. She took it with raised eyebrows. "You wouldn't be trying to get me tipsy, now would you?"

"Guilty as charged. I was hoping we could try out the whirlpool tub." He took a sip from his glass before wrapping his free arm around her and escorting her back into the house. "Since you do happen to smell like onions..."

"Ooh, I'm going to get you for that!" she promised, pinching his backside.

Mike stopped at the foot of the stairs and turned her in his arms. He gazed down, eyes smoldering, and said, "I do love you, Sara. And I swear I'll never let you down again."

Sara's eyes filled with tears. "And I love you. Now take me upstairs so I can wash the smell of onions from my hair."

He grinned. "My pleasure."

Author's Note

Thank you for reading Mike & Sara's story. *There's Only Been You* is the book of my heart, and I sure hope you enjoyed reading it as much as I enjoyed writing it. If you found yourself drawn to Sara's hotheaded brother, Garrett, please check out his story...

MEANT TO BE

JAMISON SERIES: BOOK 2

She's running from her past, he's unsure about his future. Maybe together they can figure out what was MEANT TO BE...

Officer Garrett Jamison is at the lowest point in his life. He's lost faith in his ability as a police officer after unwittingly setting his sister up with a dirty cop. Garrett ended up getting shot, and his sister's son kidnapped right out of his own bed. He takes a leave from the force, in need of some time to make a decision about his future. Too bad he can't get a decent night's sleep thanks to his sexy new neighbor and her howling cat.

Jessica McGovern moves halfway across the country to start a new life in Green Bay, Wisconsin after her ex-husband is convicted of involuntary manslaughter in the death of their young son. Her new neighbor is as infuriating as he is handsome, but when her ex is released from prison early and shows up in town, Jessica discovers she's never needed anyone more.

"Witty and heartfelt, with an unforgettable cast of secondary characters, MEANT TO BE is a definite page-turner!"

~ Lori Foster, NY Times bestselling author of
BACK IN BLACK

"Remember, you promised to be good," Garrett reminded his nephew as he pulled open the door to the restaurant. "Any sass-mouth and I'll take you right home. I mean it."

Ethan frowned, but wisely nodded his head. He stomped through the door and stood next to the PLEASE WAIT TO BE SEATED sign. Garrett couldn't help but grin. Even annoyed, Ethan had better self-control than his uncle.

The hostess, a busty, middle aged woman with a humongous salt-and-pepper beehive hairdo, walked up and winked at Ethan. "Hey, good-lookin', would you like a table or a booth?" She grabbed a menu, placemats, and a few crayons off the hostess stand.

"We'll take a booth," Garrett said. "In Jessica's section, if that's all right."

She cast him an appreciative once over and smiled. "She has a booth open in the corner. Follow me."

Ethan dragged his feet the entire way, then climbed in and crossed his arms, his little face screwed up in a mutinous scowl. Garrett let out a resigned sigh.

The hostess handed him the menu, set down the paper placemats, and dropped the crayons in front of Ethan. "Jessica will be with you in just a minute."

"I ain't no baby," Ethan muttered as soon as she walked away.

"You're seven, sport. There's nothing babyish about coloring when you're seven." Garrett flipped open his menu, hoping a decent meal might sweeten Ethan's disposition. Hell, who was he kidding? The only cure for his nephew's foul mood would be if Jessica disappeared from the planet. And *that* would surely put *him* in a foul mood. The thought of never seeing her again was enough to make his blood run cold. Damn, when did he become so attached?

He blew out a frustrated breath and glanced over the menu. "Hey, they have chicken quesadilla appetizers. Want to split an order?"

Ethan shrugged. "I s'pose." He picked up one of the crayons and started doodling.

Garrett felt a glimmer of hope. He certainly didn't need the little squirt's permission to date Jessica, but it would be nice if he could at least be civil to her.

"Well, I didn't expect to see you two here."

Jessica approached the table, and Garrett had to clear his suddenly dry throat. Jesus, what in the world was wrong with him? It hadn't been *that* long since he'd gotten laid.

He shrugged. "We have to eat lunch, and this is as good a place as any." *Did that sound nonchalant enough?*

"So, what can I get you?" She pulled the pad and pen from her pocket before craning her neck to see what Ethan was drawing. "Wow, that's amazing. A dog?"

His nephew looked up with utter disdain. "It's a horse. Don't you know anything?"

Garrett's face grew hot with embarrassment. He slapped his menu shut and yanked the crayon from Ethan's grasp. "That's it, sport, I warned you. No lunch and no movies tonight. You can sit in your room and pout until you learn how to treat people with respect." His gaze moved to Jessica. Jesus, what she must think. "I'm sorry. I honestly thought his manners would've improved by now."

Ethan's eyes grew red and his chin quivered. "But it's a horse! Anyone can see that!"

Garrett had had enough. He started to push himself to his feet when Jessica laid a placating hand on his forearm.

"Please, he's right. Anyone can see it's a horse. I don't know what I was thinking." She then turned to Ethan. "You know, we make one of the best cheeseburgers in the city, and it comes with a big plateful of curly fries. *And* if you finish your food, you get a free sundae. What do you think? Are you up for it?"

Ethan shrugged a shoulder, but remained silent.

"If you don't think you can do it..." Jessica added, letting her words trail off as if in silent dare.

Garrett watched in wonder as most of the hostility faded from his nephew's eyes. The thrill of possible victory even brought a smug grin to the little shit's face. A free sundae? There wasn't much Ethan wouldn't do for that.

"Well, sport, it's up to you. Do we stay, practice our manners, and have one of the best cheeseburgers in the city, or go home for some of Uncle Luke's Spam casserole?"

Ethan shivered in revulsion. Garrett and Jessica both laughed.

"I guess that settles it. And I think I'd like to try that challenge as well." He handed Jessica both menus as he mouthed the word "thanks".

She winked. "Okay, so that's two cheeseburger challenges. What can I get you to drink?"

Ethan glanced at Garrett who nodded. Those bright blue eyes lit up. "A large orange soda. And no onions on my cheeseburger."

"Make it two sodas." Garrett leaned back and laid his arm along the back of the booth. "And no onions on mine either." He returned her wink.

She rolled her eyes, but he caught a hint of a smile as she turned away.

Thirty minutes later, Jessica set two huge, cherry-topped hot fudge sundaes on the table with a flourish. "I have to say, I'm impressed. You boys sure can eat." Of course, she'd never admit she'd seen Garrett filching curly fries off his nephew's plate. The kid was, after all, only seven.

And while Ethan wasn't exactly smiling and friendly, he *had* managed to refrain from hurling insults at her. For that, she was grateful.

"Yeah, but nobody can eat as much as Uncle Danny," Ethan informed her. "I saw him eat a whole cake before."

Jessica widened her eyes dramatically. "No way! A *whole* cake? He must've had a bellyache for a week."

He nodded, warming to his subject. "Yep, and he puked his guts up, too."

"Ethan, we're in a restaurant," Garrett warned in a low tone. He met her gaze and shook his head. "Sorry."

Jessica waved his worry away. Although a typically indulgent and caring uncle, Garrett didn't let the little stinker get away with bad behavior, which, she had to admit, was another check in the man's 'pro' column.

She slid the check face down onto the table and said, "Well, I'm glad you guys stopped in for lunch. Have a great time at the movies tonight. Eat some popcorn for me."

Garrett cocked a brow at his nephew whose little face screwed up in resignation. "If you wanna come, you can come," Ethan grudgingly invited. "But you have to eat your own popcorn."

He earned a wink and smile from his uncle, which seemed to please him.

Jessica knew the last thing Ethan wanted was for her to tag along, though, and decided there was no point in pressing her luck. They'd be neighbors for at least five more months, and it would certainly be easier for everyone if Ethan didn't think of her as the Wicked Witch of the West.

"Thanks. I appreciate the offer, I really do. But the last thing I want to do is intrude on a guys' night out."

Garrett raised both brows at his nephew this time, and Ethan set his spoon down with a resigned sigh. But when he glanced back up at her, his smile seemed almost genuine. "It's okay. My mom even comes with us on guys' night out sometimes. And she's a girl, too."

Jessica could barely hold back a giggle. She looked over and met Garrett's gaze with a you-don't-have-to-do-this look. But the truth was, she hadn't been to a movie theater since she was a kid, and, darn it, she wanted to go.

"Come on, it'll be fun," Garrett said. "We're going to see that new superhero movie. And it'll be my treat, popcorn and all."

She glanced back and forth between them. "If you're sure I'm not intruding, I'd love to come. I haven't seen the inside of a theater in years."

Ethan shoved a heaping spoonful of ice cream into his mouth and shook his head. "We're not going to the theater," he said after gulping it down. "We're going to the drive-in!"

Foolish Pride

Jamison Series: Extra Peek Short Story

(Available wherever e-books are sold)

Youngest brother Danny Jamison has a lot to learn about women, and even more to learn about himself...

When God was handing out pride, Danny Jamison must have gotten in line twice, because he's about to let the best thing that's ever happened to him slip away—Emily Harris.

Emily is head-over-heels in love with Danny, but she's not sure she can take his jealous mood swings anymore. Something has to give or his Foolish Pride is going to be the end of them.

Sinking down until submersed to her neck, Emily bent her knees and closed her eyes, letting the steaming water work its magic. It seeped into her bones, relaxing her from head to toe as her worries seemed to melt away.

By feel alone, she grabbed her two-in-one shampoo, squeezed a small amount onto her head, and scrubbed like a mad woman. Once rinsed, she reached for the washcloth and bar of soap. She lathered up her face first, washing away her dried tears and every trace of make-up. She ran the washcloth over her shoulders, under her armpits, over her breasts and stomach. She moved the washcloth between her legs—

"I'd be more than happy to take over for you."

Emily squealed and sat up in a rush, splashing water all over the floor. When she realized it was Danny leaning against the doorframe, she threw the wet washcloth at him. "Dammit, you scared me half to death!"

He pushed away from the door and strode forward. "Sorry. I knocked, but you had Metallica blaring so loud you couldn't hear me."

"I find Metallica extremely relaxing!" she snapped. "Now give me back my key and get the hell out of my apartment." She held out her hand.

Danny knelt beside the tub, but instead of handing her the key he brushed his knuckles down her cheek. "Look, Em, I know you're royally pissed at me right now, but if you'd just give me a chance to explain, I—"

"Are you kidding me? 'Royally pissed' doesn't even begin to describe how I feel." Suddenly more angry than upset, she crossed her arms over her breasts and brought her knees up in an effort to preserve a little modesty. Which she knew was ridiculous since they'd been sleeping together for more than a year.

"You have no idea how sorry I am for what I said. It was completely inexcusable. But...if you could just give me one more chance..." He grabbed her hand and brought it to his lips, holding it against his cheek as he said, his voice raw with emotion, "Em, I love you. And I know you love me, too."

Her eyes filled with tears. Damn him! Now? He waits until things are over between them to finally say those three little words she'd been waiting so patiently to hear him say? But...as much as she wanted to believe him, she couldn't, she just couldn't.

She jerked her hand from his. "I'm sorry, too, Danny, but I can't do this anymore. Your jealousy has gotten crazy lately and that temper...sometimes I'm afraid..."

Shock twisted his face into a mask of incredulity. "My God, I would never hurt you. How could you even think—"

"I don't know! That's the problem. It's like I have no idea who you are anymore. You're angry all the time, you've become so possessive." She reached up to swipe at her eyes. "It seems like the only time you're in a good mood anymore is when we're in bed."

"Then let's crawl in bed right now and stay there forever."

"Danny, please, just go. I can't do this right now. *Please*."

With a deep sigh, he pushed to his feet, head hung low, and turned to leave. Looking back over his shoulder, he said, "Fine, I'll leave. Give you a couple days to get over your anger. But eventually we're going to talk about this. Because there's no way in hell I'm just going to just let you go."

Also by Donna Marie Rogers

GOLDEN OPPORTUNITY

Golden Series: Book 1

(Available wherever e-books are sold)

"Deliciously sweet...with plenty of heat!"
~ Norah Wilson,
New Voice In Romance award-winning author

James McMillan is a third generation owner of the most prosperous horse ranch in Golden, Colorado. When a gorgeous little filly shows up at his door waving what she claims is the deed to half his ranch, James tries to send her packing. But the document is authentic, according to his lawyer: Reese McMillan sold the little opportunist his half of the Double M during a poker game in Atlantic City. So not only must James find a way to buy those shares back, he needs to fight his growing attraction to his luscious new business partner—who turns out to be a lot more than just a pretty face.

Angela Roberts, having been on her own since she was a teenager, has never wanted anything more than the security of a real home. Her dreams come true when the chance to own half of a Colorado horse ranch falls into her lap. If Reese McMillan is too blind to appreciate what he has, that's his loss. Only she hadn't counted on the hostile reception she receives from his brother. Surly as a bear, James McMillan is also much too handsome for her peace of mind. Refusing to be intimidated, Angela sets out to win him over by proving she has what it takes to help him run the ranch—and ends up losing her heart to both.

One

"I'm telling you I bought it fair and square. This deed proves it."

James McMillan glared down at the crazy woman waving a document under his nose. So his fool baby brother had finally done it—he'd gambled away his half of the ranch. James' biggest fear had come true, and she barely reached his shoulder.

He blew out a silent breath and thumbed his Stetson back. "Look, Miss...?"

"Roberts. Angela Roberts."

"It'll take me a few days to raise the funds to buy it back. In the meantime, there are several hotels in downtown Golden—"

"Sorry, Cowboy, but you're not getting rid of me that easily. I'm staying right here at the Double M. Reese said—"

"Reese is an idiot, and I don't give a damn what he

said. I'll be dipped if some gold-digging opportunist is gonna set one foot inside the home my great-grandparents built with their own hands. Now, I'll pay for your hotel room if you can't afford one, but either way, you're leaving."

She huffed out a sigh of frustration and crossed her arms over her ample chest. Big blue eyes clear as the Colorado sky gazed up at him, and for a brief moment, James became lost in them. He gave himself a mental shake, ignoring her full pouty lips and shiny auburn hair, which hung in loose waves down to her waist. Lord, did he love long hair on a woman.

Damn you, Reese.

"I told you, I'm not going anywhere. I own half this ranch, whether you like it or not. And if you insist on making me leave, I promise you I'll be back with the sheriff."

Great. Just freakin' great. Sheriff Martin would pounce like a mountain lion on a chance to make James miserable. And if she got that vindictive old cuss involved, the story of Reese's stupidity would be all over town by nightfall.

His frustration must have shown on his face because a knowing smile curved those luscious lips. James propped his hands on his hips in defeat and took a step back. "Fine. You wanna play house, lady, be my guest. Just don't get too comfortable."

With a toss of her head, she picked up her suitcase, her high heels clicking on the tiled floor of the foyer as she strode past him. It took all James' self-control not to give her denim-clad ass a swat as she passed by.

Angela gazed around the surprisingly modern log ranch house, nearly overcome by emotion. Her heart swelled with hope as she took in the vaulted ceiling, large stone fireplace, and overall rustic charm. So beautiful...and by being in the right place at the right time she was now half-owner. Reese had said the place was nothing special. Big brother was right about one thing; Reese was an idiot.

She turned to face Mr. Tall, Dark, and Incredibly Handsome, feeling a sudden pang of insecurity. "I've never seen a more beautiful home. Reese made it sound...well, I didn't know what to expect."

"Reese always preferred bright lights and the big city over the hard work of running a horse ranch."

She met his gaze. "I can't imagine why. I'd have done anything to get out of the city."

The hostility in those whiskey-brown eyes returned. "Is that a confession?"

Angela set her suitcase on the foyer. "You can think whatever you want, Cowboy. The fact is, Reese was about to put his half of this place up as collateral with some high rollers who, trust me, you wouldn't have wanted showing up on your doorstep. I had a pretty decent nest-egg saved, so I offered to buy it outright. He got more than he would've as a bet, and I got a ticket out of the city."

"And how did you happen to be at this 'high rollers' card game?"

She understood the resentment and anger that laced his words. Hell, she still couldn't believe Reese had nearly put up his half of this gorgeous paradise to match a fifty-thousand dollar bet, even if the pot had been worth twenty times that. And big brother may not think so now, but Angela was most definitely the lesser of two evils. She could only imagine the look on his face had Vinnie the Butcher showed up at the door with his goons. "I was the dealer."

He lifted his Stetson and raked his hand through thick, dark brown curls. Angela swallowed the urge to sigh like an infatuated schoolgirl. Reese was a hottie in a dimples and suave charm sort of way, but big brother was easily the best-looking man she'd ever seen. She much preferred his brooding sexuality to Reese's boyish charisma.

"Come on, I'll show you to a guest room." He picked up her suitcase and headed toward the winding staircase that led to the second floor. Angela decided to keep her trap shut about the 'guest room' dig. No sense pressing her luck. At least she was in the door.

She followed him upstairs to the last room on the left. When he swung open the door, she sucked in a breath. The room was stunning—and huge—ten times nicer than anything she'd ever imagined. A king-sized sleigh bed sat against the far wall, the rich burgundy bedding and matching curtains looked like they belonged in a queen's room. The dark oak mirrored dresser, chest, and armchair all appeared to be antique.

He set her suitcase down and glanced around the room, as if lost in memories. "Pretty, ain't it? Belonged to my grandmother. She passed last year."

Before Angela could process that bit of news, he strode to the door and said over his shoulder, "Supper'll be served in about half an hour. If you wanna eat, don't be late."

She winced when the door slammed shut behind him. Okay, so he had reason to be upset—he'd just lost half of his ranch to a stranger. And since he didn't know her from Eve she could let the 'gold-digging opportunist' comment slide, too. But dammit, she was a hard worker, willing to do anything necessary to prove she belonged here. If he'd give her half a chance, she could win him over no problem. She'd worked two and three jobs at a time since she was fifteen years old; no one who knew her would ever accuse her of being lazy. And hell, at least she was here, which was a lot more than could be said about his brother.

Angela did a quick bounce on the bed before hurrying over to look out the window. Miles and miles of lush green hills were dotted with trees and fuchsia wildflowers against a backdrop of the majestic Rocky Mountains and crowned by the bluest skies she'd ever seen. Tears burned her eyes. This was the kind of home she'd always dreamt of having, the kind of home she'd read so many wonderful stories about.

No way in hell would she give it up without a fight.

After trading her pumps for a pair of white tennis shoes, she ran a brush through her hair and headed downstairs, feeling like a little kid on Christmas morning. She was hoping to get a quick look at the horses before supper. Angela had never been on a horse, had never even touched one, but she'd always hoped to learn to ride one day. And thanks to a little thing called kismet, it looked like that day had finally arrived.

That is if James let her anywhere near them.

The house was fairly quiet, although she could hear faint sounds coming from the back. Probably whoever was making supper. She had no idea whether or not they had servants, but she figured they at least had a cook since James didn't exactly look like the chef type, and Reese had mentioned his brother was single.

She slipped out the front door and followed a stone

path that led around back. A fenced in area she believed they called a corral was set maybe a hundred feet behind the house, with a structure directly to the left which she assumed was the barn. A lone horse trotted inside the enclosure, and Angela's fingers itched to touch its shiny, chestnut brown coat and matching mane. She hurried over and whistled to the beautiful creature, hoping she could tempt it to come her way. Too bad she hadn't thought to buy a box of sugar cubes. She'd read that horses loved them.

The gorgeous creature turned her way and made a snuffling noise. It tossed its head, and then proceeded to saunter over. Angela clapped her hands, just barely holding in a squeal of delight. The horse stuck its muzzle through the fence, and Angela gently rubbed the bridge of its nose. "Well, aren't you just the prettiest thing I've ever seen. Got a name?"

"His name's Lucky."

Angela swung around in surprise; she hadn't heard James approach. He strode up beside her, propped a boot on the bottom rail, and leaned over to pat Lucky's nose. Again, she couldn't help but notice how attractive the man was. "I suppose there's a story behind his name?"

He shot her a quick look, then returned his attention to Lucky. She figured he meant to ignore her, but after a few moments he said, "I came across him just as a mountain lion had taken him down. If I'd been a minute later, he'd have needed burying, not saving."

Angela gave a delicate shudder. The thought of this beautiful animal being eaten alive was a horrific one. Something she could barely fathom having grown up in the city. "You're a hero then."

His mouth crooked up at that. "Hardly. Just happened

to be in the right place at the right time." He stood up and stepped back, gazing past her as if something more important had caught his eye. "Supper's ready. And trust me when I say Meara doesn't like to be kept waiting."

"Is Meara the cook?"

His gaze swung to hers and that coldness she had come to expect returned. "Meara's as close to family as a body can get without being blood related."

"Sor-ry, I was just curious. You know, you really need to do something about that attitude."

"I'll be back to my cheerful ol' self just as soon as you're gone."

Angela made a face at his retreating back. *Good luck with that, Cowboy, 'cause I'm not going anywhere.*

About the Author

USA Today Bestselling author Donna Marie Rogers inherited her love of romance from her mother. Romance novels, soap operas, *Little House on the Prairie*—her mother loved them all. And though it wasn't until years later Donna would come to understand her mother's fascination with Charles Ingalls, Donna's love of the romance genre is every bit as all-consuming. Donna's books have received rave reviews and finaled in numerous contests, including the Aspen Gold, EPIC Awards, and her chapter's own Write Touch Readers Award.

A Chicago native, Donna now lives in beautiful Northeast Wisconsin with her husband and children. She's an avid gardener and home-canner, as well as an admitted reality TV junkie. Her passion to read is only exceeded by her passion to write, so when she's not doing the wife and mother thing, you can usually find her sitting at the computer, creating exciting, memorable characters, fresh new worlds, and always happily-ever-afters.

Website and Blogs:

http://www.DonnaMarieRogers.blogspot.com

http://novelfriends.blogspot.com/

Made in the USA
Lexington, KY
14 July 2013